The Girl in the Mask

D0068004

ALSO BY MARIE-LOUISE JENSEN

✳

Between Two Seas
The Lady in the Tower
Daughter of Fire and Ice
Sigrun's Secret

The Girl in the Mask

MARIE-LOUISE JENSEN

OXFORD
UNIVERSITY PRESS

OXFORD
UNIVERSITY PRESS

Great Clarendon Street, Oxford OX2 6DP

Oxford University Press is a department of the University of Oxford.
It furthers the University's objective of excellence in research, scholarship,
and education by publishing worldwide in

Oxford New York

Auckland Cape Town Dar es Salaam Hong Kong Karachi
Kuala Lumpur Madrid Melbourne Mexico City Nairobi
New Delhi Shanghai Taipei Toronto

With offices in

Argentina Austria Brazil Chile Czech Republic France Greece
Guatemala Hungary Italy Japan Poland Portugal Singapore
South Korea Switzerland Thailand Turkey Ukraine Vietnam

Oxford is a registered trade mark of Oxford University Press
in the UK and in certain other countries

© Marie-Louise Jensen 2012

The moral rights of the author have been asserted

Database right Oxford University Press (maker)

First published 2012

All rights reserved. No part of this publication may be reproduced,
stored in a retrieval system, or transmitted, in any form or by any means,
without the prior permission in writing of Oxford University Press,
or as expressly permitted by law, or under terms agreed with the appropriate
reprographics rights organization. Enquiries concerning reproduction
outside the scope of the above should be sent to the Rights Department,
Oxford University Press, at the address above

You must not circulate this book in any other binding or cover
and you must impose this same condition on any acquirer

British Library Cataloguing in Publication Data

Data available

ISBN: 978-0-19-279279-2

1 3 5 7 9 10 8 6 4 2

Printed in Great Britain
Paper used in the production of this book is a natural,
recyclable product made from wood grown in sustainable forests.
The manufacturing process conforms to the environmental
regulations of the country of origin.

For Tom

Acknowledgements

With thanks to Anne Buchanan, Local Studies Librarian at Bath Central Library, living proof that libraries need trained, paid librarians. Also to Victoria Barwell of the Bath Preservation Trust. And as always to Liz Cross, my brilliant editor and Kate Williams for her invaluable copy-editing.

CHAPTER ONE

✳

I didn't hear my cousin's voice at first. It wasn't until the library door was flung open with a bang, making me jump, that I came back down to earth.

'There you are, Sophia!' exclaimed my cousin Jack loudly, bursting into the room. He was a tall, gangly young man with laughing blue eyes, ruddy-faced from many hours spent outdoors. 'I've been looking for you everywhere. Didn't you hear me calling?'

'Vaguely,' I admitted. 'But I didn't realize it was me you wanted.'

'Well, who else would it be?' demanded Jack, exasperated. 'If I'd wanted the servants, I'd have rung for 'em.'

'Sorry. This arrived by carrier this morning . . . ' I showed him the play I was reading, knowing he'd understand. 'It's *The Rover* by Aphra Behn!'

Jack rolled his eyes and looked disapprovingly at the trail of discarded brown paper and string that led to the settle where I now sat curled up by the empty fire grate. I'd spent the past hour chuckling with glee at the wit on the crisp, new pages.

'Another book!' he exclaimed. 'What do you see in them? As if we don't have enough of books with the tutor. You'll be doing your Latin homework next!'

'I've already done it,' I said with a grin, nodding to the desk on the far side of the library where my volume of Virgil lay still open on the desk, my scrawled notes discarded beside it. Also on the desk lay scattered several volumes of poetry, with markers at the pages of my favourite verses.

'Come now, Sophia,' exclaimed Jack, disgusted. 'Put that dull stuff away. I've much better sport to offer you.'

'But it's so funny!' I told him. 'Listen. I must just read you this passage . . . !'

'No!' cried Jack, stuffing his fingers in his ears as I leafed through the play. 'No book nonsense! We've a day off studies and we're going to have some fun.'

'Please!' I begged. 'Just this one joke!'

'Not even one!' Jack risked unblocking his ears long enough to twitch the beautiful, leather-bound volume out of my hands. He cast it carelessly onto the settle and pulled me to my feet.

'Wait!' I said crossly, resisting his efforts to drag me out of the room long enough to check he'd not damaged the pages. Then I allowed myself to be towed away. 'Where are we going?' I asked.

'To the orchard. I've pinned up some playing cards and thought we'd have some sport with my pistols,' he said.

'Oh, all right then,' I agreed, willingly enough.

The overnight rain had cleared away now, leaving a chilly spring day with a fresh wind blowing. I hesitated in the porch wondering aloud whether I needed my cloak. But Jack pulled me impatiently onwards. We passed through the shrubbery, crossed the damp lawn and went through the gate into the walled orchard. A few geese feeding on the grass amongst the apple trees, bright just now with pink blossom, honked and waddled hastily out of our way.

'Here, you take this one,' said Jack, passing me one pistol as he took up the other. 'Take care now, mind those geese!'

I grinned, but handled the weapon gingerly, knowing it could go off at the lightest touch. Jack loved his pistols, and kept them in prime order. He thought himself a fine shot, and it was a sore point with him that I could shoot nearly as well as he could.

'I'll challenge you to a match. Whoever can blow the pips out of three cards with the fewest attempts. I've set us each an ace, a two, and a three.'

I looked across at the posts where Jack had nailed the cards, trying to gauge the difficulty of the task. 'Very well,' I said at last. 'And the stakes?' Neither of us had any money to speak of, so the wager was always a dare or agreement.

'The winner chooses the afternoon activity,' said Jack promptly. 'I want to take the dogs ratting in the barn.'

I pulled a face. I loathed rats with their thick, wormy tails, but I didn't much care for seeing them torn apart by Jack's dogs either.

'I propose,' I said, and hesitated, unsure of my own inclinations.

'No books, Sophia!' warned Jack.

'Oh very well. How about an expedition to South Farm?'

'What the devil for?' demanded Jack, an expression of outrage on his face.

'I have estate business there. I need to speak to the tenant about draining his bottom meadows. They're under water half the year.'

'I can hardly contain myself,' interrupted Jack, sarcastically.

'And it's a fine ride across the moor in this weather,' I continued as though he hadn't spoken. 'We could gallop the horses.'

'I suppose so,' said Jack with a weighty sigh. 'It's all irrelevant anyway, as I shall win.'

'Don't be so sure,' I warned him, straightening my shoulders and bringing my pistol up to aim my first shot. The report echoed in the walled orchard, a tendril of smoke curling from the barrel.

'By Jove, cousin, you're getting to be good,' confessed Jack admiringly, looking at the hole blown clean through the ace of my card. 'It puts a fellow on his mettle, so it does!'

He stood ready himself, sized up the distance to his own card and in one smooth movement brought his arm up and fired. The shot was as clean and accurate as mine, the ace holed neatly.

'Now it gets trickier. Your turn,' he said.

We reloaded and shot on, neck and neck. I missed one shot, then so did Jack. It was all on the last diamond of the three. Jack missed, and cursed fluently. I covered my ears in mock horror.

'Mind your language, cousin, when there's a lady present,' I objected.

Jack snorted, amused. 'What's so funny?' I demanded. 'Do you forget I'm a young lady?'

'You don't often give me reason to remember it,' said Jack frankly. 'I suppose at least you're dressed like one today. Unusual. Haven't you been out riding, then?'

'Yes, of course, hours ago, whilst you were still enjoying your beauty sleep. But it was still raining then. I was soaked when I got back, so I changed.'

'Just as well. You're scandalizing the good people hereabouts. They call you the Squire, you know.'

'Someone has to manage the estate business. Anyway, it interests me, and I have plenty of time on my hands after all.'

'Only because you never sleep! No one has the right to as much energy as you. Damn, it's not decent!'

'I can't help your notion of what's decent! It's a wonder to me that you can slumber so many hours away.'

'Huh,' retorted my cousin scornfully. 'Your shot, cousin.'

'Yes, let's finish this. I'm looking forward to that gallop,' I said provocatively. I took careful aim, steadying my breathing and my hand, confident I could win the match.

'So-*phia*!' exclaimed an outraged voice behind me. Startled, I jumped. The gun exploded in my hand, the shot going wide and burying itself in a nearby tree. I dropped the pistol unheeded into the grass and turned, my limbs turning to water.

'No,' I whispered, horrified. I caught sight of my cousin's face beside me, looking as white and shocked as mine felt.

Striding towards us through the blossoming fruit trees was a tall man, who looked strange and yet at the same time appallingly familiar. He was dressed in what looked, to my untrained eye, to be the very height of fashion. A long, green velvet coat fell in graceful folds around him, turned up in great cuffs at the wrist, and open at the front to reveal a lavishly embroidered waistcoat. The hilt of a sword was just visible through the vents in the coat skirts. He was booted, spurred, and wore a travelling wig. In one hand he held a whip, in the other a three-cornered hat. His guise suggested he'd come straight from a journey, which indeed he must have done, as I'd thought him at least a thousand miles away.

I took in these details as the man walked swiftly towards us. All the time my brain was thinking frantically, no, it cannot be. It cannot possibly be. It was the sight I dreaded above any other. He was burned brown from the tropical sun and had new lines in his face which betrayed the years that had passed since I'd seen him last. But there could be no doubt. Without warning, with no word of announcement, my father had returned. I didn't know what had brought him all the way from the West Indies, but I knew that from this moment, everything was over.

CHAPTER TWO

My father stood staring at me, outrage on his face. His eyes travelled slowly from my windblown hair down to my shabby gown and patched shoes. I flushed painfully under his scrutiny, feeling suddenly awkward and clumsy. Finally, he glanced at the pistol at my feet.

'Can you explain the meaning of this?' he demanded coldly.

'Of what, sir?' I faltered, uncertain what was annoying him most: my apparel or my occupation. My most haunting memory of my father was that I always earned his displeasure, and had often stood before him, as now, afraid, but unsure what exactly I'd done to anger him.

'It's my fault, uncle,' Jack broke in. 'I suggested to Sophia that we might do a little shooting, and . . . '

'Silence, boy,' snapped father, not taking his eyes off me. 'I'll deal with you in your turn.'

Jack subsided at once. I was sure he felt the threat in those words just as I did. 'Have you nothing to say for yourself, Sophia?' my father asked once more. At a loss for what he wanted to hear, and afraid of provoking him, I merely hung my head and shook it slightly.

'Then go to your room. Stay there until I call for you!'

I turned, and Jack took a step to follow me, but was

stopped by my father raising his whip and blocking his way. 'I hadn't dismissed *you*,' he said, and his tone sent a shiver down my spine. I looked back at Jack, and he met my eyes for a moment, his own lacking their usual merry twinkle. He looked afraid.

I walked across the orchard on legs that felt numb. I stretched my hand out to open the door that led out into the park, and saw that it shook. Behind me, I could hear the murmur of my father's voice as he spoke to Jack. I forced myself to keep moving. I closed the door carefully behind me to keep the geese from escaping. As I did so, I heard the first crack of my father's whip and winced. I knew that there was a good chance I would feel the lash myself later, and shivered as I made my way back towards the house.

A large travelling chaise and four horses stood in the sweep of the carriageway before the house, and servants were carrying trunks and valises from the carriage to the house. A figure that resembled, at first glance, a giant crow was standing by the front door overseeing the operation. As I drew closer, I saw that it was in fact a female. A voluminous black gown swayed about her with every movement she made. Her large travelling bonnet was heavily trimmed with black crepe, denoting mourning. My heart sank even lower. I thought I recognized her. Could it be that my aunt Amelia had come to stay?

There had been some huge row, I dimly recalled, at the time of my father's departure. The details were vague in my mind; perhaps I had never quite known them. But I was sure my aunt had refused to take charge of me during his absence. So I'd been left alone here, with Jack, in the charge of a particularly strict and joyless governess.

At that moment, my aunt turned towards me. I backed into the cover of the trees, and then swiftly skirted the house before she caught sight of me. After the shock of seeing my father, I couldn't face Aunt Amelia. We'd always disliked each other.

I ran swiftly up the servants' staircase, arriving two storeys higher, unseen and only very slightly out of breath, at my bedchamber. Restlessly, I paced the small room that had once been my nursery. Jack and I were in trouble. Was there anything I could do? Hurriedly, I pulled open my closet door. There hung my breeches and riding coat. My father certainly wouldn't approve of those. I rolled them up into a bundle and stuffed them up the chimney. They would get sooty, but that was the least of my worries. I tried to anticipate the other things that would put my father in a rage, but my mind was strangely blank.

It was because absolutely everything I'd done would enrage my father. I could hide my breeches, but that was it. As soon as he looked through the paperwork, called for his steward or for my governess, all would be revealed.

Had I not known my father would return some day? In a vague and insubstantial way, I had. But I'd always dreamt he might stay indefinitely on his plantations. Then there was always the possibility he might succumb to some tropical disease, or even be shipwrecked on his return voyage. Then we might never have had to face the reckoning.

My life had begun properly four years ago, when my father left for the West Indies. Freed at last from his long rule of oppression and tyranny, Jack and I had swiftly made a few vital adjustments to the household he'd put in place, and then we'd flourished. The house that had once been sombre, filled with fear and brooding, became a home. We pulled back the heavy curtains to let in the light, ransacked the library and ran through every room shouting with life and joy. We ate our meals in the kitchen, haunted the stables, and rode all over the estate. I'd never known such happiness, not even when my poor mother was still alive, and I was just a small child.

Jack, the orphaned son of my mother's brother, had come to live with us at Littlecote a year before my father had left. He had been here long enough to be as thankful as I was that my father's tyranny had been so completely and miraculously removed.

But he was back. I leant my forehead against the painted wall and groaned aloud. What would my life be now? Any hope my father's nature might have been softened by his long stay abroad had been put to flight in that brief glimpse I'd had of him in the orchard.

I waited in my room to be called, but no call came. My father had always known that the punishment itself could never be as bad as the anticipation, and the long wait brought back dark childhood memories. The sun passed slowly over the noon and crept towards the west. My tummy began first to growl with hunger and then to cry out. I'd eaten nothing today except a hunk of fresh bread and smoked ham in the kitchen at five o'clock this morning.

What could my father be doing all this time? I imagined him questioning the servants, looking through the estate books, and my hands sweated with fear. Dusk came. I lay on my bed, chilled and weak with hunger, unused to being so inactive, and yet unable to think of anything to do to occupy myself. I wished I'd at least had my new play here, and a candle to read it by.

At some point I must have dozed off, for I was startled awake by a noise. I sat up, staring into the pitch darkness wondering what it could be. The sound came again: a soft scratching. A glimmer of light showed through the gap at the bottom of the door. Someone was standing on the other side holding a candle.

I got off my bed, my body stiff with cold, and tiptoed to the door. 'Who is it?' I asked.

'Hush! It's me, Jack.'

I tried to open my door, but it didn't move. I tugged on the handle, but it was locked, the key missing from the keyhole. 'Who's locked my door?' I whispered, shivering at the thought that someone, probably my father, had crept into my room while I slept.

Jack didn't answer, but said instead: 'I've come to bid you farewell.'

'What?' I asked frantically. I tugged at the door handle, heedless of noise, but Jack hushed me again, urgently this time.

'Sophia, I'm not allowed to be here. If I get another beating because you've made a damned racket, I'll never forgive you,' he hissed through the door.

There was a long silence. 'I'm sorry,' I whispered at last. 'Are you running away? I want to go with you.'

'No, I'm being sent away,' replied Jack. 'You can't come where I'm going.'

'Where?' I felt a wave of fear and sadness engulf me at the thought of losing my cousin, my best and only friend since he'd come to live with us six years ago.

'Into the army,' said Jack. 'Your father is to purchase me a commission in a cavalry regiment.'

This news sank in slowly. The thought of Jack being posted to some foreign land to fight battles made me feel sick.

'Sophia?' asked Jack when I said nothing. 'Did you hear me?'

'I heard you. Did you have any choice?' I asked.

'Yes. It was the army or the church. I'm not one for studying and preaching, you know that. A fellow needs some adventure.'

I leant against the door, dazed and lost. The army would suit Jack, of course. He'd look dashing and handsome in his red coat, and would relish the danger. I didn't need to feel sorry for him. 'What of me?' I whispered. 'What shall I do? Has father said?'

There was a long silence on the other side of the door. 'He hasn't. I didn't rat on you, Sophia. You know I wouldn't do that. But he knows pretty much everything.'

I felt fear rise in me again. I nodded, but then realized Jack couldn't see me, and whispered, 'Yes,' because there was nothing else to say.

'Look, Sophia, I have to go. I'm supposed to be in bed.'

'When do you leave?' I asked forlornly.

'At dawn tomorrow. I'm being sent to catch the London stage.'

I felt the loneliness of his departure preparing to

crush me, but I knew I had to stay strong. Besides, Jack wouldn't welcome an emotional scene. I tried for a little humour: 'Don't get yourself shot, cousin,' I said.

The sound of muffled laughter reached me through the oak door. 'Not I,' said Jack jauntily. 'I'll be the one shooting the other fellows.'

'That dandy uniform will make you a fine target,' I retorted.

'I'll be a blur,' Jack promised. 'Sophia . . . '

'Yes?'

There was a pause and then a shadow blocked some of the light beneath the door. I looked down and saw Jack's fingertips reach through to me. I crouched down and touched my fingers to his. It was the nearest we could get to a farewell hug.

'Don't do anything I wouldn't do,' whispered Jack.

'Nothing sensible, then,' I replied. 'Only mad, irresponsible things.'

He laughed softly once more, and then choked slightly. I felt tears spring to my own eyes, and blinked them back fiercely.

'You'll be all right,' Jack said gruffly. 'We've had good times. I won't forget.'

'Nor me. Now go,' I said. The warmth of his fingertips left mine. The glimmer of light faded as his footsteps receded along the passageway. I was alone now.

CHAPTER THREE

I rose heavy-eyed at around six the next morning and splashed my face in yesterday's tepid water in the washstand. It was a grey day out. I had nothing to do until someone let me out, apart from pacing the room and establishing in my mind over and over again that there really was no possibility of escape from the high, narrow window.

It was my aunt Amelia who came to me at last, unlocking my door and opening it. She stood on the threshold, looking me over. 'Your father wishes to see you,' she said. 'If you wish to please him, you won't appear before him in that outmoded gown.'

'But I don't,' I said shortly. My aunt stared at me, and I wondered if she hadn't understood me. 'Wish to please him, that is,' I explained.

Aunt Amelia stood gobbling like a turkey, unable to give expression to her indignation. 'It sh-should be every daughter's earnest desire to please her father,' she stuttered at last.

'Even if I wished to,' I continued, ignoring her stupid remark, 'I have nothing newer.'

Aunt Amelia ran her eyes over my shabby blue wrapping gown one last time before she gave up and led me from the room. 'I wonder if you will be so brave when you stand before your father?' she asked over her shoulder. I wondered too, feeling my legs shake as I descended the stairs. It was hunger, I thought, rather than fear. But it was hard to tell the difference at this moment.

My aunt ushered me into my father's study and left, closing the heavy door softly behind her. My father sat behind his desk writing and didn't look up. There was no chair set out for me. There was never a chair on such occasions. Instead I stood meekly before his desk, hands folded. There was a set routine, a ritual almost, that preceded any punishment he had chosen for me.

A fire burned hot in the grate, filling the room with a stifling heat; a complete contrast to the chill bedchamber I'd just left. I wondered my father could bear it. I reminded myself he'd spent four years in the tropics. For me, however, used to small fires and many hours outdoors, it was sweltering. I was tired, very hungry and quickly started to feel unsteady on my feet. This was the test; a sort of endurance. I fought the dizziness, gripping my hands together and breathing steadily.

After an interminable length of time, and several sheets of closely written paper, my father at last put down his pen. He shook sand over the paper to dry the ink and with great deliberation folded the sheets. With the help of a candle, he melted red wax, dripped it and then pressed his ring into the liquid to seal it. He put the letter to one side, dusted his fingers with a lace-edged pocket handkerchief, and then at long last he looked up.

His features were sharp, aquiline, and his eyes were ice cold, somewhere between blue and grey. I met them for a moment, and then dropped my own, my breathing unsteady. He always confronted me when I was weak. I understood, with sudden insight, what I hadn't comprehended as a child: that this was deliberate. I connected standing in his office with weakness, dizziness, and fainting. He'd gained a strong hold of fear over me. I felt a surge of hatred for the man who had so cruelly dominated my early life.

'First of all, Sophia, I would like an explanation of where my steward is.' His voice was quiet and menacing.

'He was cheating you, father. He put up our tenants' rents and . . . '

'I didn't ask you how he ran my estate. I enquired as to his whereabouts.'

'I . . . don't know,' I confessed.

'I see. But he is demonstrably not here.'

'No, father.' I squirmed under his incredulous gaze.

'In fact, I understand he is no longer in my employ? Dismissed under your orders?'

'I wrote to you! I tried to explain to you how he . . . '

'Yes, you did. And I wrote back and said I was happy with the man. And yet he is gone. I assume you forged my signature?'

I hung my head, feeling my face flush hot. 'But, sir! Since then the accounts for the estate have made such improvements . . . '

'I do not desire to hear justifications. You're a girl. Your head is too weak for such matters. Then there is the governess I employed to teach and chaperone you while I was gone. She was to instruct you in watercolours and fine embroidery. I assume she went the same way as the steward?'

'She had nothing more to teach me, sir, and I needed to finance . . . '

'Silence!'

I halted abruptly, a wave of giddiness threatening to overwhelm me. Breathe, I reminded myself. Stay calm.

'I have found no examples of your watercolours in the house.'

'Sir, I . . . ' I thought of my botched attempts and squirmed again. 'I have no aptitude,' I finished lamely.

'I see. So instead of applying yourself, you gave up?'

I judged it wisest not to reply.

'And embroidery? And fine stitching? Where are your pieces?'

I shook my head miserably. I hadn't done any pieces worthy of display.

'I understand that you have been studying with your cousin?'

'Yes, sir,' I replied, hoping that with this at least, he had no fault to find. I had not been lazy in the past years. Far from it.

'You have been learning Latin, Greek, and mathematics?'

I nodded, suddenly less confident of his approval.

'Can I remind you, Sophia, that your business in life is the getting of a husband? And that in order to achieve that ambition, it is requisite that you show some, if not all, of the accomplishments expected of a young lady of birth and breeding?'

I felt inclined to retort that I didn't desire to get a husband, now or ever, but I bit the words back, knowing they would anger him.

'In what way do you feel that Latin and Greek will assist you in attracting a man of sense, Sophia? A prospective husband does not wish to marry a *scholar*. A female scholar—hah! A true oxymoron! Any man would find such a woman repellent. They invariably die despised old maids.'

'Yes, father,' I whispered. His words buzzed in my head. I knew that somewhere deep inside I was angry at the way he reduced my life to the petty and the domestic, but I was too busy fighting the heat and the weakness in my body to argue.

'The most serious matter of all is that you dispensed with a chaperone. You've been living alone with a young man, and have spent your time in wild and unsuitable pursuits, scandalizing the entire neighbourhood.'

'No, father . . . ' I whispered weakly. He reached under his desk and pulled out a sooty bundle. He shook it out distastefully, and with a lurch of horror I recognized my breeches and jacket. 'The chimney always was your favourite hiding place, Sophia. You should never make the mistake of thinking me stupid. You will be punished for this. Do you understand that you deserve the severest of punishments? Do you?'

The heat and the hunger finally overcame me, and the room spun around me. I lost my balance and sank thankfully into oblivion.

I came to with a shock, the acrid fumes of my aunt's smelling salts under my nose. I pushed them feebly away, retching with disgust. They were removed, and I sat up, more dizzy and sick than ever. My father continued speaking, as though there had been no interruption: 'As you have rendered yourself utterly unmarriageable in this part of the country, Sophia, I have no choice but to take you elsewhere, where your shocking conduct is unknown. Your aunt has advised me, and has also kindly agreed to be your chaperone. Perhaps she will succeed in teaching you decorum where your governess failed. After that it will be the task of your husband to school your wild behaviour. The London season is over now, so I have taken a house at the Bath. We were extremely fortunate to find one as the season is now under way there. A superior house too! The previous tenant died a few weeks ago, leaving an unexpected vacancy. We leave here in three weeks' time.'

'A resort of the very *highest* fashion,' murmured my aunt.

'Thank you, Amelia. I believe we can now dispense with the pleasure of your company,' said my father coldly. My aunt left the room, flustered. Father waited until she'd closed the door to speak again.

'Please, father,' I begged him as soon as we were alone. 'I don't wish to be married. I can behave, I promise. I would so much prefer . . . '

'Nothing could be of less interest to me than your wishes,' he interrupted, his voice icy. 'Your punishment,' he stated. I waited in dread as the silence drew out. I was so ashamed of myself for fainting, but I knew if he whipped me, I would do so again. I felt so ill. 'Your horses, which you were not authorized by me to purchase, will be sold. Your collection of unsavoury and unsuitable books, likewise, will be burned. You will perform this task yourself tomorrow under my supervision.'

I gasped in shock. He had fastened unerringly upon the two things that mattered most to me. 'Please, no . . .' I begged. 'Take the books away, but please, please, do not burn them!'

'They will be burned,' he repeated. 'Books are bad for the female brain. They overheat and overexcite it. The subject matter you have selected is moreover highly indecorous, and not even suited to married ladies. *Poetry!* It has a most disturbing effect. Salacious *plays*!' He shuddered. 'Even worse! In future, you will restrict your reading to sermons and religious discourses. If you prove yourself more sensible of your role as a young lady, I may eventually allow you the occasional history. And if, Sophia,' he paused, stood up and drew himself up to his full height for effect, 'I say, *if* you disgrace me in any way at the Bath, I shall not hesitate to punish you much more severely. Do you understand me?'

'Yes, father,' I whispered.

'You may go. You will keep to your room except at mealtimes.'

I turned and fled. I'd rather a thousand times he'd beaten me than inflict such punishments.

The following morning was the worst experience of my life. The day began quietly enough with breakfast. My father read the newspaper and exclaimed over it, reading passages out loud to us.

'This will serve the damned Whigs right!' he swore, slamming his fist onto the table. 'Setting some blasted

German puppet-king on the English throne instead of a true Stuart. Listen here, Amelia! There were riots in London on the first anniversary of the death of Queen Anne . . . ' He read on in silence, before muttering: 'Constables injured, property damaged, fires started. Whatever next?'

Aunt Amelia was studying her plate with great interest, and only assented half-heartedly. I made no response at all. I knew there had been a new king crowned last year, King George the First, but nothing more. My mind was occupied instead with my punishment and dread of the projected journey to Bath.

I didn't have long to wait. Breakfast was scarcely over when my father ordered the head gardener to have a bonfire lit. Once it was burning fiercely, he made me carry all my precious books to it. I begged, I pleaded. I even wept, but he was unmoved. In fact, I'm certain he enjoyed my distress.

He stood over me, a look of smug satisfaction on his face as he compelled me to put one much-loved book after another onto the fire. The plays of Wycherly, Congreve, and Aphra Behn, even the new one which I'd only half read, all followed one another into the flames. The poetry of Pope, Dryden, Shakespeare and others followed swiftly after. As each beautiful volume curled, blackened and was consumed by the greedy flames, I recalled the sacrifices I'd made to buy it; doing without new clothes, shoes or fires in my bedchamber. Many small hardships that had meant I could save enough of the small household allowance Father had left us to collect the wonderful stories, plays, and poems that were now being destroyed. I felt the pain of each loss like a physical blow.

After that, I was permitted to say farewell to my two horses: my hunter and my hack. I stroked them and hugged them, whispering words of affection and apology, knowing I would never see them again. It almost broke my heart.

I vowed then and there that I would be avenged. It would be my only aim and ambition. The only matter to be resolved was *how*, and I hoped time would provide an answer.

CHAPTER FOUR

The chaise lurched down into a huge dip in the road and swayed violently. I caught at the strap to steady myself, certain that we were to be overturned this time. Miraculously, the carriage righted itself and continued its slow, lumbering progress towards the Bath.

I'd never travelled post before. Sitting still in such a confined space was driving me to desperation. I cast a jealous glance out of the chaise window at my father who was riding on horseback beside us. His manservant was armed with pistols, mounted on a second horse and rode a respectful distance behind. To ride would have been an adventure. This was intolerable.

I'd begged and begged to be left behind this morning to no avail. 'If I *must* go, might I at least not ride?' I'd asked at last. My aunt had given a small scream of horror and a thunderous expression had descended on my father's face. 'I thought I'd told you,' he said awfully, 'that these signs of wildness and ill-breeding in you will not be tolerated. Your suggestion is highly indecorous.'

How I hated that word 'decorum'. It was synonymous in my mind with dire boredom and restrictions. I'd had to endure a long lecture from my aunt on the impropriety of females riding on long journeys. 'Only think of the state you would be in after the first few miles!' she exclaimed as the chaise swayed and bumped. 'Hair tangled, habit muddied, and a spectacle to every yokel who wishes to eye you on the public highroad.' She fell silent for a while, before finally adding, 'Besides, you would find such a long ride quite exhausting.'

'Aunt, I'm never tired,' I told her. I glanced at the book of sermons my father had placed beside me in the carriage and gritted my teeth with anger. Even if I'd been able to swallow my pride and obey him, even if they had not been mind-numbingly dull, it was impossible to read while the chaise pitched and rolled like a ship on the high seas. 'Is there not a better road we could have travelled on?' I asked in exasperation.

'This is the main road from Devon to London, Sophia,' she replied with a titter.

'Good Lord, are all the roads in England so dreadful?' I asked.

'I haven't travelled on them all,' she replied unhelpfully.

'What fun it's going to be, Aunt Amelia, for me to spend several months in a city house with such delightful relatives as you and father,' I remarked. 'I imagine the conversations will be scintillating, don't you?'

My aunt glanced at me, looking flustered and uncertain as to whether I was being intentionally rude. 'You are fortunate to be taken to the Bath,' she replied at last. 'It's a place of the very highest fashion, the very best company, and it would be any girl's dream to spend time there.'

'Any *other* girl, perhaps,' I replied. 'What makes you

suddenly so keen to take charge of me, Aunt? I seem to remember there was a time when you'd rather eat slugs.'

Aunt Amelia gave a stifled shriek and stuttered: 'I . . . what nonsense! Slugs indeed! I . . . I have always cared for you . . . but, my husband, you understand . . . '

'Not a word, I assure you,' I told her. 'What was that about your husband?'

'My *late* husband,' said Amelia, a reproving note in her voice, 'was ill before he died and couldn't have supported the noise and disruption of a young person in the house . . . '

Her voice trailed off, and she failed to meet my eye, instead dabbing at hers with a scented pocket-handkerchief. I felt sure she was lying. Such interest in my welfare after having ignored me for years was odd, to say the least.

My thoughts turned to our destination. 'I'd always understood Bath was a place for old, sick people; a spa for treating gout and dropsy and the like,' I observed.

'Oh!' scoffed my aunt, pleased to be on safer ground and to show off her superior knowledge. 'No, indeed. *That* is a very out-of-date notion. To be sure, people still take the waters, but it is become the first city for refined entertainment after London. And you will find, Sophia, that it is referred to as *the* Bath.'

'Refined entertainment,' I murmured, looking out of the window once more. I could form no picture in my mind of what that might include. How did people of refinement entertain themselves? Having grown up in an isolated manor house, I had no idea.

The countryside crept slowly by. The views transformed gradually from moorland with heath and gorse, to rolling, fertile hills. Towards evening it began to rain, a fine, misty drizzle that would have been a pleasure for me to feel against my face. My father called a halt at the next posting house where he'd booked two bedchambers and a private dining parlour. 'How far is it to the Bath if we must stop overnight?' I asked my aunt, as we climbed the rickety, creaking staircase to our shared bedchamber.

'Do *try* not to be so ignorant, Sophia,' she replied impatiently. 'The journey will take three full days if we are fortunate with the roads and the weather.'

Her words stunned me into silence. Two more days, perhaps longer, in that stifling, cramped post-chaise? I would go mad.

We washed our hands and faces and tidied ourselves by the light of one shared candle, and then my aunt lay down on her bed, her petticoats billowing about her legs. I stared, wondering what it was that made them stand out and sway about so much.

'It's an hour until supper, Sophia,' she told me. 'You should take the opportunity to rest after such a fatiguing day.'

'I would find a walk infinitely more refreshing,' I told her. 'I need to stretch my legs after sitting cooped up.' I headed for the door, ignoring my aunt's squawks of protest: '*Walk?* But where? *Why?*'

I'd had enough of accepting other people's decisions for one day. I ran lightly down the stairs and made my way out of the inn into the busy inn yard. There was a hill behind the inn that looked high enough to give me exercise climbing it, and rewarding views from the top.

It felt wonderful, after the long day of inactivity, to climb the steep slope, and breathe the fresh, bracing air into my lungs. I climbed stone walls and vaulted over gates, as my cousin had taught me, until I reached the summit. The wind was strong up here, but the rain had stopped, and the prospect across rolling green hills was magnificent. I sat on a tree stump and drank it in.

I soon lost myself in my thoughts. They began with how much I missed my cousin Jack, and concluded with endless speculations over what our stay in the Bath would be like. I was furious with my father's assertion of power over me and determined to fight back. I wasn't going to make this easy for him.

When I arrived back at the inn, windblown and out of breath, the landlady called to me. 'Your father is concerned about your whereabouts, Miss,' she said. 'He'd ordered dinner half an hour since. I'm to show you straight in.'

Cursing myself for staying away so long, I followed her into the private dining parlour. My father and aunt sat at a table laid with covered dishes. Both had dressed for dinner. My aunt looked very imposing in a fresh black mourning gown, and a black shawl, and my father had shed his riding clothes and travelling wig for a full-bottomed wig, an embroidered silk waistcoat and an expensive-looking brown velvet coat, great cuffs turned back to reveal ruffles of costly lace. I thought resentfully that he refused to spend money on essential repairs to his tenants' houses, or to invest it in improving their farms, but did not appear to begrudge any expense on his own attire. I was scruffy by comparison, but it was too late to tidy myself. A servant moved forward to remove the covers as I approached the table.

'Stand, please, Sophia,' instructed my father. 'Behind your chair.'

He shook the lace back from his wrists, pulled his pocket-watch out of his waistcoat pocket and consulted it. 'You have kept us waiting almost thirty minutes. It is an insult to the cook who prepared this meal and to your aunt and me.'

'I'm so sorry, father,' I said as humbly as I could manage. 'I didn't realize how late it was.'

'You had no business leaving the inn at all, and will not do so again.'

After that, my father didn't speak to me again. The covers were removed and he and my aunt served themselves as I stood and watched. There was roast beef, gravy, a chicken fricassee, a selection of vegetables, a basket of freshly baked white bread and a dish of golden butter. A bottle of red wine stood on the table and the level sank swiftly. I could feel my mouth watering. I hoped I would soon be allowed to sit down and eat.

I was disappointed. When the two of them had eaten their fill, the servant was ordered to clear the table. He removed the half-eaten dishes as I looked longingly at them. Once, as he passed me, he caught my eye and made a sympathetic grimace. He was a friendly-looking young man and he reminded me of Jack.

Dessert was put on the table next. A curd pudding, a fruit jelly, and a dish of marzipan sweetmeats. My stomach gave a loud rumble. I could see from my father's satisfied expression that he'd heard it. The servant removed my untouched plate and laid a dessert bowl and spoon in their place.

'She won't require those,' said my father, waving them away. 'A delicious meal. My compliments to the cook.'

'Thank you, sir,' said the servant, bowing slightly before he left the room. I stood and watched as my aunt ate a jelly and a great number of sweetmeats, and my father ate the entire pudding.

My back was aching now. I cultivated a look and pose of indifference, even though I would be so hungry tonight I'd be unable to sleep. At last my aunt rose, and left my father to his brandy. I accompanied her back upstairs where she locked our door behind her and put the key under her pillow. 'Your father's orders,' she explained, seeing me watching her.

I walked to the window and looked down the sloping roof at the posting yard, now quiet for the night, the horses stabled and resting. 'I'm so fortunate,' I sighed.

Aunt Amelia looked bewildered. 'You are, if only you realized it,' she said.

'I do, truly, Aunt. With such a wise father, so devoted to my discipline, I'm sure I shall learn to behave well in no time at all.' I spoke earnestly, keeping all trace of laughter from my voice. I could see I'd thoroughly perplexed her.

I changed and got into bed, lying meekly beneath the linen sheets. I watched Aunt Amelia undress with a horrified fascination: all those layers of petticoats she wore.

And at last the secret of the swaying skirts was revealed. Beneath her petticoats, attached to her waist, my aunt wore what looked like a huge birdcage of wires, bone, and tapes. I sat up, staring in astonishment. 'What *is* that thing you're wearing, Aunt Amelia?' I asked, quite forgetting it might be rude to watch someone undress.

Amelia looked round. 'This?' she asked, unfastening the cage. 'This is a hoop, Sophia. Dear me, how is it possible to be so ignorant? Anyone would think you were a savage from the Americas, and not a baronet's daughter from Devonshire.'

She stepped out of the hoop, laying it aside, pulled a nightgown over her head and climbed into her bed, blowing out the candle with a puff. I lay back, wishing I were indeed a savage, so that I wouldn't have to go to the Bath and be a fine lady. A dreadful thought struck me. 'Aunt, you are not expecting *me* to wear such a contraption?' I demanded. 'For it is utterly out of the question.'

'Go to sleep, Sophia,' was all the response I got.

Despite all that wine and good food, it seemed to take an eternity before my aunt finally fell asleep and began to snore rhythmically. Restless with hunger, I got out of bed and cautiously pulled my gown and shoes back on. I stood looking down at her sleeping face for a moment. 'Start as you mean to go on,' I murmured to myself. Then I threw up the sash window and climbed out.

CHAPTER FIVE

The roof tiles were slippery with the rain that had fallen earlier in the day, but I managed to keep my balance as I descended carefully as far as the gutter. From there, it should have been an easy drop down to the yard, but unfortunately my gown snagged on a broken bracket as I tried to jump. I dangled there for a moment or two, kicking helplessly, cursing the loss of my breeches, before finally freeing the fabric with an ominous tearing sound. Then I dropped to the ground.

I straightened up, brushing myself down, and looked around. I was shocked to see what looked like half the servants from the inn sitting on upturned crates, staring at me, their faces a picture of blank astonishment.

'You really need to get that guttering repaired,' I remarked, to hide my embarrassment. 'It's a menace to guests who are compelled to use the roof as an exit. Just look what it's done to my gown!'

There was a moment of shocked silence, and then one of the young men began to laugh. I recognized him as the waiter who had served dinner. 'It must have escaped our notice, Miss,' he said. 'For some reason, our guests usually prefer the stairs.'

'Even on such a fine night?' I asked, feigning amazement.

The kitchen maids giggled, and I found myself relaxing, the blush fading from my face. Now that I looked more closely there were only four servants: two young men and two girls.

'I don't know how it comes about, after the fine supper that you serve here,' I told them, 'but I find myself quite famished.'

The servant lad chuckled. 'I thought it might be hunger drove you down here,' he remarked. 'It fair broke my heart to see you standing there, not allowed to touch so much as a morsel.'

'It broke mine too,' I agreed. 'I came down in the earnest hope of remedying the situation.'

The servants glanced at one another uncertainly. 'We've finished serving now,' explained the lad. 'The tables have been set for breakfast. I don't think you'd be comfortable in the tap room, neither. There's only men in there tonight, two of 'em your father's coachman and groom.'

'Oh, that wouldn't do at all. But as we already agreed, it's a fine night, and starlight makes a grand setting for a meal. I'd be grateful for anything: a hunk of bread, an apple, whatever you can spare. You can add it to my father's bill, naturally.' I smiled at the thought of how furious my father would be when he saw how I'd tricked him. It would be worth any punishment, I thought recklessly.

The servant lad disappeared into the inn, reappearing a few minutes later carrying a bundle wrapped in a clean napkin. 'Here you are, Miss,' he said handing it over. 'This should keep the wolf from the door. And the land-lady don't know I took it, so no need to bother with the bill.'

I took the bundle gratefully, sat down on a spare box and unwrapped the feast. There was a slice of fresh white bread, lavishly buttered, a thick slice of ham, a square of cheese, an apple and a generous selection of the sweet-meats that I'd not been allowed at supper.

'This is wonderful! Thank you,' I exclaimed, sinking my teeth eagerly into the bread. The servants watched me eat. 'Does your father make a practice of starving you?' asked one of the maids.

'Well, he's been away in Jamaica for four years,' I said between mouthfuls. 'So I'd almost forgotten it's his favourite punishment. He's been back less than a fortnight, and this is the third meal I've been deprived of.'

'Who helped you out the other times?' asked the sec-ond girl, a plump lass with red cheeks and bright eyes.

'No one. I starved!' I said with a sigh.

'Oh! I couldn't bear that,' said the girl. 'I love my food!'

The others laughed and began teasing her a little. I lis-tened to their banter, enjoying my late meal and gradu-ally feeling the weakness fade. One by one, the servants were called back in to work, until only the young man who'd brought me the food was left. I ate everything in the napkin, shook the crumbs out, folded it carefully and returned it to him.

'I'm more grateful than I can say,' I said. 'You deserve a handsome tip, and I'm very sorry I can't give you one.'

'Consider it a favour,' he replied. 'So where are you journeying to?'

'We're going to Bath,' I told him. '*The* Bath, I should say.'

'You'll be going to catch a fine husband then,' he said with a mischievous grin.

'Not if I can avoid it,' I retorted. 'I have no opinion of husbands!'

The young man laughed out loud, and then broke off with a quick glance behind him to check his merriment hadn't been overheard. 'How's that then?' he asked.

'Well, just imagine the type of man my father is likely to select for me! Older of course, sober, and strict enough that my father will consider him able to tame me . . . ' I shuddered at the vision my words had conjured up.

The young man's eyes twinkled with amusement. Then his smile faded. 'My old man took my sister off to the Bath over a year ago. I've been thinking for some time I should go check on her, if only I could get the money together. See how she's doing. He promised he had an opening for her in a respectable line of work, but I don't trust the old rascal.'

'You have father trouble too?' I asked, raising a sympathetic eyebrow.

'Of a different kind,' he said.

'Have you not had letters from her?' I asked curiously.

He shook his head. 'I could read 'em, just about, but she can't write,' he explained.

'I could look out for her, if you like?' I offered. 'I could write you a letter if I meet her, then you'd know she was safe.'

34

'You'll be consorting with the fine ladies and gents in the city, not working girls,' he objected.

'I shan't care for that,' I said swiftly. 'I'll ask for her if I get the chance, I promise you. It's the least I can do. What's her name? And your name too?'

'I reckon you'll not be allowed to,' he replied. 'But if you wish to know my name, it's Bill Smith. And my sister's Jenny.'

I put out my hand. 'Pleased to meet you, Bill Smith,' I said. 'I'm Sophia Williams.' After a moment's hesitation, Bill took my outstretched hand and shook it.

'If it so happens that you should have a chance to look for Jenny,' he said, 'you'll know her by her little finger on her left hand. Half of it's missing.'

'I'll remember that. Now I have one more favour to ask of you,' I confessed.

'You need to get back into your room?' he guessed. 'Can you climb back up if I boost you up as far as the gutter?'

'Definitely,' I agreed. 'I have some experience of climbing.'

'I'll bet you do,' he said. 'I reckon you're a rare handful. If I hadn't seen what your father's capable of, I'd feel right sorry for him.'

I slept deeply and woke early the next morning feeling much more cheerful. The scramble back up the roof and in through the window had been accomplished easily, and my aunt never knew I'd left the room.

We breakfasted and then four horses were put to our chaise. As we rumbled over the cobbles out of the yard, Bill was at the gate, and waved a discreet farewell to me.

I gave him a smile and a small wave, and then we were under way; another long day of lurching through ruts and potholes. The following day was no better. In the afternoon, it began to rain heavily, turning the roads swiftly into a quagmire.

'As if they weren't bad enough already!' exclaimed my aunt, when the chaise got stuck for the third time, and we had to get out and walk while the coachmen freed it. I was glad to escape the confines of the carriage, and strode ahead happily, ignoring the rain and the mud.

A little further on, I came upon a commotion. A stage-coach had overturned and crashed into a stone wall on one side of the road, leaving the horses injured, and passengers scattered across a wide area, nursing cuts and bruises. I ran forward to see if I could help, but there was already a doctor in attendance, splinting a broken leg and bandaging the worst cuts.

Just at this point, the road ran between two walls, narrow, muddy and treacherous, and was now completely blocked. The accident was clearly recent, and no one had yet had a chance to think about shifting the coach. I looked at the way it was jammed between the walls and judged it would be hours before the road was clear again.

'Here's a fine mess,' said my father riding up behind me. 'Just as I'd hoped to reach the Bath tonight. What do we do now?'

We were told there was an alternative route to the Bath. With difficulty, we turned our chaise in the narrow road and by early evening we reached the steep hill that led down to the city from the north.

CHAPTER SIX

Dusk was falling, and the road ahead of us plunged down the steepest hill I'd ever seen. The chaise came to a slow, hesitant halt. The coachman pulled the door open and let down the steps. 'You're going to have to walk,' said my father from where he sat astride his horse. 'This hill's too steep for the horses.'

I got out at once. My aunt sighed, complained that her shoes pinched and finally emerged clutching her vinaigrette. 'What a fatiguing journey,' she murmured, casting a look of horror at the road that dropped away into the evening gloom ahead of us. '*Such* a steep hill; I really don't know how I . . . ' She gathered her heavy black petticoats in her hands and took a few hesitant steps. Impatiently, my father turned away and spoke to his man. 'Ride ahead now, will you, Brown,' he ordered. 'Announce our imminent arrival and make sure supper will be ready for us. We shan't be long now.'

Brown hesitated and then nodded and rode on down the hill. Father rode ahead more slowly. Our groom was already at the offside leader's head, holding his bridle, so I went to the nearside horse to help.

'I don't know if you can manage, Miss,' the groom said, uncertainly. 'It'll be hard work. You'll need to hold tight to stop 'im speeding up as we go down. The carriage is heavy with all this luggage, otherwise it wouldn't be so bad.'

'I understand,' I nodded. 'Let's go.'

We set off slowly, one step at a time down the steep road, feeling the push of the heavy chaise in the harness, holding the horses back hard when they were tempted to move forward any faster. It was back-breaking work, especially whenever the chaise wheels lurched forward out of a rut in a rush, threatening to propel us off our feet. I found myself frequently leaning back against my horse, forcing him to slow with my own body weight.

We descended into a bend in the road, overshadowed on either side by tall trees. It was darker under their profuse spring foliage, and the evening air seemed damp and stale somehow. As my father rode back to see how we were doing, the stillness of the evening was abruptly shattered by a gunshot. We all jumped, Aunt Amelia screamed, and the horses plunged and reared in their traces, fighting to bolt forward down the hill.

'Hold them!' yelled the groom desperately. I tried, but my small weight was no longer enough, and I was dragged along the stony ground by the terrified beasts. My father flung himself off his own horse and grabbed my horse's reins at the bit, forcing it to stand still with brute strength. As we all struggled, our attention completely engrossed in our dangerous task, two horsemen rode out of the trees, straight at us.

'Halt!' they shouted, as though we were not already putting every ounce of our strength into doing just that. The horses were finally brought to a stop. Weak with relief, I turned to see who these travellers were, to be confronted with two masked riders and the muzzle of a pistol. 'Stand and deliver!' shouted the bigger of the two men in a rough voice.

It went through my head even at that very moment, facing the gun and the possibility of death, how pathetically melodramatic and worn-out that line was. It was every child's playtime cry, and I wondered they could think of nothing more original to say.

I had no money on me; not so much as a farthing and not a single trinket. Indeed, I owned nothing at all of any value. So I merely stood there, waiting for the scene to unfold. My father let go of the horse and raised his hands, backing slowly away. I guessed he had a pistol strapped to his saddle and was trying to reach it.

'Stand still!' ordered the masked rider, clearly suspecting the same.

Father froze, looking furious, hands raised. My aunt was shaking like a leaf and whimpering. I looked quickly away, hiding a smile, delighted to see *them* humiliated instead of me for a change.

While the large highwayman kept us covered with his pistol, the small one slipped off his horse to pocket our valuables, taking care not to step between us and the gun. He took a purse from my father, some coins from the servants, and a necklace and two rings from my terrified aunt. He patted their pockets, their hats and their sleeves for hidden valuables. When he came to me, I saw that below the mask the freckled face was scarcely more than that of a child.

'You're welcome to search me, but I have nothing,' I

said. As he reached forward to check anyway, I thought there was something incongruous about him. I looked closely at his slim figure and what I could see of his face as he patted my clothing expertly and saw smooth skin with no hint of down on it. This was not a youth at all, I realized; this was a girl, her gender hidden behind a mask and a black coat. I confess: I was impressed. The thought that a young girl had the courage to rob travellers on the king's highroad gave me a thrill. The fact that it was my own father she was robbing added spice.

The girl reached up to check the neckline of my gown for a necklace, and that's when I saw her left hand. Or, more precisely, I noticed the little finger, the end mutilated, and I caught my breath with shock.

'Jenny?' I murmured. I could hardly believe the coincidence. The girl blinked, but showed no other sign that I'd spoken. 'Your brother Bill's worried about you,' I said softly. The girl didn't reply. She turned away from me without another glance and climbed inside our chaise, presumably searching it for more booty. But if she found anything, I didn't see it when she emerged. The two riders made off, disappearing into the gathering darkness under the trees as swiftly as they'd appeared.

I wondered whether it was possible there were two girls in Bath with part of their little finger missing, and concluded it was more than likely. For all I knew, it could be a common injury. Probably I'd been mistaken, and the girl wasn't Bill's sister. It was just as well; I was pretty sure he wouldn't have considered highway robbery remotely respectable.

I expected rage from my father at being so outwitted. Imagining our whole trip might be ruined if he'd been robbed of all his money, I waited gleefully to hear what he would say. But, to my disappointment, he merely disappeared briefly inside the chaise and then emerged with a satisfied look upon his face.

'Pull yourself together, Amelia,' he said sharply to my aunt who was sitting by the road, rocking backwards and forwards, close to hysteria. 'They're gone now, no one's hurt and there's no harm done. Drive on,' he nodded to the coachman. Just like that, the excitement was all over, leaving us to resume our tortuous descent to the city. I puzzled over my father's calm. The robbery hadn't upset him, and for the life of me I couldn't work out why.

The lanterns at the city gates were in sight before the coachman considered the road level enough for us to climb back into the chaise. My aunt leant back against the cushions, sighing with exhaustion, her eyes closed. I was not in the least tired and waited with eager anticipation to see the city.

Brown was waiting for us at the archway, leading his horse. As we came into sight, he mounted and led us to the right. 'Trim Street is outside the city walls, sir,' he told my father. 'Follow me.'

We rumbled on, skirting the walls. In only a few minutes we pulled up in a narrow street between two rows of pale buildings. Torches flickered outside them, giving me a glimpse of tall, gracious town houses, all joined together in a long row. The façades were plain and yet elegant.

When we halted, I didn't wait for the steps of the chaise to be let down, instead jumping down into the cobbled street and looking around me, consumed with curiosity. In the distance I could hear the deep chime of heavy church bells ringing.

'Impetuosity is a grave fault in a girl, Sophia,' said my father coldly. 'Strive to curb it.'

'Yes, sir,' I said automatically.

The door of number seven, the finest house in the street, opened, light spilling out of it. We'd arrived at our new home.

CHAPTER SEVEN

At breakfast the next day, which we ate in the ground-floor dining parlour, I noticed my father pull out his pocket watch and consult it. I stared at it, puzzled.

'How did the highwaymen miss that yesterday?' I asked.

My father regarded me ironically, and his eyes flickered towards the new butler who was clearing dishes from the table. I became sure there was some secret. I left my father reading a London newspaper, and followed my aunt upstairs to the main room, a handsome apartment on the first floor, with huge south-facing windows letting in the bright spring daylight. As my aunt sank onto the settle with a sigh and declared herself delighted with the house, I took note of her pearl necklace and matching bracelet.

'How fortunate that the robbers didn't find your pearls either, ma'am,' I said, knowing my aunt was far more likely to be forthcoming than my father.

'Isn't it indeed?' she exclaimed. 'I thought your father was mad wanting to conceal our valuables in the chaise! I've always kept them on me before, feeling certain that was safest, but just think! They would all have been stolen to feather some scoundrel's nest by now!

Instead, he advised me to wear only paste and worthless trinkets, and to keep a purse filled with coins of small value as a decoy. So clever! Those men got little enough from robbing us.'

I smiled and nodded, as though admiring my father's wisdom, but all the while thinking: *So, he has a hiding place somewhere in the chaise, does he? I can find that.* Not that I had any reason to do so. It merely seemed like good sport to know my father's secrets.

'Can I go out and see the city this morning?' I asked.

My aunt shrieked with horror. 'Dressed as you are? Sophia, really, have you no sense at all?'

I thought that was fine talking coming from the person who'd just betrayed my father's secret hiding place to me. I said with as much politeness as I could muster: 'But no one knows me here. What can it signify?'

Aunt Amelia shuddered. 'They soon will know you, and think if anyone remembered seeing you in such a dowdy, outmoded gown. Pray, do not think of it.'

'Then . . . ?' I began, wondering how I should pass a whole morning shut into such a small house without even books to occupy me. I was interrupted by a loud knock at the front door. I ran to the window, wondering who could be calling on us in a city where we knew no one. There was a bustle and the sound of voices, footsteps on the stairs and the door was opened.

'Mr Richard Nash, Master of the Ceremonies!' announced the butler.

My aunt jumped to her feet, flustered, and sank into a deep curtsey, her black petticoats billowing about her. 'Mr Nash!' she exclaimed. '*Such* an honour.'

The visitor bowed with exquisite elegance to us both. 'On behalf of the Bath Corporation, may I welcome you to the city and wish your stay here will be a pleasant one? I shall certainly do my best to make it so.'

'Thank you!' cried my aunt, overcome. 'Allow me to present my niece, Miss Williams. Please forgive her appearance. She urgently needs to visit a dressmaker.'

I curtseyed awkwardly, stunned by the appearance of our visitor. I'd thought my father richly dressed until this moment. I now realized that he was but a pale shadow compared to this man. Nash's heavily-powdered long-bottom wig fell about his shoulders in a mass of carefully-arranged grey curls. The tails of his cravat were not worn loose as my father wore his, but instead tucked neatly through a buttonhole. A diamond pin glinted among the rich lace. A pink waistcoat, intricately embroidered with navy and silver thread, his buttons a gleaming silver to match, contrasted with a navy coat with absurdly large cuffs folded back to reveal a quantity of expensive lace at his wrists and jewelled rings on his fingers. Nash wore no sword at his side, which surprised me in such a fine gentleman, but instead carried an elegant walking-stick. Clocked silk stockings were fastened neatly above his knees, and square-toed black shoes with large, sparkling buckles and high red heels completed the vision.

I fear I gaped. Nash noted my gaze and smirked, clearly pleased by the attention. He no doubt consid-ered it admiration, and his rightful due. I don't know if I admired him or not. I think I was mainly taken aback that any man would spend so much time and money on his appearance.

At that moment my father came into the room, still attired in his morning gown and nightcap as he had been at breakfast. I blushed for him, but neither he nor Mr Nash seemed the least concerned at his state of undress. They exchanged conventional greetings. My father complained about the robbery last night, and Mr Nash was suitably shocked and sympathetic. He warned him against the men who carried the sedan chairs in the city and then began speaking of the baths, the pump room, and instructing my father in how he should set about subscribing to balls at the Guildhall and to Harrison's tea rooms and private gardens. It all sounded insufferably dull. My attention soon wandered to the window. It was a fine day out and I was just wondering whether there was any way I could escape and enjoy it when I realized a silence had fallen in the room. I looked round and found everyone staring at me. My father looked angry.

'I'm sorry . . . ' I began automatically, wondering what I'd missed. Mr Nash kindly put me out of my misery:

'I was just asking, Miss Williams, if you are not looking forward to the balls at the Bath? All young ladies love to dance, do they not?'

I hesitated, uncertain how to reply. Under my father's frowning stare, I couldn't tell the truth: that I'd never danced, knew no other young ladies, and would rather die than appear at a ball. 'It will be . . . a new experience for me,' I mumbled at last. There was another uncomfortable silence, broken by a loud peal of church bells.

'More visitors,' said Mr Nash with every appearance of delight. 'We welcome every new arrival of note with bells. Did you hear them ringing for you last night?'

'That was for our sake?' asked my aunt, apparently overcome by the thought.

'Yes, indeed,' said Mr Nash. 'I'll leave you now, if you'll excuse me, but please do speak to me if there is anything you need to know or if I can assist you in any way.' He rose, bowed low with great dignity and took his leave.

'Who the *devil* was that pompous, self-important ass?' demanded my father as soon as we heard the front door close downstairs.

'Oh, Sir Edward!' exclaimed Aunt Amelia. 'That was Beau Nash! Such an honour that he should call upon us personally!'

'Who is Beau Nash when he's at home? *Beau* Nash, indeed,' scoffed my father. 'An under-bred fellow if ever I saw one!'

'You quite mistake the matter, my dear brother,' Aunt Amelia assured him. 'That is to say, I believe his origins *may* be quite low, his father was a glass manufacturer from Swansea or some such thing. But he is king of Bath!'

'King?' cried my father, and although he clearly hadn't liked Mr Nash, I could see now he was simply enjoying contradicting my aunt. 'If the place has crowned that confounded, jumped-up nobody king, then I say we should pack our bags and leave at once, because it won't be at all the sort of place I want to stay in! What the deuce did you mean by dragging me here, woman?'

'But, Sir Edward,' my aunt wailed, thinking he was serious. 'We've only just arrived! And I assure you all the best people come here, and the entertainments are quite the finest outside London. And Beau Nash is *very* respected, although, I confess, I thought his linen not quite clean, but truly . . . '

'I'll give it two days!' said Sir Edward. 'And if they're all like him, we're leaving and you can pay the bills.' My father slammed out of the room and my aunt dissolved into floods of tears. I took the opportunity to slip quietly away, fetch my cloak and leave the house.

I walked along Trim Street, thinking how new and clean it all was; the sandstone of the houses such a pale yellow it was almost white. To my great excitement, I found a building with *Trim's Theatre* painted onto a sign. I resolved to ask my father about seeing a play there at the first opportunity.

There was a slight whiff of rotten eggs in the air but I couldn't track down where it was coming from. One end of the street led into fields and the other into a building site, so I took the only other route, a short street called Trim Bridge running at right angles to Trim Street, which took me across the city walls and into the city of Bath itself.

The city was a crowded, bustling maze of narrow streets, alleys, and jumbled old houses of all shapes and styles, mostly built from the same pale-yellow stone. I roamed through the crowds, avoiding the piles of rubbish lying in the streets, looking around me with great curiosity. I'd visited towns before, once or twice, but Bath was bigger, dirtier, and busier than anything I'd seen. It smelt bad too, over and above the rotting refuse that lay about; that rotten-egg smell grew stronger the further I walked into the city.

Two men pushed roughly past me, carrying a huge, heavy box slung on poles between them, and I was surprised to see a lady in a fine gown sitting inside it. This must be one of the sedan chairs Mr Nash had spoken of. Before long, I realized I'd reached the fashionable part of the city. Instead of beggars, workmen, and traders, the streets were filled with ladies and gentlemen in absurdly fine clothes, sauntering at their leisure and gazing into the shop windows. The windows truly drew the eye: colourful displays of all kinds of luxuries which I was certain I'd never have a use for.

I reached a square where one building dominated: a fine abbey built of the same pale stone soared above the buildings around it, dwarfing and outclassing them. It was quite the most beautiful church I'd ever seen, and I stood admiring it for a moment before a noisy crowd caught my attention. Finely-dressed people, and a few less fine, were wandering in and out of a building. Inside was a kind of gallery where they were leaning over a balustrade, laughing and pointing at a scene below.

I'd finally tracked down the source of the smell. Here below me was one of the famous baths that the city was named for. I looked down and saw bathers of both sexes, dressed with great modesty in some yellowed canvas garments, floating around in the murky waters below us. As I watched, one spectator threw an apple core into the bath, causing shrieks of laughter among those around him.

'Here, let's throw something bigger in,' cried a young man. 'How about you?' he asked, grasping a young lady around the waist.

'Ooh, don't you dare!' she shouted and began shrieking in the most vulgar way as he hoisted her into the air.

I couldn't believe he'd really do it, unless perhaps he was drunk this early in the morning; it was a long drop and the young woman could be hurt.

'No, wait!' cried another young man. 'I've a better idea!' So saying he darted out of the building, grabbed hold of a dirty stray dog that was gobbling scraps off the pavement, ran back in with it and flung the poor creature bodily over the wall.

The dog fell with a great splash, and then thrashed wildly in the waters. The bathers were all screaming and fighting each other to get out of its way.

It was very childish, but mildly amusing, to see such finely-dressed people behaving so badly. I grinned a little, left the gallery and walked on around the abbey. There were coffee houses here, people sitting inside eating and reading newspapers and books. I saw ladies eating syllabubs and jellies in cook shops and everywhere I could smell the aroma of freshly-baked, buttery bread. I soon felt hungry. After all, it was some time since breakfast. I asked a sooty chimney sweep the way back to Trim Street and followed the directions he gave me.

Walking along Trim Bridge, I was suddenly seized from behind and dragged under an archway into a deserted yard. A firm hand was clapped across my mouth and another held a knife to my throat. I was so astonished it didn't even occur to me to resist.

'Don't even think about hollerin'. This knife's sharp and I ain't afraid to use it,' said a girl's voice in my ear. A thrill of excitement ran through me. I'd expected to be bored to tears in a city, but I'd been completely mistaken. The hand was removed cautiously from my mouth. I was silent and still, awaiting events. 'Tell me what you know of Bill Smith,' said the voice.

I almost laughed. 'Jenny? However did you find me so quickly?' I demanded. 'You could just have come up and asked.'

The hand was clamped back over my mouth and the knife pressed tighter. 'I didn't say as I was called Jenny,' the girl hissed in my ear. 'I jest asked what you know of Bill. And you didn't take much finding. I asked around where you lived and here you is, wandering about like a reg'ler green 'un. Now keep yer voice down.'

As the hand released me cautiously once more, I said: 'I'm not saying a word at knifepoint.'

'I'll make yer!' said the voice fiercely.

'How? By cutting my throat?' I asked calmly. 'I won't be able to say anything then. I don't mean you any harm, you know.'

'I'm supposed to trust you, am I?'

'I really don't care,' I replied. 'I liked your brother, but this is the second time you've held me up. You haven't made a good impression so far.'

'All right then,' said the girl, loosening her grip. 'But you don't look round.' The knife was withdrawn, and I breathed freely again. I could feel my heart beating fast in my chest, but it was with excitement rather than fear. 'Bill was working at the Golden Lion on the post road here,' I said. 'We got talking and he said he had a sister called Jenny at the Bath. He's thinking of coming to look for her.'

There was a sharp intake of breath behind me. I had to master an impulse to look round. It was frustrating not being able to see who I was talking to. 'I promised him to look out for her,' I added. 'I said I'd write to him and tell him how she was.'

'You can tell him she's fine. He don't need to come here. Right?'

'He's concerned,' I said carefully, 'that her father might have put her into a line of business that isn't respectable.'

'Tell him,' the girl said, 'that she's set up jest fine and dandy; nothing he wouldn't like. He's not to bother with such a long journey.'

'Can I give him your direction?' I asked.

There was a long silence behind me. 'Jenny?' I asked. I suddenly had the feeling there was no one there. Turning round, I found I was quite right. I was standing alone in the yard, talking to myself.

CHAPTER EIGHT

'Where *have* you been, you troublesome girl?' demanded my aunt, seizing me and shaking me the instant I got home. 'You're lucky your father's gone out or you'd be shut in your room for a week!' Aunt Amelia dragged me into the withdrawing room and rang the bell. A footman appeared at once.

'Call two sedan chairs, will you?' my aunt demanded. 'And hurry!'

'If one is for me, I can walk,' I said at once.

'Walk around the city? In those clothes?' My aunt shuddered.

'But, Aunt, I've already done so, and indeed, no one stared at all.'

'You've been walking . . . ?' my aunt began faintly, and groped at once for her smelling salts. 'Please, don't tell me. I'd far rather not know. For goodness' sake, Sophia, go and put a comb through your hair and wash your face! You look a perfect fright. Hurry!'

By the time I came back downstairs, two chairs await-ed us outside the front door. 'Where are we going?' I asked, as my aunt propelled me out to them. 'I want some luncheon. I'm starving!'

'You should have been here when it was served.' She

pushed me towards the sedan chair, but I dug my heels in. 'I'm not getting in that thing, until you tell me where we're going,' I said loudly.

'Hush, girl! We're going to the dressmaker's. We both need new clothes before we can make an appearance.'

'No,' I said at once. 'I've seen the sort of clothes ladies wear in the city, and you're not dressing *me* like that.' The chairmen were sniggering, but I didn't care. I turned and began to walk towards the house, but my aunt grasped my arm with unexpected strength. 'You'll regret this, Sophia,' she hissed. 'And you *will* go to the dressmaker's sooner or later, whether you like it or not.'

I twisted away from her and went into the house. From the window, I watched as she climbed into the chair, and the two men bore her away. I grinned, rang the bell and asked the footman to bring me some food. He looked embarrassed. 'I'm sorry, Miss. It's the master's orders. We're not to serve food to you outside of meal times.' He bowed. 'Would there be anything else?'

'No, thank you.' I dismissed him, and flung myself furiously onto a settle. I was humiliated at being refused food. How *dared* my father treat me like this?

An hour later my father and my aunt both returned, she in a chair, he walking beside it. I was thoroughly bored, still angry and had been considering going out again, to make my rebellion complete.

'Well, Sophia,' said my father as he entered the room where I stood looking out of the window. 'I hear you have not yet learned sense or compliance with my orders.'

I looked at him silently, wondering what he would do.

His voice grew soft and dangerous. 'The dressmaker is calling here in a few minutes' time. You will see her and make no fuss, do you understand me?'

The menace in his voice had the effect of drying my mouth in fear, but I gathered my courage to answer him back: 'I don't wish to wear such gowns, or to appear in society, father. You cannot force me to do so.'

He came closer so that he loomed over me. 'You understand very little about me if you think that I cannot force you to do anything I like,' he said softly.

There was a knock at the door downstairs and the bustle of an arrival.

'You'll see the dressmaker now,' said my father. 'If there is any trouble at all, I shall come in here, forcibly strip you of your clothes and hold you still while she measures you for new ones.'

I wanted to tell him that he could scarcely make me attend balls, even if he could force me to dress, but somehow I couldn't reply. My tongue cleaved to the roof of my mouth, and I had to grit my teeth to stop myself shaking. My old fear of my father was reasserting itself. Every capitulation I made reinforced his power over me, but the violence in him brought back so many hateful, half-suppressed memories from my childhood. I could feel my resolve crumbling.

So it was that when the elegantly-attired dressmaker entered the room in my father's wake a few moments later, I stood silent and still while he explained to her that he wished me to be fashionably dressed, clearly the daughter of a wealthy nobleman. 'Her gown should befit a modest maiden making her début,' he said.

The dressmaker curtsied: 'You'll be pleased with the result, sir, I promise.'

My father bowed and left the room. In a daze, I allowed myself to be measured, draped about with fabrics and discussed, all without a word of protest. I was furious with myself, but I couldn't overcome my fear of my father. Terms such as brocade, point lace, flounce, tuck, and pleat flowed over me in a gentle stream, and the most I managed to do was nod and shake my head silently when required.

'The gowns will be ready in a week. I venture to hope you'll be very pleased with them,' said the dressmaker at last, packing up her tapes and pins. 'And the bill . . . ?'

'Is to be sent to my brother, Sir Edward Williams, at this address,' said my aunt.

The dressmaker withdrew, and my aunt looked sharply at me, assessing my mood. 'I think we may as well get the linen and hats today too,' she said, clearly wanting to make the most of my compliant state. 'It's three hours until dinner.'

'So long?' I whispered. Hunger had me in its grip once more.

'Four o'clock is the dinner hour here in the city,' replied my aunt.

When the sedan chairs arrived, I no longer had the strength to argue that I would prefer to walk. Instead, I climbed in meekly. With a lurch, the men lifted the chair off its legs, and I was carried through the streets. It was a strange sensation.

Our visits to the milliner's and the other shops passed in a blur of noise and confusion. My aunt did the talking, the ordering and the choosing. I wasn't even sure what she'd bought, though I'd had gloves pulled on and off my hands, shoes on and off my feet, shifts and lace petticoats held up against me, and, in yet another shop, hats placed one after another on my head. I was as helpless as a rag doll, and I loathed the feeling.

When it was time to leave the last shop, it was pouring with rain. The shopkeeper sent a boy running to find us chairs. When they arrived, he escorted us to them under an umbrella. I was still in a trance-like state, barely noticing anything all the way home. When we stopped, however, and I came to climb out of the chair, the door was shut fast. I shook the door. I was hungry, tired, sick to my very soul with my own weakness and just wanted to go home. The sounds of an altercation reached me through the heavy splashing of the rain on the cobbled street.

'Aunt?' I called, hearing her voice. There was no reply. 'Hey, open the door!' I called, thumping on the wood. The door remained fastened, but abruptly the roof above me opened, revealing the grey sky. The heavy rain poured straight in on me, drenching my hair in seconds.

'What's going on?' I cried. I heard my aunt screaming. I was wide awake now. The cold rain had roused me from my torpor. Struggling in the confined space of the sedan chair, I climbed onto my seat and looked out through the open roof. The two chairmen were lounging at their ease under the stable-yard archway while both my aunt and I were locked into our chairs, roofs lifted off to expose us to the elements. If this was some kind of practical joke, I wasn't amused.

I pulled myself up and out of the chair and dropped lightly onto the streaming cobbles. The chairmen hadn't noticed me. They were watching my aunt's chair, from which sounds of great distress were issuing. I splashed through the puddles to the door of her chair, lifted off the wooden latch that secured it and opened the door. My poor aunt sat inside, weeping, soaked through; her hat with its handsome black feathers a ruined, bedraggled mess on her head.

'Come!' I cried, grasping her hand. With a sob of relief, she let me tug her out of her chair, and we managed to take one step towards our front door before both chairmen blocked our way. 'Not without payment!' one of them demanded indignantly. He was an ill-favoured rogue with a wart on his face.

'Carry us home without soaking us and we'll pay you!' I told him fiercely, seeing that my aunt was too upset to speak. 'Now get out of our way or I'll scream so loudly everyone will come out to see what's going on. And then I'll ask them to call the constable.'

He confronted us for a moment, a mixture of anger and doubt on his face. I filled my lungs ready to scream, and he stepped back reluctantly, allowing us to pass. I knocked loudly on the front door; it was opened and we rushed in out of the downpour.

My father had already changed for dinner and was awaiting us in his evening clothes. 'What the . . . ?' he asked, drawn out into the hall by my aunt's noisy sobs. He stared in astonishment at our drenched state.

'The chair . . . men!' sobbed my aunt. 'They . . . oh . . . oh!' She began wailing again. My father rang the bell vigorously and sent for her maid to take her away, dry her off and calm her.

'A rational tale, please, Sophia, and a brief one,' he ordered me. I retold the incident in as few words as possible, and the butler coughed discreetly behind me.

'What is it, Watson?' asked my father, brusquely.

'A common trick in this weather, I'm afraid, sir,' he said apologetically. 'The Bath chairmen are rogues, I'm sorry to say. I'm certain they asked the mistress for a fantastic sum, she refused, and they simply opened the roof and awaited her capitulation.'

'But that's a scandal!' exclaimed my father.

'Yes, sir. Mr Nash has been waging war on them for years, but there's still plenty that will cheat you as soon as look at you.'

He bowed and withdrew to the dining room. My father bent his eye on me.

'Climbing out of sedan chairs!' he exclaimed angrily. 'What the devil will you do next? Go and get changed and be quick about it. I want my dinner.'

My aunt was subdued over the meal, saying little. Every now and then she drew a shaky breath that still had something of a sob in it. I concentrated on appeasing my hunger, partaking of an entrée of woodpigeon in a sauce, followed by a roast of mutton, served with potato pie and a selection of vegetables.

'You will be pleased to hear I've been busy,' announced my father as the servants removed the main course, bringing in dishes of blancmange and jelly as well as sweetmeats and nuts. 'I've been to Harrison's and have subscribed. There's a pretty tea room there, as well as a card room, and there's also a private garden down along the river, which seemed a pleasant sort of place to walk. I've also subscribed to the balls at the Guildhall. Everything's run by that damned fellow Nash,' here my father cast a disparaging glance at my aunt, who looked nervous again. 'But I'm told he does a decent job of conducting everything, and all's proper, so there we are.'

'You're *very* good to us, Sir Edward,' said my aunt, brightening at this news. 'What a delightful time we shall have, to be sure.'

'I imagine so,' said my father drily. 'You may make your own choice of coffee house, Amelia, as I have made mine, but take great care that Sophia doesn't get hold of unsuitable books. I gather the coffee houses have libraries and booksellers attached.'

'Yes, Sir Edward,' said my aunt obediently. 'Girls are not allowed into coffee houses in any case. Though they may browse the bookshops. And the concerts are . . . ?'

'Also at the Guildhall, I understand,' replied my father. 'No one has, as yet, tried to get me to part with any money for those.'

'There is a theatre here in Trim Street too, father,' I said. 'I should dearly love to see a play.'

'Out of the question,' said my father. 'Playhouses are hotbeds of vice.'

I sighed deeply and ate a jelly, trying not to think about the sort of life that awaited me as soon as my new clothes were ready. Only the theatre had roused a spark of enthusiasm within me, but plays were forbidden, of course.

'Sophia,' said my father abruptly. I couldn't help myself starting. 'I take it you are not proficient in dancing?'

'No, sir,' I replied, very disappointed that he was asking now. I'd very much hoped to drop this bombshell at the first ball.

'Then you'll be delighted to hear I've engaged a dancing master to attend you every morning for the next two weeks,' he said. 'That should keep you out of trouble.'

I retired to my bedchamber on the top floor that night completely dispirited. Dancing, balls, promenades, tea parties, and at the end of it a husband of my father's choosing. I could see no escape from my grim future and it seemed I didn't even have the capability to rebel. I needed to do something disobedient at once, or my courage would fail me entirely. I climbed out of my window. It gave onto a low stone parapet that ran the length of the terrace of houses and came to a dead end. It was far too high to jump, indeed the long drop made me quite dizzy, and there were no convenient trees.

I scrambled up over the slate tiles onto the peak of the roof and slid down the other side to the back of the house, and here I was more fortunate. On this side the terrace ended in a block of stables built right up against the end house. After a walk along the parapet and a short but tricky descent of a drainpipe, I dropped lightly onto the stable roof and from there it was easy to climb down into the coach-house yard. Finding the door unlocked, I went in and found our own chaise standing with several others.

I climbed inside, thinking I'd look for my father's secret hiding place. I felt carefully over all the seats and seams, and looked under the seats, exploring the wood for hidden compartments. I found nothing. 'It's definitely inside the chaise, though,' I said aloud to myself. 'Because this is where he came and checked.'

I ran one hand along the back shelf above the seats again, pulling the fabric aside, and at last found a small catch. I pressed it and the seat came loose in my hand. As I pulled it forward, I could see in the dim light of the coach house that a sizeable compartment had been revealed. It was empty now, of course, but it must have been packed with valuables on the way here. I whistled silently, thinking how nervous my father must have been when Jenny was searching the coach. But it was too well hidden to be found in a hurry. I'd only succeeded because I'd had plenty of time and because I knew it was here.

Storing the knowledge up for an unspecified future occasion, I slipped out of the coach house, under the arch, and walked towards the city.

CHAPTER NINE

The city by night was a different place. Torches flickered outside many houses, with pools of deep darkness between them. Sedan chairs hurried to and fro, carrying the well-to-do to their places of amusement. There was drunken singing from the taverns, and groups of young men lounging in doorways.

I was out of place in my petticoats as I hadn't been by day, and mourned the loss of my boy's clothing. I kept out of the lights, stayed mainly in the back streets and the quiet alleys and avoided people. As I explored, I found the city was a small, overcrowded, jumbled maze of streets, alleys, and squares, confined by the city walls.

Despite the labyrinthine maze of narrow ways, I gradually got my bearings. My wanderings led me at last to the river. I sat down upon the bank, stared at the still, black water, thinking about my cousin Jack. Where was he now? He couldn't possibly be as miserable as I was. I missed him badly. I wished I could talk to him about what I should do.

Running away would have been my preferred option, if only I'd had somewhere to run to. But the only place I knew was my home, and even that was to be let to strangers. I sighed. I was trapped here. I had an escape from my room, which was better than I'd hoped. But by day I was at the mercy of my father and aunt. I gritted my teeth. 'I won't let them get the better of me,' I muttered. 'I won't submit to my father. I won't let him marry me off. And I *will* punish him. I haven't forgotten my vow to do so.'

I threw a stone into the dark water, by way of confirming my resolution. It fell with a dull splash. A breeze stirred, wafting the rancid scent of the river towards me. I longed for my country home, where the air and the streams were clean and fresh.

The memory of home stirred some half-forgotten words of my father's in my mind. He'd brought me here . . . what had he said? Because I'd disgraced myself so that no one at home would marry me.

The implications of this dawned on me: to prevent any offers of marriage being made for me, I needed to disgrace myself publicly at the Bath. How hard could that be? Of course, I didn't yet know exactly what kind of things would be considered most shocking here. But I could soon find out.

The dancing master arrived at six o'clock the next morning. He was short with thin legs and a weak chin. I disliked him on sight. He was ushered into the downstairs drawing room by the butler and bowed to me. I made an awkward curtsey in return. His eyes fixed on my feet for a painful moment. Raising his eyes to mine, he said: 'You need to wear *shoes*, Mistress Williams, to learn to dance. Not . . . whatever *those* are.' He indicated my footwear with a wave of one limp hand and an exaggerated shudder. I looked down at my flat, patched shoes, scuffed and dirty with climbing over roofs and walking about the city.

'I don't have any oth— Oh yes, I do. Must I wear them now?'

'If you wish to benefit from my expertise, certainly,' he said.

'Please wait a moment,' I asked him, and ran swiftly back upstairs. My aunt had bought me new shoes, hadn't she? I hadn't seen them since, and couldn't remember anything about them. I rummaged in my closet and found neat stacks of cardboard boxes one of the servants must have placed there. I pulled them out and tipped them higgledy-piggledy onto the floor in my hurry not to keep the master waiting.

The first boxes contained a selection of gloves, shawls, brushes, fans and cosmetics. The shoes were stacked at the bottom: leather shoes, damask shoes, kid slippers, shiny buckles, ties, bows, red, pink, cream, beaded and stitched and all with monstrous high, waisted heels, two or three inches at least. I searched in vain for a flatter pair. Which ones were for dancing? I had no idea.

'What a waste of good money,' I said aloud, 'to buy such impractical shoes.' I selected a pair at random, left everything else in a heap and ran downstairs in stockinged feet to present them to the dancing master. He nodded his approval and I buckled them on. I stood up and nearly fell over again. 'Must I truly learn to dance in these?' I asked, perturbed. 'I can scarcely walk in them.'

'You must,' was his curt reply. The master led me through the steps of the minuet without music in the impossible shoes. I added bad breath to his list of faults and kept my distance from him as much as was possible, and my face averted. I had barely memorized a single step of the minuet before he switched to a country dance. I gave up concentrating, simply wobbling and stumbling through the sequences without trying too hard. I had no wish to learn to dance.

My father and aunt returned from an early morning bathe in the famous waters just as the dancing master was leaving. 'How did my daughter do?' asked Father as he climbed from the sedan chair.

'She has some natural grace and rhythm, sir,' the teacher replied waspishly, his temper sorely tried by his time with me. 'But she wants application and must learn to *walk* in the correct footwear before she can *dance* in it. Until tomorrow.'

He bowed and left, and father turned his frowning gaze upon me. 'You want application, do you, Sophia?' he demanded, pulling off his nightcap. His closely-shaven head looked very naked without its usual covering, giving him an altogether more menacing aspect. 'You try my patience too far. I think you'll find missing breakfast will give you all the motivation you require for tomorrow. Go to your room.'

'But, father, truly, I tried as hard as I could,' I protested. 'But he went through the steps so fast and it was all so new to me!'

'I'm not interested in excuses,' was his answer. With a dragging step, I climbed the stairs. My father had won again. I was condemned to more hunger. And what was worse, I'd never been so bored in my life. Shut in this tiny bedroom with no books and no exercise. There were so many things I'd love to be doing. Walking, riding, shooting, or managing the estate. I wondered how our tenant farmers were getting on without me. No doubt my father had frozen all expenditure on the estate, perhaps even raised the rents, and in effect our tenants were paying for our stay here.

I kicked off my uncomfortable new shoes, climbed out onto the roof, and lay on the tiles in the sunshine watching the comings and goings far below in the street. I didn't dare go further afield, in case my absence betrayed my escape route.

In the late afternoon there were footsteps on the stairs followed by a sharp rap at my bedchamber door. I only just had time to scramble back in through the window before the door opened and my father stood before me. He looked at me suspiciously before standing aside and saying: 'This is Dawes, your new lady's maid, Sophia. She is to begin at once. Show her your room and your wardrobe, such as it is, and then . . . '

His voice tailed off as he noticed the mess in my bedchamber, all my new possessions tumbled and kicked all over the floor and my spare gown lying on the chair where I'd dropped it. He surveyed it all in undisguised disgust and then brought his gaze to bear upon me.

'I wasn't aware that you chose to live like the pigs, Sophia,' he said. 'If we had a sty here at the Bath, I should send you out to sleep in it for the night. I'm sure you'd feel very much at home. Meanwhile, you'll eat your dinner in your room tonight; a simple dish of bread and milk will suffice. That will give you a chance to tidy this disgraceful mess and to reflect on the virtues of orderliness.'

I groaned inwardly at the thought of another hungry night. Meanwhile, father turned back to the maid: 'Dawes, remove any unfashionable shoes from this room and dispose of them in the fire, would you?'

My heart jumped into my mouth. My shoes! I couldn't possibly do without them. My climbing and night-time wanderings would be at an end. I wondered where they could be in all this mess, and resolved to hide them the moment the new maid had left the room.

'I'll leave you to sort things out,' said my father and left us. Dawes and I stared at each other as his footsteps receded. I felt compelled to speak:

'There isn't much dressing to do just yet, as you can see, Dawes,' I said, indicating my shabby gown and my bare feet, annoyed to find my voice apologetic. 'To tell the truth, I've never had a maid. I've always looked after myself.'

'So I should suppose, Miss,' she said with barely-concealed disdain. 'But I can see that gown you have on wants mending. I'll take that now, if you like.'

'Oh, yes,' I said, surprised. 'Yes I tore it on a . . . well, yes, I tore it a few days ago. Thank you . . . ' I untied the gown and handed it to her, picking up my spare brown one and wrapping it around me instead.

'And the shoes your father mentioned, Miss?' asked Dawes, unsmiling. She was a large woman with a sour expression on her face. 'I'll take those with me now too.'

I froze in horror. I glanced involuntarily towards the pile of scattered belongings. My colour rose as I spotted the toe of one shoe sticking out of a jumble of boxes in front of the closet. I looked away again quickly, praying she wouldn't see it.

'Oh . . . I . . . you see, my father was mistaken, Dawes,' I faltered. 'The shoes he so dislikes have already been thrown away.'

We stared one another out, and eventually Dawes dropped her eyes. 'If you say so, Miss,' she said. I knew she didn't believe me. She would almost certainly search my room at the first opportunity, but that would give me the chance I needed to hide my valuable footwear.

I didn't dare use the chimney and there were no loose boards in such a new house, so I merely laid the shoes outside on the parapet, out of sight of the window. I would need to find a box or a piece of oilskin to protect them before it rained next. But Dawes certainly wouldn't climb out there looking for them; she had enough trouble with the stairs. I grinned to myself at the image of Dawes attempting to squeeze herself through my small window.

My days resolved into a pattern for the rest of the week. Dancing for an hour and a half before breakfast was a regular torture, my meal dependent on my teacher's comments at the end of the session. The first few days I had no breakfast, and found myself forced to concentrate hard on pleasing the dancing master to avoid the long, hungry days that followed if I didn't. The rest of my tedious waking hours were spent deliberately wrecking some piece of stitching foisted on me by my aunt or leafing through the book of religious discourses my father had given me in the vain hope of distraction.

My nights on the other hand were entertaining, out roaming the city which I began to know well. I explored every alley and path until they were all familiar to me. Once I thought I spotted Jenny, and called after her, but she ran from me and disappeared over the city wall. Every night I wished I had money so that I could satisfy my hunger with the wares from one of the street vendors or taverns, but I had not a single coin and no way of obtaining any.

'Father,' I asked with as much politeness as I could muster over breakfast one morning. 'I should like to write a letter to my cousin Jack. Will you post it for me?'

My father finished the last of his egg and toast and then laid down his cutlery neatly. He dabbed his mouth on his napkin and looked across at me. I could read his answer in his eyes before he spoke. 'You have nothing to write to young men about,' he said. 'The suggestion is indecorous.'

'But father . . . ' I began to protest. He rose from the table abruptly, pushing his chair back and speaking to my aunt as though I wasn't present: 'Amelia, a word with you in my study when you have finished eating, if you please!' He swept out of the dining room.

'You shouldn't cross your father, Sophia,' said Amelia accusingly as she followed him. 'He is so good to you! New gowns, dancing lessons and all the expenses of a Bath season. You're a lucky girl.'

I wished for none of the things my father was providing me with so lavishly. He wanted me well-married and off his hands. It was an investment.

If father was so strongly opposed to my writing to my cousin, I dreaded to think what he would say to a letter to Bill Smith. With no money, I was completely in his hands and he knew it. It was a problem that urgently needed solving.

We were just finishing breakfast a week later when there was a knock at the door. We heard the butler open it, and the voice of the delivery boy: 'The goods ordered for Miss Williams.'

'Sophia! Your gowns have arrived!' cried my aunt in great excitement. 'You must try them on at once!'

'I shall leave you to it,' said my father hastily, seeing mountains of boxes and packages being carried into the house. He disappeared upstairs to dress, saying he was going out to his coffee house and would be back for luncheon.

My aunt was in raptures. I watched her unpacking the boxes, radiant with delight. 'Look at this pink brocade!' she exclaimed holding it out to me. 'Isn't it exquisite? Oh, and this primrose walking gown, for the promenade— quite ravishing! How I envy you, my dear!' She unpacked and exclaimed, but some of the boxes she just glanced into and laid aside without showing me the contents. I caught a glimpse of a soft grey fabric in one and a pale lilac in another.

'What are those?' I asked curiously.

'Oh, those are just a few trifles I was obliged to order for myself,' she said deprecatingly. Her pile grew as we went through the boxes.

'Goodness, Aunt Amelia!' I exclaimed. 'I'm sure you have even more new clothes than I have!'

'Nonsense, child! No such thing! But, if I am to launch you, it is important I'm correctly dressed too. I can't go to balls in my blacks. These new gowns are half mourning, you see; it's six months now since my dear husband passed on.'

'Ah, I see,' I said, watching her as she laid her own gowns aside. 'So my father has paid for these too, has he? Does he know?'

My aunt quickly changed the subject.

The dressmaker arrived to help us try on the gowns and to see if any adjustments were required. Dawes was called and together they fastened the hoop around my waist. I bore it in rigid silence, my fists clenched. When I'd first seen my aunt's hoop, I'd thought that it looked like a cage. Now I was wearing one myself, I knew that my first impression had been correct. I was trapped inside it, my movements restricted. Once the layers of petticoats had been tied around my waist and the heavy, open-fronted brocade gown pulled over my head, I could barely move. I walked a few steps with difficulty.

'Do you like it?' asked the dressmaker eagerly. 'You look very fine.'

'I feel utterly ridiculous,' I said bluntly.

'Oh, hush, Sophia,' exclaimed my aunt, scandalized. 'It's a *beautiful* gown. You don't know how lucky you are! Indeed this all works out *most* fortunately, for there is a ball tomorrow, and now we shall be able to attend.'

I had to admit Dawes had some skills the following evening as she dressed my soft, brown hair simply but elegantly. She pinned it up with just a few locks arranged with curling irons to tumble down to my shoulder. Then my hair was powdered. Dawes helped me into my new linen shift, my dancing shoes, my hoop, my layers of laced petticoats and my ball gown of cream brocade, tugging and adjusting them so they sat just right. She fastened a pearl necklace about my neck and I exclaimed in surprise. 'Where did that come from?' I asked.

'From your father, Miss,' said Dawes. 'I'm to tell you it was your mother's, like the other jewellery in this box.'

I touched the necklace lightly. I could barely remember my mother. It was a strange thought that this had belonged to her. Dawes dusted my face with powder to whiten it, applied a hint of rouge to my cheeks, fixed a patch high on one cheekbone, and said: 'There. You'll do nicely now, Miss.'

I regarded myself gravely in the mirror. I didn't recognize myself in the least. The hairstyle I didn't dislike, though the powder made me look like an old lady. The gown was ludicrous, but I could see it had a certain beauty, especially the way the short train fell in shimmering folds to the floor behind me. The front of the gown was open, the fabric caught back on either side to reveal layers of cream and gold petticoats in front; a froth of lace.

The patch on the other hand was monstrous. I pulled it off and put it on the dressing table. 'I don't want to wear such a thing,' I said. 'There's no need for me to look like a ghost, either,' I said, critically regarding my face before rubbing it clean of cosmetics with a damp cloth. 'I'm quite pale enough after all these days indoors.'

Dawes didn't argue, and I descended the stairs, ready to face the people of Bath. My aunt and father awaited me, attired in evening finery, powdered, painted and patched. My father looked at me critically, but then nodded his approval. 'A natural look. Yes, you judged rightly, Sophia. It suggests youth and innocence. Good. Let's go.'

Annoyed at having inadvertently won his approval, I vowed that I would behave as badly as I dared tonight.

CHAPTER TEN

The upstairs ballroom at the Guildhall was far smaller than I'd expected; less grand and extremely crowded. When we arrived, a group of musicians was already playing, though no one was dancing yet. I moved warily into the room, my heavy, unfamiliar gown and petticoats swaying and quivering about me.

'Take smaller steps, Sophia,' my aunt ordered under her breath. 'Don't stride about like a man!'

I tried to do as she said, noting how the other ladies appeared to glide effortlessly about, as though they were in skates rather than shoes. I sighed a little and looked around me at the sea of faces and figures in bright garments that made up the world of high fashion, gathered at the Bath for the summer months. I knew no one. This was nothing I ever wanted to be a part of.

Beau Nash made us personally welcome and promised me a partner for the first dance. I felt my courage draining slowly away. The first dance began, the minuet, very slow and formal. Only one couple danced at a time, in order of social rank, while everyone else stood crowded against the walls and watched. I dreaded having to perform under the gaze of so many pairs of eyes, and clutched my hands together in their cream kid gloves, twisting the strap of my fan until it snapped. My aunt scolded me in a whisper.

I had a long time to wait, as there were far more exalted guests present than us. At last all the dukes, marquises, earls and viscounts, of whom there appeared to be an extraordinary number, had taken their turn. My father was presented to a partner and danced down the room with her. My aunt was excused dancing on account of being in half-mourning, but the Beau brought me an elderly gentleman, who bowed stiffly and offered me his arm.

'Miss Williams, may I introduce Mr Bedford to you?' he said with a bow. 'He is a widower and spending the summer at the Bath.'

My intention had been to refuse all offers to dance. But under the stern yet kindly eye of the Beau, and the curious gaze of the rest of the room, I found I couldn't do so. I curtseyed, placed my fingertips on my partner's arm as the dancing master had instructed me, and allowed him to lead me to the top of the room.

I stumbled more than once in my high heels and was several times late on the turn, but I somehow got down the room without absolutely disgracing myself. I ignored the giggles and whispers I could hear each time I made a mistake. My partner bowed deeply to me. 'Thank you for a most charming dance, Miss Williams,' he said, eyeing me in a way that made me uncomfortable. 'You dance most delightfully, if you will permit me to tell you so.'

I flushed and didn't reply, embarrassed by compliments I certainly didn't deserve. 'You were clearly born for no other purpose than to grace a ballroom,' he continued, kissing my gloved fingers. 'You should never do anything but dance.'

I snatched my hand away. His words struck me as so false and insulting, I was moved to retort: 'Indeed, sir, I consider dancing a pitiful waste of time. There are far more useful occupations. As for my dancing, if your eyesight were sharper, you might have noticed my wrong steps. Excuse me,' I said, walking off without curtseying, and leaving my partner standing, his mouth half open in shock.

I was relieved to be rid of him and glad to be putting my plan into action at last. *Social disgrace*, I reminded myself, when my conscience pricked me, telling me it wasn't fair to treat an elderly man so disrespectfully. *If I make everyone dislike me, no one will want to marry me.*

Screens were removed from behind us, revealing food. There was quite a spread. I took ham and bread and ate it with relish. My aunt gasped disapprovingly when she caught sight of me. 'Ladies take a jelly or a syllabub at a ball, Sophia,' she whispered fiercely. 'The meats are for the men. It looks so . . . unladylike to eat so eagerly.'

'But I'm starving!' I objected. It was always wise, I was fast learning, to take the opportunity of food when it was offered.

'You shouldn't *show* it!' exclaimed my aunt, exasperated.

I decided I'd been too docile so far this evening. What could I do to misbehave more? I had to disgrace myself as soon as possible.

Before I'd thought of anything definite, the food was cleared and the musicians struck up for the country dances. Couples took to the floor, a line running the length of the ballroom. I saw Beau Nash walking towards me, a slender man mincing on ludicrously high heels beside him and had to hide a grin. He was dressed all in pink satin and silver lace. His face was white, his lips painted red and he had three large patches on his face. His powdered wig was monstrously tall and the long skirts of his coat were whale-boned and stood out from his body as stiffly as a lady's hooped gown. He sported an ear-ring in one ear, and, worst of all, he carried a fan which he fluttered as he walked. He stopped in front of me; bowed deeply with a flourish of a scented pocket handkerchief.

'May I present Mr Wimpole to you, Miss Williams?' Nash asked. 'He's eager to meet you.' He bowed politely and moved away.

'May I be so fortunate as to beg the honour of the next dance, Miss Williams?' Mr Wimpole asked with a flutter of his fan. He clearly considered himself to be bestowing a great honour on me rather than requesting one. He glanced at my aunt as he spoke and she nodded and smiled her approval.

'I'm very sorry, sir,' I said seriously. 'But that's not possible.'

He looked taken aback. 'You are promised to someone else?' he asked. He looked around as though expecting a partner to materialize suddenly.

'No, sir, but I can't dance with you,' I told him, being sure to speak in a clear, carrying voice. 'You see, I've learned only the lady's part.' I paused and looked him up and down, 'And we cannot *both* dance it.'

It took the dandy a moment to understand I'd insulted him. A flush of anger flooded his face; he turned on his

extremely high heel and walked away. Some ladies nearby had overheard and were giggling behind their fans. A
handsome young man in black satin laced with gold half
turned away to hide a smile.

I glanced at my aunt, and saw her looking bewildered,
but it was otherwise with my father. Judging by the look
of fury on his face, he'd not only heard but also understood what I'd said. He walked towards me, gripping me
painfully tightly by one elbow.

'I think, Sophia,' he said in a carefully controlled
voice, 'that we'd better leave now, don't you? And have
a little 'chat' together at home?'

A shiver of fear ran down my spine, but I'd deliberately provoked him and was ready to take the consequences. I had to show him that he couldn't force me to
do his will. My father propelled me several steps towards
the door, but we were stopped by the same gentleman
in black and gold, standing between us and the way out,
executing a very graceful bow. 'Could I beg the indul-
gence of a dance with your daughter, sir?' he requested
politely. 'I would consider myself honoured.'

I was astonished. He'd heard my rudeness. Why
was he asking me to dance? My father hesitated, then
pinched my elbow to ensure my obedience, bowed and
passed my hand to the man.

'Miss Williams, is it not?' the stranger asked me, leading me away, fixing me with a disconcertingly clear stare.
There was just a hint of a smile in his dark eyes but I didn't
know whether he was being friendly or laughing at me.

'Yes, sir,' I replied. 'But I don't believe we've been
introduced.'

The man raised his brows ironically. 'Now, I didn't have the impression that such social niceties would trouble you.'

I blushed. 'They don't,' I said defiantly. 'I don't care what your name is.'

The young man merely smiled at my rudeness and led me to the top of the hall where we took our places ready to begin. He moved with ease and grace, wearing his fine clothes casually, almost negligently, as though neither the heavy, opulent fabrics nor the high heels of his shoes restricted him in the least. I tried to be as calm and unconcerned as he, but my father's fury, briefly glimpsed and still to be unleashed, had given me a shock and my hand on his arm shook a little.

The dance began. Unnerved as I was, I started on the wrong foot and had to shuffle quickly to retrieve my mistake. My partner politely ignored my clumsiness.

'Tell me, Miss Williams, how are you enjoying the Bath?' he asked courteously.

'Not at all,' I replied, struggling with the steps. They were a blur, and my only advantage was the firm lead my partner offered.

'I'm very sorry to hear it. The fault must lie with us, for I'm quite certain you came determined to love the place.'

I was quite certain now that he was making fun of me. 'No, I came determined to hate everything about it,' I countered.

'And to insult its inhabitants. How very original,' he observed.

Thrown by this, I took a wrong step and accidentally

trod hard on my partner's foot. A pained expression crossed his face. We were parted and then came together again. I looked up at him. 'Why did you ask me to dance, sir?' I asked bluntly.

'It was curiosity, I believe,' he said, as though considering the matter. 'I wanted to know why you chose to insult Mr Wimpole so grievously. Do you lack both manners and sense, I wondered, or was it deliberate?'

'And your conclusion?' I asked, feeling uncomfortable under his cool scrutiny.

'You can't expect me to make up my mind about you after one conversation, Miss Williams, however quickly *you* may judge people. But I shall look forward to pursuing my acquaintance with you,' he concluded as he restored me to my father. 'Thank you for a most delightful dance.'

He bowed gracefully, kissed my gloved hand lightly and left me. I tucked my hand into the folds of my petticoats, my heart beating uncomfortably fast. What did he mean by it?

My father escorted me briskly from the ballroom, hurrying down the steps to where a great crowd of sedan chairmen awaited the guests, jostling for position to get our custom. I wished I could tell the men to carry me away from Trim Street. I didn't care where, as long as I didn't have to return there. But the men's fare sat snugly in my father's pocket, and they carried me inexorably home after him. I entered the candle-lit house first and already had my foot on the bottom stair in an attempt to flee a scene, when my father called me back.

'Sophia, stay! Amelia, you must be exhausted and will wish to retire.'

My aunt swept past me and on up the stairs. I longed to follow her. My hand on the balustrade was trembling a little, so I clasped it behind my back, awaiting my father's orders. 'Wait for me in my study,' he said curtly. I walked slowly to the downstairs room he'd adopted as his own. As I went in, he gave all the servants orders to go to bed. 'That includes Miss Sophia's maid,' he said. 'She won't be needed tonight.'

I wondered with a kind of fearful fascination what punishment he had in mind. Sending the servants away sounded like a beating. I wasn't afraid of that. Or at least only a little afraid.

CHAPTER ELEVEN

I sat upright and very still at breakfast the following morning. I'd put on my comfortable old blue wraparound gown, but even so, every movement rubbed the fabric against the welts the lash had raised on my back, causing exquisite pain.

Despite this, and despite the fact that I'd not been out for my usual nocturnal ramble, I made a good breakfast. Battle was joined and I'd shown my father I wouldn't obey him meekly.

I found it slightly disconcerting that my father was in such a good mood this morning. His trip to the baths and the pump room had cheered him greatly, it seemed. Or perhaps he was hopeful he'd got the better of me at last. When he sent me a gloating look, I was certain of it. I felt suddenly sick. I pushed away my cup and rose from the table.

'That's right, Sophia,' said my aunt. 'You go and get changed ready for the promenade.'

'The promenade?' I asked faintly. 'Must I . . . ?'

'Yes, indeed!' she said enthusiastically. 'We take chairs to the Grove directly after breakfast.'

I nodded gloomily and left the room, walking carefully. The butler bowed me out and then went back inside, leaving the door ajar. I leaned my forehead briefly against the cool wall, conquering a wave of pain that had swept over me, breathing deeply. Before I could move on, I caught my name.

'Who do you think that fellow was who danced with Sophia last night, Amelia?' my father asked.

'Well?' she prompted curiously.

'Damn it . . . what's the fellow's name again? Can't remember. But he's the son of some earl, so I hear. Younger son, more's the pity, so he's not likely to succeed to the title, but still.'

I heard the sound of liquid splashing and pictured my father pouring himself another mug of ale. I scarcely dared breathe in case I missed anything.

'I'm told he rarely dances, so apparently it was an honour.'

'But a younger son, Edward,' objected my aunt. 'There may be no fortune at all! He was very young.'

'There'll be money somewhere in the family. What's more the fellow's popular with the ladies. You make sure you encourage him. And stay within earshot of the girl when you can. She's not to be trusted. We can't have her being rude to . . . '

The knocker on the front door hammered suddenly, right near me. Before I could leave the hallway, Watson emerged from the dining room to answer the knock and caught me listening. I flushed with embarrassment, but he only gave me the ghost of a wink as he passed by.

The caller had brought a note for my aunt, but I didn't wait to hear what it contained, instead fleeing upstairs to my bedchamber. Hunting through my closet for a suitable gown, I realized I had no idea what should be worn to the promenade. Reluctantly, I rang for Dawes, who soon came lumbering up the many flights of stairs from the basement, breathing heavily.

'We're going to the promenade, Dawes,' I said to her. 'What should I wear?'

She glanced out at the patch of sky that could be seen from my small window. 'It's a fine day, Miss, for the time of year. Would you like to wear the primrose gown with the white petticoats? Or the pink gown and cream petticoats?'

Life at the Bath had begun in earnest for me if such were the decisions around which my day was based.

The paths and walkways of the Grove were crowded with fashionables in exquisite clothes, and I recognized faces from the ball the previous night. One or two of the other girls pointed me out to one another and giggled. I was glad to think that I was becoming notorious already, and tried to ignore the slightly uncomfortable feeling it gave me. I walked with my aunt with slow, tripping steps that had no aim or purpose to them other than to show off our gowns and while away the long morning.

My aunt seemed to know a great many people, and was bowing and smiling to them as we passed, sometimes stopping to exchange dull conversation, which forced me to suppress yawns of boredom. 'I thought you hadn't visited the Bath before?' I asked her at last. 'How do you know everyone?'

'My dear girl, the whole world is here. If you've spent a season in London, as I have done, then this is the same crowd. They come here the better to enjoy each other's company, to win each other's money and gossip, just as they did in the winter.'

'I see,' I said, feeling depressed. A thin, sallow gentleman paused to greet my aunt at that moment, bowing over her hand and casting a covert glance at me. They drew apart, enjoying a low-voiced exchange, and he discreetly passed my aunt a note which she concealed in her reticule. I fidgeted uncomfortably, unsure what to do with myself. I glanced around me, and saw my partner from the previous evening, the desirable *parti*, in conversation with several ladies nearby. They were chatting to him, casting him worshipping looks that turned my stomach. He was smiling and listening to them, but his eyes were intent on my aunt and her companion. When he saw me watching, he gave me a polite bow. The ladies looked daggers at me and I smiled a little to myself.

My aunt broke off her conversation. 'Sophia, you must be bored! You don't want to spend the day with a dull matron like me,' she said. 'Now, I had a note this morning . . . friends of ours from home are here at the Bath.' She began looking around her, as though seeking someone. 'My dear Jane!' she said, beckoning to a stout older woman and a plain young one. They approached and my heart sank as I recognized them. The girl was Mary Welland, my least favourite neighbour. Her mother and my aunt had grown up close friends, but we'd spent the majority of our childhood disliking one another cordially.

My aunt kissed them both and turned to me with a smile. 'I thought it would be lovely for you and Mary to spend some time together while Jane and I enjoy a cosy chat about old times.'

I scowled. Mary simpered, looking scarcely more pleased than I was, but my aunt was already fishing in her reticule for something, and a moment later held out some coins and a ticket to me. 'Why don't you girls go and treat yourselves to a bun or a syllabub in the pastry-cook shop and then meet us at Harrison's Assembly Rooms in an hour or so?' she suggested.

My impulse was to refuse indignantly to do any such thing. *I* spend an hour or so in Mary's company? No, thank you. But the precious coins pressed into my hand made me think differently. So I allowed the obnoxious Mary to tuck her arm through mine and lead me off to her favourite pastry-cook in the nearby High Street.

'Dear me, Sophia,' Mary said. 'You seem to have succeeded in making yourself a figure of fun in Bath in no time at all. I thought you might want to make a new start if you came away here. I know that was your aunt's hope.'

She looked up at me, pretending sorrow and sympathy at my waywardness, but I wasn't fooled. I could see the malicious gleam in her eyes.

'I care nothing for a parcel of Bath dandies,' I said contemptuously.

'Clearly not. Only one evening in public and you've offended two gentlemen already!' She sniggered behind her hand.

I pulled my arm out of hers. 'As I said, I really don't care.'

'How *brave* you are, Sophia!' she said, mock-admiringly. 'As for me, I should hate to be a figure of fun. I prefer to please.'

'How very galling it must be for you then, to fail so dismally,' I said spitefully. I regretted the words at once, but didn't know how to say so. An angry flush darkened Mary's features and she sent me a look of pure loathing. Then she schooled her features into a pious resignation that made me want to slap her. 'You always were unmannered,' she said. 'But I *forgive* you. This is the cook house.'

We entered together, and Mary chose a table by the window. 'So we can see everyone passing by,' she said. 'It is quite the best seat in the place!'

I disagreed. To sit in full view of the street and to be ogled by every gentleman that passed by might be Mary's idea of fun, but it wasn't mine. I didn't argue, however, still feeling guilty at my nastiness. I sat down quietly and very cautiously, so as not to hurt my sore back.

'What can I get for you, ladies?' asked the waiter.

'Order anything you like,' I told Mary. 'It's my aunt's treat.'

She ordered a jelly, but I said I wanted nothing. 'I couldn't eat a thing,' I excused myself to Mary. 'One is fed so heartily here, I find.' I clutched the coins tightly in my hand, already planning the letters I wished to write.

'Strange then, that you're looking so thin,' said Mary with a false smile.

I got up abruptly to look at the newspapers that were available; it was a shame that Mary had not chosen to go to the bookstore, but the London newspapers were better than nothing.

I joined her at the table again, flicking through the paper, pretending to be engrossed, but actually bored. I'd never been one for news. Plays, tales and poetry interested me far more. The only story that caught my attention was an account of riots: they had spread outwards from London. People had been smashing things, toasting the late queen, the Stuart heir, and shouting for the Church and the Tories. Oxford, Wolverhampton and Chippenham had had their share of mobs and violence in recent weeks. 'Chippenham . . . is that not close to Bath?' I asked Mary.

'Oh, Sophia, you are so ignorant,' she sighed.

I went back to reading, ignoring Mary. She watched the passers-by, chatted sometimes to the other guests and ate her jelly.

Harrison's Assembly Rooms were set in gardens down by the river. I presented my ticket, Mary presented hers, and we were admitted to the enclosed area that was for subscribers only. It was prettily laid out, with a smooth lawn in front, the rooms fresh and attractive. We entered the tea room, which was already crowded with visitors, and Mary left me at once, going back to her mother. I looked around for my aunt, but couldn't see her.

I walked through to the second room. Here, tables were set out for cards, all of them full. I spotted my aunt in a far corner, engrossed in a game with some other ladies. My father sat at another table, cards fanned in his hand and a glass of red wine at his elbow. I was completely useless at all card games, so I sighed and wondered whether I should walk home. But there was nothing to do there either.

I wandered back into the tea room and was offered tea, which I accepted, and a small cake too. I stood alone, drinking my tea, wishing my back would stop smarting. Although the room was crowded, there was plenty of space around me; the other visitors avoided me as though I had some infectious disease. Mr Bedford passed by and moved on quickly without looking at me. The dandy from last night stared insolently and then pointedly turned his back. I held my head high and told myself I didn't care.

After a long, awkward wait, a familiar figure approached me and bowed. It was last night's mysterious dance partner, and I greeted him uncertainly. I supposed it was a relief to know there was one person here willing to talk to me.

'Good day, Miss Williams. All alone, I see.'

'That's how I prefer it,' I told him.

'Really? It's one thing to despise and dislike the people of Bath, but a different thing altogether to be despised and disliked *by* them, wouldn't you say?'

'If you despise and dislike me so much, sir, I wonder you acknowledge me at all,' I said as disdainfully as I could.

'I wasn't one of those you insulted yesterday,' he pointed out.

'That can be remedied,' I told him swiftly.

'Please. Feel free to insult me all you like,' he said with a mischievous look that I confess appealed to me. His face in repose was rather stern, but when he smiled it transformed it, making him look much younger. 'You're with your aunt?'

'My aunt is playing cards, sir,' I replied.

'You're not a card player?' he enquired politely.

'No. Cards bore me. Besides, I have no money to gamble.'

'You are very wise,' he said. 'I'm no card player either. You haven't seen the gardens yet. Would you like to accompany me out to view them?'

'You tell me everyone hates and despises me,' I said indignantly, 'and then you ask me to walk with you! Why would I want to?'

'Curiosity?' he suggested. Again, there was just a hint of a smile in his eyes. Almost against my will, I nodded. It was no part of my plan to form friendships at the Bath, especially not with young men my father considered eligible, so it was difficult to account for my acquiescence.

My companion offered his arm, and after a moment's hesitation, I laid my hand on it. As we went out through the door, my companion let go of me for a moment and placed a guiding hand on the small of my back. His touch was too light to hurt, but I flinched instinctively and caught my breath. The man said nothing, however. I made some remark, I hardly know what, about the mild weather and the moment passed.

The gardens were laid out in a formal walk that led down along the river. It was much more spacious than the Grove. I took cautious steps, the fabric of my gown chafing my tender back. 'This is the famous Harrison's Walk,' said my companion. 'What do you think of it?'

'It's very pleasant,' I said. 'Although I should prefer somewhere less formal. Up there perhaps.' I pointed to the wooded hills that rose steeply on the far side of the river.

'The Beechen Cliff? It's a fine place with grand views, but few ladies venture so far.'

I shrugged, and then winced, regretting the incautious movement. I decided I should certainly explore the Beechen Cliff before I was much older. 'Do you know, sir,' I said, changing the subject, 'that I still do not know your name? Are you as disinclined to part with it as you were yesterday?'

A slight smile touched his lips and I regretted my words. 'I'm delighted to hear that you are so interested in me,' he remarked.

'Oh, I'm not,' I countered hurriedly. 'But I can't keep calling you 'the arrogant man from the ball'.'

'You confuse arrogance with poise, Miss Williams,' he told me.

'I'm not sure that I do,' I replied thoughtfully.

I felt the arm my hand rested on shake with laughter, and risked a swift glance up at him. 'You are a worthy opponent, Miss Williams,' he said, smiling down at me. I looked away, uncomfortable at how attractive I found his smile.

'We *are* enemies then? I suspected as much,' I told him. 'But one should always know one's adversary's name.'

'For in the unknown lies fear? My name is Charleton, Miss Williams. It's ordinary enough to dispel any sense of menace, wouldn't you say?'

'Oh yes. I shall now enter the battle fearlessly.'

'I have an idea you are not prone to fear very much,' he remarked.

'My cousin Jack always says I have no sense of fear at all.' I bit my lip, immediately regretting my confidence. We reached the far end of the walk and paused a moment, looking across the brown river to the shadowed, misty cliffs opposite.

'So where is your cousin Jack now?' Mr Charleton asked. 'He's not with you at the Bath?'

'He's gone into the army,' I replied briefly.

'And the lady in whose care you are is your aunt, I understand?'

'My aunt Amelia is my father's sister.'

'And has she lived with you long?'

'No, not long. She's recently widowed.' Seeing he was about to ask another question, I interrupted him: 'I had no idea that my family interested you so much.'

'I'm merely making polite conversation, Miss Williams. It's what people do.'

'There's a difference between conversation and inter-rogation,' I pointed out.

He paused, looking up at the hills, a slight frown creasing his brow. 'Do you read the newspapers much, Miss Williams?' he asked abruptly.

'Not often,' I replied, taken aback. 'I prefer plays, poetry and stories.'

'Ah! Such as?'

'The poems of Pope and Dryden among others.'

'Have you read *The Rape of the Lock*? That is Pope's latest and very popular.'

'Not yet. I will as soon as I can obtain a copy. But

my absolute favourites are the plays and tales of Aphra Behn. I love that she was a spy for King Charles the Second, and led such an exciting life. I wish I could live as she did.'

'You wish to be a spy?' He smiled enigmatically. 'The king rarely paid her, you know. A fate common to spies, I believe. She was thrown into a debtor's prison. I imagine such lives are more exciting to read about than to live. Alexander Pope is staying here at the Bath; you will meet him, I daresay. But to return to the newspapers. Have you read them recently?'

'Yes, just this morning,' I said. 'Why?'

'Then you will have seen an account of the riots around the country.'

'I read about them, but I don't pretend to understand them.'

Mr Charleton lifted mildly incredulous eyebrows, and I felt irritated. 'It makes no difference to me who the king is,' I said.

'Mobs fighting in the streets might concern you, however. People have died. Does that not trouble you?'

I turned puzzled eyes on him. 'I suppose so. But it's all a long way from here, after all. What does it have to do with me?'

'That's what I should like to know,' he said, puzzling me further. 'What if the unrest were to come closer? Right into the city of Bath itself?'

I shook my head in bewilderment. 'Could it do so?'

Mr Charleton subjected me to a searching gaze. His eyes were hard, I would almost have called them suspicious; only what could he possibly suspect me of?

But then he changed the subject abruptly. 'You hold yourself very regally today, Miss Williams,' he observed.

'What?' I asked blankly.

'Or perhaps merely carefully. Do your shoes pinch your feet perhaps? Or is your gown uncomfortable?'

'Ladies' gowns are always uncomfortable,' I said, disconcerted. I was sure no one else had noticed anything amiss. Had he seen me flinch after all? He could scarcely guess the cause. But before I could myself change the subject he lowered his voice and spoke again.

'Miss Williams, I had too many beatings myself as a stripling, not to recognize someone with a painful back,' he said. 'Does it hurt you very much?' His voice had changed. It was softer, no longer harsh. It was almost kind. I experienced a rush of emotions in reaction to his sudden gentleness. My throat tightened and I found myself unable to speak.

Embarrassed to be receiving sympathy from a stranger, and terrified I might be about to cry, I snatched my hand from my companion's arm and fled back along the walk, my skirts swaying around me, heedless of the pain in my back. It was not my nature or my habit to confide my troubles, and certainly not to someone I barely knew, who seemed only a moment earlier to have been hostile to me.

To defeat my father, I needed to stay alone, aloof. I couldn't afford to feel weak as Mr Charleton had just made me feel, no matter how kind his intentions were. Not that I was convinced he *was* kind. Some motive or other he had, I thought, in befriending me.

CHAPTER TWELVE

I was up at dawn the next morning. While my father and aunt were at the baths, I went through my father's papers, and found Jack's direction. He was based in a training camp near Windsor with his regiment. I felt better simply knowing where in the country he was.

I helped myself to my father's writing paper, pen, and ink, and wrote letters to both Jack and Bill and then walked into the city. There was a very pleasant young postmaster at the post office who kindly explained the complicated system of cross-post charges to me. It seemed it was going to cost Bill a great deal to receive the single sheet I'd written and that made me anxious. The postmaster smiled kindly when I told him my worries. 'The letter to Windsor can go with the London post,' he told me. 'But I think it will be better to send the Devon letter by private carrier. There's a carrier in Cheap Street who passes that way every week and would probably only charge you a penny to deliver it. He's very reliable and he won't charge your friend.'

'Thank you for your trouble,' I said, holding on to the letters still.

'It's never trouble to give good service,' said the man with a friendly smile.

I hesitated. A swift glance around me told me that the middle-aged woman who worked at the postmaster's side was busy with another customer and there was no one to hear what I said. 'If I were to be sent replies to these letters,' I said, speaking low, 'is there any way I could receive them without my father knowing?'

An expressionless look descended on the postmaster's face. He regarded me for a moment in silence, and I held my breath. Would this nice young man merely scold me or would he find a way to report me to my father? But his words were reassuring.

'Of course. You can have them sent care of Mr Allen here at the Bath Post Office,' he replied. 'In that case I would hold them until you came to collect them. I can assure you of my discretion.'

I sighed with relief and wrote the return address as he had directed on the back of my letters. At last I handed the letter to Jack to him, offered him my heartfelt thanks and left. The negotiations with the carrier were straightforward enough and with a feeling of satisfaction, I hurried back to the house before my relatives returned, pink-faced and damp from their emersion in the hot spa water.

'You really should come with us and try the waters, Sophia,' said Aunt Amelia, as she took her place opposite me at breakfast. 'Now you're no longer taking dancing lessons. It does one so much good.'

'Thank you, Aunt, but I'd prefer not to,' I said, recalling the stray dog in the water and the stench of rotten eggs.

My father entered the room and sat down, signalling that we could start eating. I helped myself to porridge and stirred some cream into it, while my aunt reached for the buttered rolls. My father poured himself a mug of ale, carved a slice of ham, but then laid down the knife with something of a snap and sat back, looking at me. 'It seems Sophia has business she attends to while we are out,' he remarked in a silky voice. I froze in the act of lifting my first spoonful of porridge to my mouth and stared at him, my heart beating uncomfortably fast.

'I've had an interesting word with the servants. Sophia has been in my study and has been out of the house this morning.' My father's cold eyes rested on me. 'Where did you get money from, Sophia? Not from me.'

My aunt gave a muffled shriek, and through her mouthful of buttered roll, said: 'Did you not spend that money on jellies, Sophia?'

'I bought Mary a jelly, Aunt. I wasn't hungry,' I said. I didn't dare look at my father, certain he would see the guilt in my face. At least the letters were safely in the post. He couldn't stop them now.

'I have sent the butler to the post office to retrieve the correspondence,' said my father, dispelling my hope. 'I told you not to write to your cousin, Sophia. You have been dishonest.' He paused a moment, looking at me. 'What punishment do you think you deserve,' he asked in a soft voice, 'for such disgraceful disobedience?'

When I didn't reply, he got up, picked up the mustard pot, took a generous dessert spoonful out and walked towards me. My heart thumped with momentary dread, wondering what he was going to do with it. He stirred the spoonful thoroughly into my porridge, and then sat back down and looked at me.

'Eat your breakfast up, Sophia,' he commanded quietly. 'Otherwise you will be hungry by suppertime. There is no luncheon for girls who engage in clandestine correspondence.'

I felt my stomach protest at the mere thought of the strong mustard taste. I hated it of all things. Under my father's pitiless gaze, I took a spoonful, put it in my mouth and swallowed. I gagged. The bitter taste burned. But I took another mouthful and another. My eyes were watering now, but I carried on eating until the bowl was empty. Then I sat back and looked defiantly at my father, choking down my nausea.

'Thank you, father,' I said. 'That was delicious.'

He stared back at me, his eyes unreadable. Then he turned to my aunt. 'Amelia, I'm desolated to have to inform you that I'm obliged to go away next week. My solicitor has found tenants for Littlecote and there are some formalities to see to. I shall be gone some time. On my return, I shall of course look forward to hearing a *detailed* account of how you and Sophia got on in my absence.'

He threw his napkin upon his plate, rose from his chair and left the room. I reached for the milk, pouring some into my glass and drinking it, in the hope it would slake the fire in my throat and in my belly. For a second it eased, but then I was forced to rush to the outdoor privy where I threw up violently. I leaned against the rough wooden wall, feeling some relief, though my insides still burned. I was shaking; growing weak. My father was defeating me. I needed to fight back, before I turned into the quivering, cowardly kind of weakling I despised.

My father had taken the letters back, but I would write more. All I needed was money. At that moment, an idea so daring, so completely outrageous, came into my mind that I caught my breath: had my father not said he was going away? What if I were to find a way to hold up his chaise and rob him? A shiver of horrified excitement ran through me. I could scarcely believe such a desperate thought had crossed my mind.

I passed my father as I went back into the house. His smug grin showed he knew he'd made me ill, despite my bravado. Well, he could just wait. I no longer felt so helpless.

My aunt dragged me out to a service in the abbey and then to Harrison's rooms, where I was mildly disappointed to see that Mr Charleton was absent. I told myself I didn't want to see him, but nonetheless I couldn't help but find the rooms dull without his presence.

'Fetch me a dish of tea, would you, Sophia?' Aunt Amelia asked hurriedly as the same sallow-faced man wove his way through the busy throng to speak to her. I kept an eye on them as I did so. They conversed in hushed tones, their heads close together. Then he left the rooms, and my aunt looked around uncomfortably, as though checking whether anyone was watching her.

'Who is he, Aunt?' I asked her, when I returned with her tea.

'Oh, no one!' she said nervously, almost snatching her dish from me, so that some of the liquid splashed out. I looked at her, puzzled, as she sipped her tea, her colour heightened. Feeling my curious gaze, she explained:

'One collects some acquaintances, Sophia, over the years . . . My dear departed husband had many friends who . . . Well, never mind.'

She rose, shaking out her petticoats. 'Why don't you go and take a walk in the gardens, dear? I'm going to play a hand or two of loo before we go home.'

My heart sank. My aunt always said a hand or two and then lost all sense of time, while I waited, bored rigid, surrounded by the crowd of frivolous fashionables whom I didn't want to know, and who didn't want to know me.

I walked with a lagging step to the door, and then happened to glance back at my aunt. On her way to the card tables, she had paused, and I could have sworn I saw her discreetly hand something to a swarthy gentleman with whiskers and an ill-fitting black coat. My curiosity was now awakened. But she joined a group of ladies and had a hand dealt to her. There would be no moving her for several hours now.

Bored and resentful, I decided I would certainly not restrict myself to the gardens, but would go further afield whilst I was unwatched. Walking out of Harrison's, I left the city by the South Gate and crossed the river by way of the road bridge. From there it wasn't far to the wooded hillside of the Beechen Cliff. Kicking off my shoes and stockings and hitching up my petticoat in a satisfyingly unladylike manner, I threw myself into the steep climb.

I met no one on the ascent. As I grew warmer and more out of breath, I could feel how much good the climb was doing me. I needed to move, to exert myself. I wasn't made for a dawdling, sedentary life. I missed my horses and the outdoor activities I'd enjoyed in the country.

I stood at last at the top of the hill, panting and exhilarated, enjoying the vista before me. The sound of the abbey bells rose faintly to me. The city, its ancient walls hugging it close, lay nestled in the bottom of the valley, the brown river partly encircling it in a lazy embrace. Only Trim Street spilled out over the city walls to the north. From here, it all looked small and insignificant, and I could believe that I could defeat both its intolerable life and my father's plans for me. I was far above them both, almost high enough to touch the clouds.

My pleasant reverie was interrupted by a cough nearby. I turned swiftly to see a quietly-dressed young man in a plain tie-wig a short distance from me. He looked familiar. I dropped my petticoats to conceal my grubby feet and hid my shoes and stockings hurriedly behind my back. The young man bowed respectfully and approached me. 'Pardon me,' he said. 'But weren't you the young lady who came to the post office this morning?'

I remembered him, of course. 'My father had the letters returned, did he not?' I asked, embarrassed.

The postmaster smiled. 'No, Miss Williams. He did not. Ralph Allen at your service, by the way,' he said, holding out his hand. I didn't hesitate to shake it.

'So what happened, Mr Allen?' I asked eagerly.

'The letter to Windsor had already been sent with the mail coach before your servant arrived.'

'And the other? The one to Devon?'

Mr Allen bowed and grinned. 'What other letter would that have been, Miss Williams?' he asked.

I laughed with relief to think that both my letters had gone safely after all, and my father had been unable to prevent it. 'Of course! He guessed I'd written to my cousin,' I said, 'but had no notion of the second letter. Mr Allen, you've done a good deed, and I thank you.'

'You're welcome. It's a grand view from up here, isn't it? I walk here whenever I can.'

We both turned to contemplate the view. I wondered how I could get my shoes and stockings back on without making a spectacle of myself.

'One ought to build a house up here,' Mr Allen remarked. 'Something really spectacular that can be seen from the city. And from the house, one would have the view of the Bath. It would be remarkable.'

'But think of bringing the stones and timber up here!' I exclaimed. 'The poor horses!'

'Ah, Miss Williams. That is the beauty of it. In the hills behind us lie the finest reserves of stone, just waiting to be lifted out. There is enough to rebuild the city many times over; or something grander by far. It's a golden fortune awaiting the man who has the vision to cut the stone and market it.'

I looked at him curiously. 'Is that what you're doing up here? Planning to make your fortune?'

Mr Allen sighed. 'I'm merely daydreaming, Miss Williams. In order to make a fortune, one must first possess a fortune, and I have none.'

'Nor I,' I agreed. 'I even had to save the carriage of my letters out of a few coins my aunt gave me for a jelly.

That was why I'm so grateful they were sent after all.'

Mr Allen smiled. 'We must both of us work to improve our situations then. Do you return to the city now? I am heading back and could accompany you if that would be agreeable.'

'Yes, indeed. I need to get back. But . . . ' I hesitated. 'I'm . . . er . . . not wearing my shoes at the moment.'

'I couldn't help observing that, Miss Williams, when I first saw you,' said Mr Allen gravely. 'Do you wish me to turn my back whilst you remedy the situation?'

'To be honest, if it doesn't shock you very much, I'd prefer to wait until I'm at the bottom of the hill to put them back on. They're city shoes and . . . '

'Quite unsuited to walking. I understand completely. I shall pretend not to notice and be thankful that I'm a plain working man who doesn't need to observe the fashions.'

I thoroughly enjoyed the walk back to the city with Mr Allen. He refrained from asking a single question about the fact that I was roaming the hills outside the city alone, but instead told me about the faults of the postal system and how he would like to remedy them if only he had the authority. He seemed an earnest and energetic young man, and I liked him very much indeed. When we reached Harrison's Assembly Rooms, we shook hands cordially. He interested me more than most of the wealthy and noble gentlemen inside the rooms put together.

One of those nobles was emerging just at that moment. 'Your servant, Miss Williams,' said Mr Charleton with a polite but distant bow that reminded me I had walked off from our last conversation. Then he turned to my companion. 'Good afternoon, Allen,' he said cordially. 'A word?'

With a quick bow and word of farewell to me, Mr Allen departed with Mr Charleton. I watched them stride away, already deep in conversation. I was surprised the two men were acquainted. The one was a fashionable fribble, the other a serious working man. It was curious.

I didn't wonder about it for long; I was in a hurry to return to my aunt. For once, I was lucky. She was still playing cards. I stood at a distance and watched her sweeping her winnings from the table. She was doing well. Behind me at a different table, Beau Nash was swearing softly but fluently under his breath and I gathered he was not so fortunate. My father, also engrossed in play, was looking strained, the sweat standing out on his forehead in the hot, stuffy room. He threw down his cards and pushed a pile of golden coins towards the winner. I ground my teeth in anger. That money, so desperately needed on the estate, was being thrown away at the gaming tables. What was this unreasoning obsession with cards and dice?

My aunt rose from her table in a very good mood. 'You're a good girl, waiting so long, Sophia,' she said. 'Your father is still busy, I see. Let's leave him to it and stop for an ice on the way home, shall we?'

She was treating me like a small child, but the day was hot and I was hungry and thirsty after my long walk, so I didn't object. The lemon ice was delicious. I had been quite unable to eat a thing at Harrison's earlier, the memory of the mustard still hideously fresh in my mind.

But now that had faded, I relished the tangy-sweet flavour. My aunt was smiling at the whole world, delighted with her success, clutching her winnings tightly in her reticule.

It was a great pity I had no skill at cards. I too urgently needed money. As I put the last spoonful of lemon ice into my mouth, the idea of robbing my father came back to me. I began to turn the possibilities over in my mind.

CHAPTER THIRTEEN

With robbery uppermost in my mind that night, I climbed down from my bedroom and explored the city in hope of finding Jenny. She was nowhere to be seen. Even if I found her, I wasn't sure how I was going to get her to listen to me.

I hunted for her every night for a week before I came across her. Dressed in a ragged gown, she was picking the pocket of a well-dressed but drunken gentleman leaving an inn. I waited around a corner and after a few seconds, she came tearing around it to the shout of 'Stop thief!'

I caught her by the neck of her gown and hung on, delighted at how fate had played into my hands. 'Say you'll help me, and I won't hand you over to the constable!' I hissed in her ear. She squirmed and fought, but I held her fast as the pursuit drew nearer.

'I'll help you!' she promised at last. We both turned and fled, heavy footsteps close on our heels. I followed Jenny as she wove her way down several alleys at a run, and then scrambled up a drainpipe and over a wall, dropping into a private garden; an oasis of greenery and fragrance in the centre of the stinking city. We stared at one another in the darkness, panting with exertion, listening as our pursuers gave up the chase far behind us.

'What do you want from me?' asked Jenny, her eyes sparkling in the darkness.

'I need to rob a coach,' I told her. 'First thing in the morning. I need to borrow a horse, some boys' clothes and a gun. And if possible, I need a second person to help me. If the robbery succeeds, I'll pay handsomely.'

'A partickler coach, or jest anyone you see?' she asked, a sarcastic edge to her voice. 'Cos they ain't all got enough on 'em to pay for all that trouble. Or if they have, it's well hid.'

'Ah, but what if one knew the place where it was hidden?' I asked.

Jenny's eyes gleamed. She was interested now. 'How would you know such a thing?' she asked.

'It's my father's coach,' I told her, my conscience pricking me uncomfortably as I spoke the words aloud.

Jenny's eyes widened. 'We're robbing your old man?' She whistled as I nodded to confirm it. 'All right then,' she said, a mischievous grin lighting her face. 'What if I say I'll go with you?'

'Not you,' I said quickly.

'You doubt me, do yer? Think I ain't brave enough?'

'No, I know very well that you are. But your brother wouldn't like it.'

Jenny was silent a minute, thinking. 'I knows a lad what'll go with yer,' she said at last. 'But he ain't so good with a gun.'

'I can handle the gun,' I said confidently. Jenny looked sceptical. 'I'm a crack shot,' I assured her.

'Ever shot at a person before?' she asked. 'Cos it makes a difference.'

'No, but I won't be shooting *at* anyone. Only over their heads.'

We negotiated the details and then left the city over the wall and split up. I crossed the river and climbed the hill to wait on the Wells Road and Jenny went off to collect the things we needed. 'It's madness robbing in daylight, mind,' were her parting words. 'We'll be lucky not to get taken up.'

I made my way on foot to the ambush she'd described. As I walked, I pondered the word 'we' in her final sentence and realized I should have made it absolutely clear once more that she wasn't to be involved.

It was a long, cold, hungry night. I huddled under a tree, and hoped my father wouldn't check on me before he left. I'd said my goodbyes to him the evening before, and hoped he wouldn't think it necessary to rouse me at dawn to repeat them.

There were no travellers on the road during the night. All was still except for the call of a few owls, and once, in the distance, the scream of a rabbit, probably caught by a fox. In the grey light of dawn, hoof beats at last approached me. I got up, stiff with cold, and waited to see who it was. Two horses emerged from the darkness, one ridden astride by a slim figure in breeches, the other saddled but led.

'All's fair!' called a low voice, speaking the password we'd agreed. Relieved to hear that Jenny had apparently found someone to assist me, I stepped out of the shadow of the tree, revealing myself. The rider slid to the ground, lifted down a pistol and a bundle and beckoned to me to approach. I did so, my heart thumping with excitement. The rider was already masked.

'Here's what we'll do,' said the slight figure without preamble. The voice was deep and hoarse. 'I'll lie hid yonder in those trees on the far side of the road. You hide here. Then when the coach comes, we'll . . . '

'Wait,' I interrupted. 'You haven't found someone to help me at all, have you? You couldn't keep up that fake voice for more than a sentence.'

The figure that was Jenny cursed and pulled off her mask. 'There wasn't no one else,' she said. 'Me pa was dead drunk, and anyways, if there's money to be made, I wants to earn it. And this bloke, your father that is, put the laughs on us last time with his bag of pennies, so now it's my turn. Our turn, I mean.'

'Jenny,' I said fiercely, 'I promised your brother I'd look out for you, not lead you into trouble.'

'I don't need no leading from a soft 'un like you,' she said indignantly. 'I was robbin' coaches when you was stuck in some fancy nursery learning your letters. Now are we goin' to do this or are we goin' to stand about arguing while the coach goes by?'

Realizing I had no choice, I sighed and resigned myself. There was no doubt that Jenny was both fearless and competent enough for this venture. I ducked back behind the tree and shook out the bundle she'd handed me. It contained breeches, a jacket complete with holes, a large black neckerchief and a battered hat. I wriggled out of my old gown and pulled on the clothes and tied the scarf around my face. They all reeked of onions. Clearly my new, fashionable life was making me fastidious. Finally, I jammed the hat down onto my head and re-emerged. It was getting light. My father was probably on his way.

A shiver of fear and excitement passed through me as I realized my dark plan was about to become a reality. I rubbed suddenly damp palms against my greasy breeches and breathed deeply to steady my nerves. Grasping the reins of the second horse, I swung myself into the saddle. The wonderfully familiar feeling of being on horseback gave me courage.

'Here you are,' said Jenny, passing me the gun. It was heavy and awkward in my hand, very different to my cousin's sleek pistols. 'It's loaded,' she warned me. 'Don't fire it unless you have to, there's people about at this time of day.'

We both looked back down the road, listening for the sound of wheels, but there was nothing yet. 'Mist's rising,' said Jenny in a satisfied voice. I looked around and saw to my surprise that she was right. A mist was materializing at ground level, thick and opaque. 'It's them hot springs, I reckon,' she said. 'A mist often comes up as the sun rises. It's in our favour. They won't see the pothole.'

'What pothole?' I asked, taken by surprise.

Jenny pointed to the road. 'If you can't see it, neither will they. Right, let's have some fun.' Jenny's eyes were alight with excitement. 'Ride out just behind 'em right before they hit that ruddy great hole, then if any of 'em got a gun, which they will have, they'll be trying to turn round and shoot behind themselves. And I'll do the talking. Got it?'

'Got it,' I said. We separated, one of us on each side of the road.

The sky paled, but the mist prevented the visibility from improving, so we heard rather than saw the coach in the distance; a rumbling that drew slowly closer. I drew my horse further back into the trees, hoping this was my father. My heart was pounding with excitement and a thrilling spice of fear.

As the chaise lumbered into view, a ghostly apparition, I tightened the reins and gripped the gun tighter. When it was level with me, I urged my horse forward and rode out just behind the two men on the box of the chaise, startling them so they ducked and half turned to see what had appeared so suddenly beside them. At that moment, the fore wheel of the coach ran into the pothole with a lurch that made the horses snort and plunge in shock. As Jenny had predicted, the rocking of the coach threw the guard off balance. He was forced to drop the heavy blunderbuss and cling to the coach to prevent himself being thrown off into the mud. Unfortunately the weapon went off as it fell, a deafening explosion in the stillness of the early morning.

In the middle of the chaos of guns, panicking horses and shouts, I heard Jenny yell in a gruff voice: 'Stand and deliver!' I winced.

'What the *devil's* going on?' I heard my father's furious voice call out, as he half-opened the door of the chaise right ahead of me and started to lean out.

I couldn't resist the temptation. I grasped the door and yanked at it. My father, who'd been leaning on it, was pulled with it, lost his balance, and came tumbling out of the carriage. As no one had let the steps down, he had a long way to fall, right down into the mud and the wet of the post road. He landed heavily, his smart velvet breeches and the fine cuffs of his coat, lace ruffles, and everything else splashed with mud. His wig fell right off his head, revealing his stubbly pate. I pointed the pistol straight down at him and said in as deep and rough a voice as I could manage: 'Don't move!'

He cowered there in the dirt, one shoe fallen off, his silk stockings soaked and filthy. Through the muffling scarf around my face, I could see the naked fear in his eyes. I understood, in a blinding realization, that he was neither brave nor strong, as I'd always thought him. He was a coward and a bully who took pleasure in browbeating those weaker than himself. He would never take on anyone who was his equal.

So intent was I on this that I forgot the task in hand until Jenny nudged me. She'd come around to my side, nodding to me to search the coach. I knew the men needed to be kept covered, but remembered that Jenny had said she didn't want to be in charge of the gun. We hadn't planned thoroughly enough. Well, there was no help for it: I was the only one who knew where the secret compartment was. I shoved the pistol into her hand, jumped down from my horse and climbed into the chaise my father had so abruptly vacated.

It took me only a few moments to run my hand over the trimmings, find the catch, release it and pull the seat open. I hadn't expected to find it so full: papers, boxes, bags and purses lay neatly stacked in the hiding place. I grabbed two heavy purses and a roll of bills and stuffed them inside my jacket. Then I slammed the compartment shut again and jumped out.

The scene outside wasn't what I'd expected; our fortunes had very nearly been reversed. Jenny was half off her horse, wrestling with the coachman who'd slipped down from the box while she was guarding my father. My father was taking advantage of her inattention to crawl through the mud, trying to reach the blunderbuss the guard had dropped.

Instinctively, I leapt on the back of the man who was fighting Jenny and got one arm around his neck, choking him. He let go of Jenny and staggered. Jenny hit him on the head with the butt of the pistol she held. He went limp in my arms and I dropped him into the mud.

Two men appeared running out of the mist, clad in rough garments; farm labourers, at a guess. Jenny was already turning her horse, kicking him into a canter. I scrambled up on mine as fast as I could and he was in full flight after her before I'd even grasped the reins or got my feet into the stirrups. A shot whistled right over our heads, making both of us duck instinctively and the horses bounded forward in fright. We thundered along the road a short way, jumped the hedge and galloped across a meadow. I followed Jenny closely as she left the field through a copse, by way of a gate she opened for us, and then cantered on into the hills. The sounds of the chaos we'd left behind us faded and gave way to the calm of early morning. When we pulled our horses up, all I could hear was birdsong and the distant barking of a dog.

The two of us looked at each other and Jenny started to laugh. 'What a ruddy mess!' she said. 'I told you not to give me the gun. We came as close as damn it to being took!'

I nodded, realizing I was shaking. But at the same time

I felt a soaring exhilaration. 'We did it though!' I said, patting my bulging jacket. Then I remembered the muck all over my father's clothes and his hat and wig lying in the mud and I started to laugh too.

CHAPTER FOURTEEN

'You have a very hearty appetite this morning, Sophia,' remarked my aunt, as I reached for my third breakfast roll.

'Oh, I'm just comforting myself for my father's absence,' I replied, spreading a generous amount of butter onto the roll, and then picking up the dish of jam. I smiled a little to myself at her sceptical sniff.

It had been touch and go as to whether I was going to get back into the house before my absence was discovered. But I'd just made it. Dawes had been surprised, when she entered my room to lay out my clothes for the morning, to find me in bed in my shift instead of my nightgown, but it wasn't her place to question me.

The morning passed slowly. I accompanied my aunt to the promenade and then ate a syllabub in a cook-shop while my aunt gossiped. Bouts of yawning kept threatening to overcome me. It had been a long night.

When we arrived home for luncheon, I was relieved to find my father hadn't returned. He must have decided to continue his journey despite the robbery. It was with a lighter heart that I set out for another afternoon of boredom at Harrison's. I would be free of my father for many days now.

In the assembly rooms, Aunt Amelia spoke to the same

handful of men she conversed with every time we went out. She never wanted me to join these conversations and these men had kept their distance when my father was with us. I was mildly intrigued, but at a loss to account for it. Then I remembered the plays I'd read over the years and suddenly believed I understood. Congreve, Wycherly and the other male playwrights: they had never interested me much, for they wrote about little else than men and women intriguing with one another. Of course! It was likely that my aunt was passing love notes and arranging secret meetings with these men. Ugh. What a nasty thought. I shook my head to clear it. I would try never to notice it or think about it again.

On the way into Harrison's I had been handed a leaflet, which I'd glanced at only cursorily at first. Then, realizing it was a play bill, I read it with excitement.

'Aunt Amelia!' I exclaimed. 'There's a performance tonight of a play by Aphra Behn! At the Trim Street Theatre. Can we not go and see it?'

'To be sure, I should not object myself,' she said, 'but your father left strict instructions on the subject . . . excuse me, dear, I think I see . . . ' and my aunt disappeared as usual into the card room.

That left me to walk up and down the gardens alone and then yawn over my tea. It was extremely dull. I preferred the mornings spent in the bookstore, where every kind of publication was available. My aunt had insisted on obeying my father's rules and banning poetry or plays, but she had no objection to the newspapers. Occasionally I slipped a collection of poetry or a play inside the newspaper and indulged my taste for literature surreptitiously. At others, I read the papers cover to cover. That was how I knew there had been another riot in London. A mob had swept through parts of the city, smashing windows and starting fires on the anniversary of the date King Charles had been restored to the throne, many years earlier.

My mind wandered as I waited, lost in daydreams of home, and it was a complete shock to me when I heard my name spoken. 'Mr Charleton!' I exclaimed, spilling tea into my saucer. 'I hadn't seen that you were here today.'

He raised his brows and smiled slightly. 'You looked for me then?' he asked.

I frowned, realizing my mistake. 'Only because it's pleasanter here without you,' I said.

He smiled, somehow making me feel very young and awkward. 'What's that you have there?' he asked, indicating the leaflet in my hand. 'Ah, yes! *The Rover*. An entertaining piece. Shall you go to see it?'

'My father doesn't like me to see plays,' I replied bitterly.

'I see. And will that stop you, I wonder?' he asked, his eyes twinkling. It was quite clearly a challenge. But before I could reply he continued: 'Your aunt is playing?'

'As you may see, sir,' I replied with a glance towards the card room where I could just glimpse my aunt dealing a hand to a group of one other lady and two gentlemen. Mr Charleton looked at the group dispassionately for a moment.

'She chooses unusual company,' he commented. I'd just been having similar thoughts, but I was hardly about to discuss something so sordid and embarrassing with a stranger. Mr Charleton smiled. 'You've made an unusual friend too,' he remarked.

I froze, feeling a surge of panic. How could he know about Jenny? Surely he knew nothing of the robbery?

'Allen is an estimable man,' Mr Charleton added. 'How did you meet him?'

I breathed a sigh of relief. 'Oh,' I said with a shaky laugh. 'Mr Allen. To be sure. I met him at the post office, of course.'

'Ah, I see. He's a man of great talents and industry.'

'I think so too,' I agreed. 'I happened to meet him again when I was out walking, and he told me something of his ambitions.'

'And do you often walk . . . ' Mr Charleton broke off as a smart young man tugged at his elbow, distracting him. With a quick bow of apology, Mr Charleton moved aside and a low-voiced conversation followed. I looked out of the window, careful not to look as though I was trying to overhear. After a moment, Mr Charleton turned back to me and bowed more formally. 'Miss Williams, I'm desolated to have to leave you, but urgent business calls me away. We can continue this conversation another time, I hope.'

I looked at him in surprise, wondering what important business a gentleman of leisure could possibly have. But it mattered little to me after all. I nodded to him and said nothing, watching as his elegant figure disappeared through the throng of fashionables. To my surprise he returned a moment later accompanied by a very small man, modestly rather than expensively dressed; he walked with difficulty, leaning on a stick. He was so bent

119

that at first I thought he was an old man, but he wasn't.
He was quite young, but crippled.

'Miss Williams, before I go,' said Mr Charleton. 'This is
Mr Alexander Pope. I know you've been eager to meet
him.' He bowed, and withdrew, leaving us together.

Mr Pope offered his hand and I placed mine in it. He
bowed. 'Pleased to meet you, Miss Williams,' he said with
a friendly smile, lowering himself into the seat beside me
with difficulty, his breath rasping. 'My friend Charleton
tells me you are a great reader.'

I blushed and stumbled over my words, shy to be
speaking to such a famous poet, but he was easy to talk
to and soon put me at my ease. We spoke of poetry and
stories and agreed on favourites. 'I see you have the playbill there,' Pope remarked. 'It's a good performance. I
was there last night. I venture to promise you'll enjoy it.'

I was in a glow after he'd taken leave of me. Even the
usual boredom of the rooms wasn't as painful as usual.
I reread the playbill, thinking over Pope's recommenda-
tion and Mr Charleton's challenge. He'd as good as dared
me to go. And he was quite right: why should I not see
the play? I concealed the playbill in my pocket and didn't
mention it to my aunt again. She'd forgotten about it by
the time she finished playing cards. Over dinner, I grew
quiet and began to close my eyes and rest my forehead
on my hand. When my aunt still said nothing, I sighed
deeply.

'What is it, Sophia?' she said impatiently. 'We must
make haste and get changed for the evening service in
the abbey. There will be cards afterwards at Harrison's.'
She put down her knife and fork with a clatter and I

winced eloquently at the sound.

'I can feel one of my migraines coming on,' I said faintly. 'Might I be excused this once and go to bed? I don't get them often, but when I do, they last all night.'

My aunt looked at me suspiciously. I did my best to look like a drooping headache-sufferer, and reluctantly she gave her consent.

It was an easy matter to send Dawes away, stuff the bed with clothes to make it look as though I was asleep and slip away through the window, pulling the shutters closed behind me. Wearing my old wrap-around gown, I purchased a ticket for the pit, hoping that would mean I was well away from anyone who knew me. But I needn't have worried; the theatre was almost empty. The audience was dispersed around the cramped auditorium in twos and threes with large gaps, and I thought how disheartening it must be for the actors. But once the first scene opened, I was spellbound by my first experience of the theatre. I was with Hellena and Florinda every step of the way as they fought the persecution by their father and brother. When the first act ended, I was breathless with excitement. A touch at my elbow and Mr Charleton's voice made me jump out of my skin.

'So you did attend after all. But your aunt surely did not let you come alone?'

'She preferred to play cards,' I said, avoiding an outright lie.

'In common with most of the nation,' replied Mr Charleton. His smile was enigmatic, and I was almost certain he guessed I was here without permission. 'But you must join me. It is not the done thing, you know, for young ladies to attend playhouses alone. Your aunt should have warned you.'

'Please, don't trouble yourself!' I begged him, but he would not be gainsaid. 'Come, Miss Williams!' he said. 'I've come tonight especially to enjoy your company, so you cannot refuse me.'

'You cannot have known I'd be here,' I objected.

'It was an educated guess, and you have proved me right.'

I raised my brows in surprise and he grinned. 'Very well, I confess I happen to live next to the theatre, opposite your house, and saw you pass by. But I was fairly sure you'd be here.' He led me to a seat beside his and insisted on purchasing me lemonade to refresh myself. I didn't know how to rid myself of him, but when he began to talk about the performance with me, I forgot about wishing him away, and threw myself into the discussion.

'Hellena is wonderful!' I agreed enthusiastically. 'She's absolutely right to flout her family's orders and try and enjoy herself before they steal her life from her!'

'No matter what the dangers may be?' asked Mr Charleton. He leant one arm against the back of my chair and looked down at me.

'What are dangers compared to experiencing life before it is snatched away?' I cried passionately. 'She may as well be dead as in a nunnery. I would do the same. Though why she should choose to fall in love is beyond me. I'd find something better to do with my last nights of freedom.'

'I'm sure you would,' agreed Mr Charleton. 'Haven't you already done so?'

I caught my breath. 'I don't know what you mean,' I stammered. I was grateful when he calmly changed the subject: 'And how did you like Alexander Pope? He's a man of great gifts, is he not?'

'Oh, yes,' I agreed, relieved to be on safe ground again. 'And I was amazed by how easy he was to talk to.'

'He's very affable. You see, Miss Williams, we shall have you making friends here in no time.'

I stiffened, annoyed that the apparently kind introduction had been part of a strategy. 'I assure you . . . ' I began crossly, but at that moment Belvile reappeared on stage. Mr Charleton laid a hand over one of mine and shushed me quietly. I snatched my hand away and sat rigid with indignation in my seat.

But the moment the players began to speak again, I forgot my anger and became caught up in the performance once more. The second act was even more intense than the first. There was some fine acting, and I was surprised at how the presence of Mr Charleton beside me heightened my enjoyment. He laughed when I laughed and then we both grew still and serious as the tragedy of the jilted courtesan played out on stage.

I had tears in my eyes at the end of the second act, so moving was the portrayal. I blinked them hurriedly away as Mr Charleton turned to me to ask how I had enjoyed my first visit to the theatre.

'I loved it,' I sighed happily. 'I could come here every night. I bought this play, you know, just a few months ago. But before I could finish reading it . . . '

'Yes?' Mr Charleton prompted as I stopped.

'To tell you the truth, sir, my father burned it. He said

it was unsuitable.' I wasn't sure what made me confide in Mr Charleton. Perhaps it was a mistake. But the sense of injustice still raged in me.

'Severe, but not uncommon,' Mr Charleton replied. 'Many girls are banned from reading such works. Hellena's first speeches against the marriage of young girls to old men are particularly outspoken and often omitted from modern productions. But when you are married you will be allowed to read more freely.'

'Won't that depend on my husband?' I asked. 'After all, my life will be ruled by the decisions men make for me, won't they?'

'How your eyes sparkle with indignation, Miss Williams,' commented Mr Charleton. 'You said earlier that any means were justified in enjoying your freedom. Would that be true even if it involved harm to others? Would you break the law?'

I sat silent, wondering again how much he guessed or knew about me. Could he possibly know what I'd done this morning? I could feel my heart hammering, and I knew a traitorous heat was rising in my face. I must keep Mr Charleton at arm's length, or sooner or later I would reveal myself. I stood up hurriedly. 'I must go.'

After a penetrating look that took in my heightened colour, he said calmly: 'Of course. You must allow me to escort you home.'

This was a fresh danger. I had to think quickly. How to shake off my unwanted companion between here and the other end of Trim Street? If he escorted me, I would be obliged to knock on the front door, and my expedition would be discovered.

'There's no need,' I told him. 'I can walk such a short distance by myself.'

'Oh, I insist,' he replied. 'Can I fetch your cloak?'

'My cloak . . . yes, indeed my cloak,' I said. 'Thank you. It's blue,' I added with a smile.

As we rose and walked to the exit together, I contrived to fall a little behind him. He went to fetch my non-existent cloak from the attendant and I slipped back into the auditorium and left it by the only other door I could see. It led backstage to a shabby maze of narrow corridors with the paint peeling off. I ran straight into Hellena, her stage paint garish in the lamp-lit corridor. We stood and stared at one another in confusion for a second.

'You were wonderful,' I told her, and impulsively I kissed her cheek. 'You've given me courage. Is there a back way out through here? In the spirit of the play, I'm escaping an inconvenient male escort.'

The young woman suddenly smiled. 'There is, but it only leads out into the back yard,' she replied, pointing the way.

'That will be perfect,' I assured her. I stepped out into the small yard that contained a privy and a number of broken props. I vaulted onto the wall and walked along it until I reached a narrow path at the end. From there it was easy enough to drop down, cross two gardens and circle back across Trim Bridge and into the stable yard. As I snuggled down into my bed, I grinned at the thought of Mr Charleton hunting uselessly for a blue cloak that didn't exist and wondering where I'd disappeared to.

CHAPTER FIFTEEN

Mr Charleton never asked me about my disappearance; he merely greeted me the next time we met with his usual politeness. I suspected he knew perfectly well why I'd run away and had only offered to escort me home from a sense of mischief. How much else did he know about me?

In the following weeks I attended breakfasts, dances, afternoons at Harrison's, promenades, and services in the abbey. Some days I had to pinch myself to be sure it wasn't the same endlessly-repeating dull dream. Aunt Amelia disappeared into the card room every afternoon. I stood at the door and watched her take her place at the tables. Obviously I was delighted to have a breathing space from her watchfulness each day, but I was surprised that gambling was becoming such a passion that she left me regularly unsupervised.

One afternoon, a lady at a nearby card table beckoned me across to her.

'You wanted to speak to me, ma'am?' I asked her as I stepped up to her table.

'Yes, dear. Miss Williams is it not?'

She was an older woman with a strong, much-painted face, a large patch on one cheekbone and an elaborate, powdered hair-style. 'That's right,' I agreed doubtfully.

'Well, Miss Williams, we need a fourth for our table. Do you care to join us? We intend to play at ombre.'

'Thank you for the invitation, ma'am,' I said, still ignorant of the lady's name. 'But I don't know how to play.'

'You don't know how . . . ?' The lady stopped, apparently speechless. One of the girls at her table tittered. Glancing at her, I saw a young and pretty blonde face. 'Lansquenet then? Or perhaps you prefer loo?'

'I'm sorry. I don't know any card game at all.'

A fresh outburst of giggles from the fair girl greeted my words, and a look of astonishment descended on the lady's face. 'But, my dear, what do you *do* all day?'

'I love to read, ma'am,' I said somewhat stiffly.

'Books!' she exclaimed. 'Don't give me books! Men and cards are all the books I need!'

'We should teach her, Lady Orkney,' cried the fair girl. 'It does not *do* you know, Miss Williams,' she said speaking earnestly to me, 'to be ignorant of cards. All the world plays.'

'Thank you,' I said swiftly, 'but I find I do well enough without cards or what you call 'the world' for amusement.'

A man nearby, hearing what I said, lounged up to us and leant on the back of the blonde girl's chair. He was dressed in brown with a waistcoat that was a vile shade of puce. He stared at me as if I were some curiosity in a travelling fair. I felt my colour rise under his scrutiny. He commented: 'How very singular!' The girls tittered again.

Blushing, I left the card room, aware of a buzz of whispers after me. I told myself I cared not. Instead I sought the tea room and accepted a cup of tea and a smile from a friendly waiter and passed some pleasant time chatting to him until a fiddler struck up outside and an impromptu dance began on the lawn. The guests crowded out of the rooms to join in. The tune was a merry one that set feet tapping at once, and I found myself drifting outside to watch. It was mildly entertaining; certainly better than sitting in a stuffy tea room on a bright afternoon.

After just a few moments, I became aware I was being watched. The same man in the puce waistcoat was staring at me once more. There were several young women gathered around him, one of them the ubiquitous Mary Welland who I avoided whenever I could. I saw the blonde from the card table whispering in her ear, her speech punctuated with giggles. They were all looking at me. I looked away, pretending I hadn't noticed. 'Lud!' the man exclaimed, loudly. 'Does she think she'll get a dance partner? Surely even she must realize that no self-respecting gentleman would be seen within ten feet of her?'

It was clear the speaker intended me to hear his words. His tone was arrogant and disdainful. There was laughter from the girls around him. I froze, unsure whether to move away, pretending I hadn't heard, or whether I should brazen it out. It hadn't occurred to me that by watching the dancing, I'd be thought to be begging for a partner. Then I reminded myself that social disgrace was my aim and steeled myself to stay where I was.

'Who'd want to dance with a girl who walks like a man and muffs all her steps?' commented another girl in a breathless voice.

'And she has no notion of the rules of ombre!' said another with a giggle. 'If ever there was a sign of no breeding.'

I glanced at the group. Mary was in the act of putting her hand on the young man's shoulder and standing on tiptoe to say in a penetrating whisper: 'At home in Devon, she rides around in breeches and they call her 'the Squire'.'

Another outbreak of mirth from the girls. 'By gad, I *thought* I caught a glimpse of a spur under those petticoats,' exclaimed the gentleman in the puce waistcoat again, pretending to inspect the hem of my gown.

'Oh, take care, Sir Oswald,' begged Mary maliciously. 'She hears you! I think she's going to call you out for that!'

I was burning with anger by now and opened my mouth to tell them nothing would give me more pleasure, but was forestalled by a hand on my arm. 'How do you do, Miss Williams? Would you care to dance?'

Distracted, I turned and found myself face to face with Mr Charleton, expensively elegant as always, in a coat of dark green velvet over a pale green embroidered waistcoat and pale breeches. 'What?' I asked.

'A dance, Miss Williams,' he said with politely lifted eyebrows. 'It's a social custom whereby we step out onto this patch of grass together, pretend it is a dance floor, follow some pre-ordained steps and try to refrain from stepping on each other's toes.'

I bit my lip, half amused by his nonsense, but my mind still on the group behind me. I heard Sir Oswald mutter distinctly: 'I've always said Charleton had no discrimination. Damn, he might be the son of an earl but the fellow has low taste.'

I stiffened angrily, ready to turn back and throw some insults in return, but Charleton took my hand firmly in his and led me towards the lawn. 'You'd do much better to dance,' he said. 'An altercation would be their triumph, believe me.'

'You heard them?' I asked. 'I'm surprised *you* aren't calling that man out!'

'When I feel my honour or yours will be better served by duelling than by ignoring him, I shall certainly do so,' he said calmly. 'But really, Sir Oswald's opinions are a matter of complete indifference to me.'

'How I wish I were a man!' I exclaimed. 'I'd call that fop out at once.'

Mr Charleton looked sceptical. 'Pistols or swords?' he enquired.

'Pistols,' I said at once. 'I'd shoot him dead.'

'I doubt it,' he said drily. I didn't reply, busy dwelling on the pleasure it would give me to see Sir Oswald's lifeless body stretched out on the cold turf of some deserted field at dawn tomorrow. 'Your eyes are positively gleaming with murderous intent, Miss Williams,' said Mr Charleton, recalling me to the present. 'Have you ever actually held a pistol, or is this a vicarious daydream?'

I frowned at him. 'Certainly, I have.'

'I see. Well, Sir Oswald had better watch out,' he remarked. 'By the way, Miss Williams, my valet has done a particularly careful job of polishing my boots this morning. Can I ask you to treat them with great care?'

'That's the second time today you've alluded to my poor skills at dancing, sir,' I said. 'If you will insist on making me dance, you must expect some damage. The other gentlemen know better and leave me in peace.'

'And have you quite decided on being a social outcast?' he asked. 'It seems an uncomfortable choice to me.'

'I have good reasons.'

'And you are certainly not going to share them with me?'

I shook my head. The dance was a country dance I'd attempted until now only with the dancing master, and our conversation died as I did my best to mind my steps. I reminded myself that I was not going to be drawn into any confidences with Mr Charleton. I'd already said too much again. It was surprising the way he could always get me to talk about myself.

'Admirable!' said Charleton as the music finally stopped. 'My boots are entirely unscathed!'

'You practically issued a challenge to me,' I explained. 'I wasn't going to give you the satisfaction of putting that long-suffering expression on your face again.'

'An excellent motivation, if I may say so,' Charleton responded. 'More of that and you may learn to dance very creditably in the end.'

'I don't care whether I do or not, and I can't imagine why you should,' I said frankly.

'Nor I, indeed. Perhaps it's the pleasure of undermining your determination to hate everything about the Bath. Can I fetch you any refreshment?'

'If that's your intention, you will certainly fail,' I said shortly. I realized with a shock that he had indeed made me forget, for a pleasant half hour, my plan to disgrace myself and to be unpleasant and rude to everyone. His humour had got under my guard and distracted me from my purpose. Across the room, I could see my aunt had forsaken the card room and was standing watching me approvingly. This was a disaster. 'I want nothing from you, sir,' I said abruptly to Mr Charleton. 'Nothing at all.'

I left him. I had to avoid him completely in future, I realized. I must keep firm to my purpose however unpleasant it was. Otherwise I might awaken expectations of wedding bells in my father's mind. Unthinkable! But I felt a pang of loss, nonetheless, at the thought of needing to avoid Mr Charleton. I was drawn to him, I had to admit. I suspected it was at least partly because he was a danger to me. I'd always liked to play with fire.

I returned to the tea room and spotted Sir Oswald with the blonde, dishes of tea in their hands. I grinned to myself and walked close by them, managing to knock the girl's elbow in passing. She cried out in distress as the tea slopped down her white gown. 'Oh, I'm so *sorry*!' I exclaimed. 'My dreadful clumsiness. I can't apologize enough.'

When we reached home, Aunt Amelia stripped off her gloves and turned to me: 'Straight to your room, Sophia. I don't want to see you until tomorrow. You are an embarrassment to me and to yourself. I despair of ever teaching you to behave like a young lady.'

Taken aback at her severity, so unlike her usual foolish

vagueness, I opened my mouth to object. But I could see she was furious and meant what she said. With a slight shrug, I decided to do as I was told. It made little difference to me whether I spent the evening in my room or my aunt's company; either was equally tedious. And now I had money, I could make up for my lost supper later.

I roamed the narrow streets that night with a particular purpose in mind. I was looking for two sedan chairmen; the two men, in fact, who had played that unkind trick on my aunt. I asked after them among the other chairmen and was directed to a tavern in Slippery Lane; a most unsavoury part of the city. Unwilling to enter the dirty, dilapidated tavern itself, I waited until the two men emerged, the worse for drink, holding on to one another for balance. They paused when I stepped out of the shadows to speak to them. I could see they recognized me. Neither of them looked remotely pleased to renew their acquaintance with me.

'I have a job for you,' I told them.

'Well I ain't working for you till I gets paid the last fare,' said the warty-nosed man pugnaciously. He was clearly the leader.

'That isn't going to happen,' I retorted. 'You should ask rather why I'd trust you when you tried to cheat us last time.'

'Fair point,' slurred the second man. 'Ain't that a fair point, Sam?'

'Shut up, you. You're as drunk as a cart horse,' said his friend impatiently. 'Let's go. I ain't about to stand here being insulted by some chit of a girl.'

'Go then,' I said calmly as they lurched off. 'I can see you're both too stupid for the job I had in mind. Which is a pity, as you'd have earned three guineas.'

The smaller man tore away from his friend at that, and stood staring at me with his mouth hanging open. 'Three guineas?' he stuttered.

The man called Sam was looking at me too now, his eyes gleaming with greed. 'What for?' he demanded.

I looked him up and down. 'No,' I said at last. 'You haven't got the guts. Besides, you're drunk.'

'Seems to me,' said Sam with a glance around him at the dark street, 'we could just take the money off you now and be done with it. Who's to stop us?'

I folded my arms and stared back at him. 'You could do that,' I agreed. 'If I'd been stupid enough to bring such a sum out with me at night. Whereas in fact if you rob me now, all you will find is a few coppers I've brought with me to buy a pie.'

All three of us stood frozen, wondering who'd give first. I was pitting my wits against two brawny, unprincipled men in a dark alley and hoping I'd planned cleverly enough not to come off badly. I loved the risk and the danger.

'Let's hear it then,' said Sam at last.

I paused, pretending reluctance. 'You have the courage to extort money from ladies,' I said at last, 'but are you brave enough to play a similar trick on a man? I'm not so sure.'

Both men looked wary. 'What sort of trick?' asked Sam.

'I was thinking along the lines of tipping him out of

the chair into a particularly muddy puddle or festering rubbish heap. Preferably with witnesses and when he's wearing his evening clothes. I don't want him hurt, merely humiliated.'

The smaller man gave a soundless whistle and his friend looked thoughtful. 'You'll pay us three guineas for that? Who's the geezer you hate so much?'

'His name,' I said with relish, 'is Sir Oswald.'

CHAPTER SIXTEEN

For the ball the next night, I wore a midnight-blue gown with white lace and silver ribbons. Dawes curled and powdered my hair, fastened my pearl necklace around my neck and draped a shawl about me.

The street was chaotic with sedan-chair arrivals when we reached the Guildhall. People were alighting with great care, the ladies holding their petticoats out of the dirt. It had been raining all the afternoon and a great deal of refuse and mud had collected in the streets and lay putrefying there. I picked my way through it to the entrance. I'd just stepped inside the pillars when a great commotion arose behind me. A crash first; a thud and the sound of splintering wood. This noise was followed by shouts and cries and the air was suddenly full of the kind of language that made my aunt shriek and cover her ears.

I looked round, curious to see the cause. A scene of chaos met my eyes. A tatty old sedan chair half-stood, half-lay in the dirt of the High Street, one leg snapped off. Its finely-dressed passenger lay sprawled in the road, his fine clothes and his wig generously splattered with filth. A grin spread across my face at the sight of the proud Sir Oswald brought low.

'Come away, Sophia,' cried my aunt, clutching my arm.

'No, Aunt, they've stopped swearing now. Let us see what happens!' Aunt Amelia didn't release my arm, but she let me stay. Truth to tell, she was probably eager to watch too.

Sir Oswald had struggled to his feet with the help of a certain wart-nosed chairman. His fine clothes were covered in muck, and he was bewailing their ruin. Quite a crowd was gathering about him and all traffic had come to a halt around the epicentre of this storm, people watching, calling out comments. 'Fetch the constable!' Sir Oswald was crying. 'These men did this on purpose!'

'No, guv'nor,' the chairman cried hoarsely. 'Accident! See—me chair's broke! And me partner here's bust 'is leg!'

For the first time, I noticed the second man sitting in the road, rocking backwards and forwards, moaning, clutching his leg. For a moment I was afraid he had a serious injury, but then I recollected that this was probably all staged to excuse themselves from blame. I was impressed. The men had worked hard for their three guineas.

'They can't have broken a chair and a leg on purpose, Sir Oswald!' exclaimed a bystander. 'Be reasonable!'

Sir Oswald cast the injured man a cursory glance. 'Curse you, you clumsy oafs!' he swore. 'I shall have to go home now. Someone get me another chair!'

I didn't quite follow what happened next, but it looked as though Sir Oswald pushed past my warty friend and then somehow tripped. I saw him stagger in a vain attempt to regain his balance and then go sprawling once more into the mud.

'Oh, the poor man!' exclaimed my aunt beside me. I didn't reply, watching joyfully as Sir Oswald picked himself up once more. This time, even his face and wig were smeared and dripping with filth.

'You tripped me, you damned cur!' he yelled. He picked his cane out of the mud and gave the chairman a blow with it. I could hear the crack of the stick across the man's back. The feeling in the crowd veered sharply against Sir Oswald and in favour of the chairmen.

'Leave the poor man alone!' people were shouting.

'I never tripped you, sir, your worship!' The chairman denied the accusation hotly, whilst cringing against further blows. 'You fell, sir!'

Sir Oswald began to swear again, and once more my aunt tugged on my arm. 'We all saw you trip, Sir Oswald,' said Mr Charleton, who had strolled up to the group on his way to the ball. 'Let these poor men get to a doctor and clear away this broken chair. The whole High Street is blocked; the traffic backed up halfway down Cheap Street.'

Charleton was as immaculate as ever in his evening clothes: a long cloak, high heels and long-bottomed wig, a sword at his side, a complete contrast to the dripping and unfortunate Sir Oswald.

'I didn't ask for your damned interference, Charleton,' swore Sir Oswald, wiping the filth from his face with a handkerchief. 'I'll get a constable on these men, I tell you.'

'Aw, take a damper, gov'nor!' called out another chairman. 'They was injured in the course o' their duty, and you oughta be sorry for 'em, not make a fuss cos you got a bit of mud on your pretty clothes!'

The chairmen rallied around now, circling their unfortunate colleagues and shielding them from Sir Oswald's anger. In his fury, he snapped his cane across his knee, threw it into the kennel, in which murky water trickled down the middle of the street, and stalked off. Except that it isn't easy to stalk in a dignified manner in high heels on a cobbled street. His departure was punctuated by stumbles and oaths. There was guilty laughter and suppressed merriment in the crowd. 'Well, that was as good as a play!' exclaimed my aunt, summing up the general feeling. 'Come, Sophia. Let's go inside now!'

I obeyed willingly, pausing at the entrance to the ballroom to shake out my petticoats. I was triumphant. First my father, then the blonde, and now the obnoxious Sir Oswald. Was anyone else keen to thwart me? I was ready to take on all comers.

The ballroom was crowded but I faced it with less trepidation than formerly, buoyed up by my victory. The musicians were busy playing at the far end of the room, but no one was listening. Everyone was gossiping as though their lives depended upon it about the incident outside.

I looked around the room. There were a number of familiar faces, but not one person greeted me with anything approaching friendliness. Mary saw me and turned her back. Several men stared at me unsmiling and the blonde girl glared at me. I smirked quietly to myself at having achieved such unpopularity in such a short space of time. And they didn't know even half the truth about me. Perhaps when my father returned to the Bath he would see the pointlessness of our stay here.

A tall, spare man with a military bearing and large grey moustaches approached my aunt and bowed before her. 'Mrs Adamson,' he said in a dry voice. 'Allow me to tell you how delighted I am to be able to resume our acquaintance.'

'Oh!' exclaimed my aunt, clearly discomposed. 'Yes indeed, how very . . . charmed, of course, to see you again.'

Looking curiously at the man, who was a stranger to me, I was certain I saw his eyes glint. He seemed pleased at having flustered my aunt. 'Harrogate, was it not? You were with your late husband. I should tell you how *deeply* sorry I was to hear of his sudden, unfortunate demise. My heartfelt condolences.'

The words ought to have been kind, but somehow they weren't. There was a sinister tone in the man's voice. Aunt Amelia's face flushed red and then white, and she choked on the reply she tried to utter. The man spoke again.

'Are you going to introduce me to your charming . . . sister?'

Why was it that so many men chose to flatter my aunt by pretending I looked like her sister? It wasn't remotely complimentary to *me* to have it insinuated that I looked only a few years younger than a stout, wrinkled matron.

'Ah yes . . . um . . . my niece, Captain Mould. Miss Williams. Sophia, this is Captain Mould.'

I curtseyed and extended one hand. The man took it in his and bowed stiffly over it. His eyes didn't leave my face as he did so, and the tip of his tongue darted quickly out over his dry lips as he examined me. It reminded me uncomfortably of the lizard Jack and I had caught in the shrubbery once. I shivered slightly and drew my hand out of his. 'Pleased to meet you, sir,' I lied.

'And I to meet you.' He took a pinch of snuff from his box and inhaled it without taking his eyes off me. 'I hope you may be persuaded to honour me with a dance later this evening?'

I felt my skin crawl. 'I'm a very indifferent dancer, sir . . . ' I began, but my aunt interrupted at once.

'Nonsense, Sophia!' She frowned heavily at me and I couldn't miss the command in her look. 'You will thank the captain prettily and accept.'

'Thank you, sir,' I said unwillingly with only the tiniest curtsey of acknowledgement. I was angry with my aunt for forcing me into this. Surely it was my right to refuse a partner if I chose to do so?

At that moment, Nash approached us with his usual elegant bow and kind smile. 'Miss Williams, may I be allowed to present you with Mr Charleton as your partner for the minuet?' His eyes twinkled at me as if with some secret complicity. As he bowed and left us, I looked to Mr Charleton for an explanation, but his look was blandly innocent. He bowed without speaking, and held out his hand for mine.

I'd been fully determined to avoid Mr Charleton tonight and to refuse him if he asked me to dance. But the Beau's introductions for the minuet were not to be set aside. So I put my gloved hand in his and allowed him to lead me away from the sinister captain to the top of the room where we would soon take our turn to dance.

'How fortunate I am to have secured your hand for this dance, Miss Williams,' Mr Charleton remarked. I remembered the Beau's smile, and frowned.

'Did you ask Mr Nash to present you to me tonight?' I asked suspiciously.

'I *may* have dropped the merest hint in his ear,' admitted Mr Charleton gravely. 'And the Beau does love an intrigue—even the merest hint of one.'

'There is no intrigue,' I said swiftly, determined not to be drawn into friendship or anything else with Mr Charleton, no matter how charming he could be.

'Ah, but the Beau believes there may be, and that is enough,' replied Mr Charleton. His light tone, his easy agreement that nothing lay between us made me relax a little.

'I fear you are unscrupulous, sir,' I said with a reluctant smile.

'Absolutely. But I had to have the opportunity of asking you how you enjoyed the spectacle of Sir Oswald in the mud just now?'

I smiled, recalling the deep satisfaction of seeing my enemy in the mire. 'The poor gentleman! Surely no one could deserve such an unfortunate incident less?' I paused in dreamy recollection and added: 'I fear his costly raiment must be quite ruined.'

'Oh, without doubt.'

'You were very quick to defend the chairman,' I said. 'Are you quite sure it wasn't his fault Sir Oswald fell a second time?'

'On the contrary,' replied Mr Charleton. 'I saw the fellow trip him. It was very neatly done.'

'But you said . . . ?'

'Really, Miss Williams. Have you forgotten already that Oswald insulted me too? Besides, he struck the chairman. One should never strike one's social inferiors. It is most unjust.'

I smiled. Mr Charleton was a man more after my own heart than I'd had any idea of. He'd found a subtle way of exacting his own revenge.

'Who is your aunt's friend?' he asked abruptly.

'A Captain Mould, apparently,' I told him, my smile fading.

'A singularly appropriate name,' said Charleton with a curious glance in the gentleman's direction. 'He must be a new arrival, for I've not seen him before.'

'How would you notice one man among such crowds? And in my opinion, Mr Lizard would be a more suitable name for the man.'

'Mr Lizard?' replied Mr Charleton with a slight smile. 'You disliked him then?'

I shuddered in reply. The couple ahead of us began to dance, and Mr Charleton led me forward so that we were ready to start once they reached the bottom of the room. 'He's a friend of your aunt?' Charleton enquired, his eyes seeking out the captain in the crowd. I looked across to where Captain Mould stood, still talking to my aunt, their heads close together.

'I don't know about friend,' I said. 'She knows him, but she didn't seem pleased to see him. She seemed almost . . . frightened.'

'How very interesting,' said Charleton, his eyes still on Mould.

'Why is that interesting?' I asked curiously, wondering why Mr Charleton always asked me so many questions about my family. Mr Charleton didn't reply immediately. It was almost as though he hadn't heard me. Then suddenly he smiled, relaxed and light-hearted again.

'Oh, no reason. Put him out of your mind for now, Miss Williams,' he recommended. 'And try to recall the steps of the minuet. I have a corn upon one toe tonight, and will suffer agonies if you step on it.'

'Oh, you are a bad liar, sir!' I retorted, forgetting all about my aunt at once. 'You don't wish me to embarrass you before all these lords and ladies!'

'Just so,' he agreed. We danced down the room without errors. Mr Charleton moved with such confidence and grace that I felt easy myself. Despite my nerves and fear of muffing the steps, I experienced for the first time a measure of exhilaration. I could almost understand that there might be something in this craze for dancing.

I felt relieved and buoyant as we reached the bottom of the room without mishap. I sank into my curtsey as Mr Charleton bowed over my gloved hand once more. He raised my fingers to his lips in one graceful movement, so that he had kissed and released them before I had a chance to object. The colour flooded my face, but before I'd thought how to react, a most unwelcome voice spoke from behind me.

'Very prettily done, Miss Williams. Now you are promised to me for supper and the first country dance.'

I turned to find Captain Mould at my elbow, an unpleasant smile twisting his lipless mouth.

'You are mistaken, sir,' said Mr Charleton at once. He took my hand and drew it through his arm. 'The lady is mine.'

'Not at all, young man. Your pleasure is over; mine is merely beginning.'

'At the Bath, sir,' countered Mr Charleton, his tone politely instructive, 'the partner in the minuet has the pleasure of accompanying his fair lady during supper.'

'I would challenge that right,' said Captain Mould, stepping forward. As he did so he thrust his sword hilt forward threateningly.

I saw Mr Charleton's eyes sparkle in response to this. 'You are offensive sir,' he said softly, dropping his free hand onto the hilt of his own sword.

My eyes flew from one to the other of the two men, my heartbeat quickened with excitement. Were they really disputing the right to take their refreshments at my side? It seemed out of all proportion.

'I'm glad you have the wit to perceive it. If we are to speak of customs, I should call your attention to the notion of a mere youngster giving way to his elders and betters,' said the captain.

Mr Charleton smiled. He bowed gracefully in acknowledgement of defeat. 'You do right to remind me, sir. What, after all, are my youth and appearance to a young lady, compared to your age and experience?' He turned to me and bowed again. 'Miss Williams, I leave you in very safe hands. You could scarcely be safer with your own grandfather.'

He couldn't have chosen a better parting shot. The captain's victory was empty, having laid himself open to that insinuation. He glared at Mr Charleton's retreating back, his jaw working. Then he recollected himself, turned and abruptly offered his arm. 'Miss Williams, that young man needs a sharp lesson. Will you come with me and take some refreshment after your exertion?'

I had no choice but to lay my hand upon his arm and follow him to the table. It was laughable to call the minuet an exertion of course; those few steps and some bobbing up and down were nothing.

I was forced to dance the next dance with the lizard. Even though I took great care to answer his attempts at conversation with rudeness and to step upon his feet several times, he hung about me for the remainder of the evening, apparently undeterred. I returned home weary and unnerved, for I felt that in Captain Mould I had met someone who would not be so easily held at a distance.

CHAPTER SEVENTEEN

✴

I felt too tired and dispirited to venture out into the city that night. But I'd barely climbed into my bed when I was disturbed by a soft scratching at the window. A dark shadow loomed on the other side of the glass. I'd made a number of unsavoury acquaintances recently, and I didn't like the idea of any of them finding their way to my bedroom window.

A hand was pressed against the glass and I noted with relief the mutilated little finger. Of Jenny, I had no fear. I threw open the window at once. 'Hello! What are you doing here?' I asked, keeping my voice low to avoid being overheard.

'Looking for you, o' course,' was the acerbic reply. 'I don't climb around on roofs for me good 'ealth.'

'*Why* are you looking for me? And how did you find me?'

'You ain't the only one as can follow folk,' she retorted. 'I needs your help.' She threw me the small oil-skin wrapped parcel of my shoes and heavy purse, and added: 'And find a safer spot for that lot if you don't want to lose it all.'

'I have nowhere,' I said, shocked by the realization that I could have been robbed by anyone who followed me onto the roof. 'I have a maid and a father who both search my room.'

Jenny sighed and beckoned me out onto the parapet. 'Look here,' she said, slipping her fingers under the tiles until she found one that was loose. Lifting it carefully, she revealed the shallow roof space beneath. I cautiously pushed my precious parcel into it. 'Now no one can't find it unless they knows it's there.'

I nodded, grateful for her help, even though it meant she now knew where I kept my money. 'So what was it you wanted from me?' I asked. We both sat crouched in the gully of the parapet. The night air was chilly. I wrapped my arms around my knees. I thought Jenny's face looked swollen, as though she'd been struck, but when she saw me looking at her, she turned her face away. In the distance a cat mewed and faint footsteps rose from the street below.

Jenny stared out across the rooftops in silence for a few moments and I wondered if she was going to answer me at all. At last with a sigh, she turned to me.

'It's like this,' she said. 'I ain't no better at hiding me money than you. Me dad caught me taking the horses back to the stable. I thought he was drunk and asleep. I couldn't've guessed he'd be there. I hadn't had no time to hide the ready. He got it off me and now he wants more.'

'I'm so sorry he took your money from you,' I said. I'd wanted it to benefit her, not her father. I pulled the purse out of its hiding place, dipped my hand into it and offered her a handful of guineas. Jenny pushed my hand away impatiently with a shake of her head. I saw her eyes flash white in the darkness as she rolled them.

'Ain't too bright, are you?' she remarked. When I still remained silent, confused, she said, 'Oh never mind! I got to get going now.'

'Jenny, wait . . . ' I wasn't sure what I wanted to say, but I didn't want her to go. I was lonely and I could tell she was unhappy. 'What do you want?' I asked.

Jenny paused and looked at me in the darkness. 'You knows all the smart folks. You know when some of them's coming and going. You could let me know.'

I was shocked. It was bad enough that I'd robbed my own father. But at least there was some justification in my own mind for what I'd done. To betray the movements of strangers to a couple of highwaymen was quite another thing. That would make me a criminal.

'I don't think . . . most of them are here for the season, you see,' I said. 'They won't go outside the city walls until the end of the summer. Besides, I don't know any of them. I'm a newcomer and not . . . not what you might call popular.'

'So you won't help, is that it?' asked Jenny flatly.

'I don't see how I can,' I said helplessly.

'I'll see you around then,' said Jenny. When I said nothing more, she got up and disappeared into the darkness. I could hear the soft rattle of the roof tiles under her feet as she climbed and then she reached the drainpipe and the night fell silent.

I felt low after she'd gone. I couldn't shake off the feeling I'd failed her. But I'd told her the truth. Even if I'd wanted to help, I really didn't know anything about the comings and goings of the people of the Bath. I hugged my knees tighter to my body and shivered.

* * *

I slept badly and was up early, hoping to go and pay the chairmen and to see Mr Allen at the post office while my aunt was at the baths. At a quarter past six, I looked through my closet and discovered to my fury that my wrap-around gowns had both been removed. I rang for Dawes at once. She took an age to appear, heaving and puffing for breath, with all the bleary-eyed appearance of the recently and rudely awakened. 'Where are my old gowns, Dawes?' I asked, ignoring her red face and shortness of breath.

'Your aunt ordered them . . . given to the scullery maid, Miss,' gasped Dawes. 'She said as how you wouldn't need them any more.'

Shaking with fury, I hurled a scent bottle against the wall. It shattered in a satisfying explosion of glass. 'How dared you remove my clothes without my say-so?' I demanded in a voice that wasn't steady.

Dawes stood rigid, her face disapproving. 'It's your father as pays me, Miss, and his and your aunt's orders I'm under. Not yours.'

'Get out,' I said, clenching my fists.

Dawes withdrew at once, closing the door with a snap. I heard her heavy tread descending the staircase. I looked around for something else to throw. There were only my hairbrushes and having hurled them at the wall, I was left with no further vent for my rage. I resorted to pulling all my expensive gowns out of the closet and throwing them one by one onto the floor. They were none of them suitable for visiting the less fashionable parts of town. In my frustration, I kicked a ball gown across the room and sat down heavily on the bed.

I was trapped in the house by fashion; how ridiculous. Meanwhile, warty Sam would be waiting for me by the tavern, hoping for his fee, as arranged. He would be angry, and justifiably so. I considered he deserved to be paid after humiliating Sir Oswald so beautifully for me last night.

After allowing despair to overcome me for nearly half an hour, I finally pulled myself together. I extricated the plainest of my walking gowns from the tangled heap on the floor and pulled it on. I didn't bother with the hoop at first, but the trouble was, without it the gown was too long and trailed along the ground. It would become soiled as soon as I stepped outside the front door. Sighing with exasperation, I pulled the gown back off and flung it on the bed while I fumbled with tapes and buckles. I was determined not to call the odious Dawes back up to help me. By the time I realized my flat shoes were still out on the roof, I was already caged in hoop and gown and had no hope of climbing through the window. Reluctantly, I picked out the least preposterous of my new shoes to wear.

It was some time later that I finally emerged from the house in high heels and swaying petticoats. I would need to hurry, at this rate, to make it back before my aunt returned for breakfast. I walked into the city, picking my way through the dirty streets, holding the petticoats of my blue gown as high as I dared. An elderly buck in velvet and lace paused in Cheap Street, to stare at me, openly inspecting my ankles. I hurriedly dropped the hem of my petticoats a little to hide them, cursing softly when the fabric skimmed a muddy puddle, picking up a dark stain.

I was attracting notice. In my shabby gown and old shoes, no one had looked at me twice. Dressed as a fine lady, people stared to see me walking by myself. I was relieved to finally turn into Slippery Lane. Sam was lounging against a wall, picking his teeth while he waited for me. When he saw me approaching, he straightened up and threw the stick into the kennel. 'You're late,' he growled by way of greeting.

'My apologies,' I responded. 'I was unavoidably delayed. Your three guineas,' I added as I handed him his fee. 'And an extra guinea for the blow Sir Oswald gave you. His downfall was a spectacle to gladden the heart of his every enemy.'

Sam's eyes gleamed as he palmed the money. 'My pleasure. But there's the question of my poor colleague.'

'What of him?'

'He's in the hospital with a broken leg. Can't walk, can't work. And him with a missus and seven little 'uns to keep. And me with no partner for the chair. Not to mention repair to the chair what got broken.' The man sighed deeply and held out his palm suggestively.

I felt a moment's real shock. I'd been so sure they'd been faking the broken leg. It had been no part of my plan for anyone to be injured, not even the vile Sir Oswald. I looked closely at Sam. His eyes shifted. I decided he was lying. 'I don't believe you. That wasn't your usual chair; I'll bet it was an old one you found especially. I've already given you an extra guinea. There's not a penny more,' I told him. 'You needed to take your expenses into account when you took on the job.'

I'd barely finished speaking before I was seized from behind. A hand was clamped over my mouth and I was held tightly. As I struggled, Sam swiftly searched my pockets and gown for money. I writhed furiously as his hands ran over my body. 'She's telling the truth,' he said to his unseen companion, who swore angrily.

'Let's have her gown then,' he growled in my ear. 'That'll be worth a fair bit.'

I was furious at myself for having been caught out. How had the man managed to sneak up on me without my noticing? And now the humiliation of being undressed and being forced to return home semi-naked stared me in the face. But the image had barely formed in my mind before there was a shout behind me.

I was released so abruptly that I staggered and nearly fell. I managed to catch hold of the wall just in time to save myself from a descent into the mire reminiscent of Sir Oswald's. As I recovered my balance, I saw the man fleeing down the street was Sam's fellow-chairman. His broken leg had made a remarkable recovery.

'Are you hurt, madam?' asked a concerned voice as my arm was taken in a strong, supportive hold. I looked up to see the kindly face of Mr Allen looking down into mine. 'Why, Miss Williams!' he cried, recognizing me.

'Mr Allen!' I exclaimed. 'No, I'm not hurt. But I'm *very* glad to see you.'

Mr Allen's companion was chasing the chairmen

with greater agility than they showed in running away. I watched him leap over a pile of refuse after Sam, keeping his balance on the slippery cobbles in his elegant boots. He caught Sam by the collar of his coat, swung him round with considerable force, and pinned him up against the wall. Swiftly, the man drew his sword and held it to the chairman's chest.

He turned briefly towards me and I saw it was Mr Charleton. I'd always thought of him as a fine dandy, and was surprised to see him so fierce. 'What did he steal from you, Miss Williams?' Mr Charleton demanded. Keeping the sword point levelled at Sam's heart, he reached into his pocket and pulled out a handful of gold guineas. 'Are these yours?' he asked.

'No, no; they must belong to him! He stole nothing from me!' I cried. The man had behaved despicably, but I couldn't rob him of the money he'd earned fairly from me. 'Indeed, he didn't hurt me at all. Please let him go.'

'Are you sure?' Mr Charleton sounded taken aback.

'Really,' I assured him. 'I'm truly grateful to you, but there's no harm done.'

Mr Charleton lowered his sword but still glared at his captive. 'You had better not approach this young lady ever again,' he warned. 'Or it'll be the worse for you.' He released him and Sam made off as fast as he could. His companion had already made himself scarce.

'What are you doing in such a street?' asked Mr Charleton returning to me. He took hold of my arm and shook it slightly, a look of black suspicion on his face. 'What have you been about, Miss Williams?'

I stood silent, afraid he'd guessed the truth. What I'd

done was bad indeed, I reflected, now I was faced with discovery. But Mr Allen interrupted: 'Come, Charleton! Miss Williams has had a fright. Don't upset her more!' He turned to me and smiled kindly. 'Did you get lost?' he asked gently.

'That's right,' I agreed, smiling at Mr Allen, relieved to have such a reasonable excuse. 'I was on my way to the post office, Mr Allen,' I explained earnestly. 'But then I took a wrong turning and lost my way.'

'I hope you'll allow us to walk you home now,' said Mr Allen at once. 'You should avoid this part of the city, it's no fit place for a lady.'

'But what are *you* doing here?' I asked. 'How did you happen to come along just in time to rescue me?' The two men exchanged a quick glance.

'We had some . . . business here,' said Mr Allen. Surprised, I opened my mouth to ask more, but Mr Charleton interrupted.

'You're a young lady and shouldn't walk alone at all,' he said. 'I'm surprised your aunt allows it.'

'You weren't carrying a purse?' asked Mr Allen offering me his arm. When I shook my head he added: 'That was fortunate, for the rogues would quite likely have robbed you of it.'

'Finding I had none, they planned to steal my gown instead,' I admitted ruefully as we began to walk towards home. Mr Charleton frowned at me.

'That would have taught you a sharp lesson,' he said sternly. Then he seemed to shake off his severity and go for a lighter note: 'And we would have had our chivalry far more rigorously tested in escorting you home, hey,

Allen? There was a real danger we'd have made a run for it instead.'

'No . . . no, indeed,' stammered Allen, embarrassed. 'I would never leave a lady to fend for herself in such circumstances.'

'Then you're a better man than I,' said Charleton.

'I do believe, Mr Charleton, that you would take escorting a scantily-clad female quite calmly,' I remarked. 'After all, there is nothing you like better than to play knight errant to damsels in distress.'

'Only the one damsel, Miss Williams,' he replied with great courtesy. I knew he was just teasing me, indeed only a moment ago he had seemed quite angry, but his words brought a little colour to my cheeks nonetheless.

It was most unfortunate that our arrival home coincided with my aunt's descent from a sedan chair outside our front door. She was astonished to see me. 'Allow us to restore your niece safely to you, madam,' said Mr Charleton with a graceful bow.

'Res . . . store? Safe . . . safely?' gibbered my aunt, pulling out her vinaigrette and taking a fortifying sniff. 'Wh-what . . . ?'

'Oh it was nothing!' I assured her, trying in vain to catch Mr Charleton's eye to warn him not to say more. 'I went for a short walk, and became a little lost. These kind gentlemen showed me the way home; that is all.'

Mr Charleton's eyes twinkled a little. 'That's right, ma'am. She assures us she was neither hurt nor robbed.'

I felt a strong inclination to kick him in the shins. 'You'll take the greatest care of her, ma'am, I know,'

Mr Charleton continued, still ignoring me. 'Perhaps Miss Williams might benefit from taking the waters with you in the mornings? You need to keep her close to keep her out of mischief, I believe.'

I gasped. 'No, by God!' I swore angrily.

'*Sophia!*' shrieked Aunt Amelia. 'Sirs, I apologize for my niece. You are absolutely right. I shall not let her out of my sight again. Thank you for your kind assistance and advice, Mr Charleton. And . . . er . . . Mr . . . ?' She looked reluctantly at my other rescuer.

'This is Mr Allen,' said Mr Charleton at once. 'Our excellent postmaster.'

My aunt looked Mr Allen over, took in his plain, modest clothing and his neat tie wig both proclaiming the professional man, not the gentleman of leisure, and accorded him only the tiniest of curtsies and a stiff nod. Clearly she would not waste her civility on a mere postmaster. I felt ashamed of her, and turned to Mr Allen, offering him my hand, hoping to make up for her rudeness. 'Thank you so much for escorting me home,' I said warmly.

Mr Allen took my hand, bowed over it and murmured something polite. I then picked up my petticoats and swept into the house without giving Mr Charleton a second glance. I couldn't help hearing him say, 'That'll teach me!' and laugh softly. I gritted my teeth in annoyance and wished I could hear what he was saying to my aunt. I realized I'd made a strategic error in withdrawing from the scene without first getting rid of the enemy.

Sure enough, I had to endure a long telling off from my aunt as a consequence of the encounter. 'Really,

Sophia, I do not know what the matter is with you,' she said crossly, seating herself on the settle and sniffing vigorously at her salts. 'You go from one scrape to another! What were you thinking of, going out alone? You know you're forbidden to do so! When I think what could have happened! You cannot be trusted to spend as much as five minutes alone. That much is clear. I shall take Mr Charleton's advice. Tomorrow, you'll accompany me to the baths!'

CHAPTER EIGHTEEN

The next morning, Dawes came to my room at a quarter to six, wrapped a morning gown about my nightgown, tied back my hair and then sent me downstairs. She was serving me in hostile silence; I wasn't forgiven for my tantrum or the wreck of my wardrobe the previous day.

My aunt awaited me, attired as I was, but with the addition of a large black turban tied around her head. None of my arguments, entreaties, or promises had prevailed with my aunt. She'd remained adamant that she could no longer leave me alone in the mornings. She'd clutched her vinaigrette and threatened a fit of the vapours, but I was becoming convinced this apparent weakness was mere affectation. Beneath it I sensed a sternness of purpose and a determination to have her own way that made me question my previous reading of her character.

As we left the house to climb into sedan chairs, I noticed a tall young man lounging against the railings of next door's house. I glanced curiously across at him. With a start of pleasure, I recognized Bill Smith. I wanted to run to him at once, but the watchful eye of my aunt made me hesitate.

Instead, I let fall my pocket handkerchief as I walked to the chair. Bill grasped the hint quickly, stepped forward to pick it up and presented it to me with a bow.

'Thank you so much,' I said aloud, then lowered my voice to a whisper. 'Bill! Can you write to me care of Mr Allen? I can't speak now.'

'Sophia!' called my aunt sharply.

Bill gave a tiny nod, and then stepped back. 'You're welcome, Miss,' he said.

I climbed hurriedly into my chair and was carried away, hoping that Bill understood my predicament.

We were greeted on arrival at the Queen's Bath by attendants who ushered us into small, cramped changing rooms. I shed my nightgown for a stiff, canvas monstrosity that billowed about me like a large tent. I objected strongly to its colour and smell: the deep yellow stain of many trips into the mineral-rich spa waters and the throat-catching stink of rotten eggs.

'Must I really?' I asked my aunt one more time as we emerged from the changing cubicles into the fog and fetid steam near the waters. 'Can't I wait for you here while you bathe?' I looked distastefully at the murky brown waters in which a number of canvas-clad men and women, most of them elderly, were already floating around. I felt sick at the thought of getting into the great stone bath.

'Nonsense, child,' snapped my aunt irritably. Then she seemed to regain command over herself and smiled at me. 'It's for your own good, Sophia,' she said in her usual tone. 'Your father trusts me to care for you and you persist in being disobedient.'

I looked at her uneasily. It was almost as though my aunt were wearing a mask. It slipped from time to time, revealing a different person underneath. She turned from me, descended carefully into the steaming water and floated away without another word.

Gingerly, I dipped one toe into the water. It was surprisingly hot. I placed one foot on the first step. The stone was repulsively slimy underfoot. Slowly, reluctantly, I lowered myself into the steaming, stinking water, trying not to think of all the diseases that were probably floating around in it. My canvas gown billowed about me. I drifted around a little, at a loss for what to do with myself. I wished this whole experience to be over as soon as possible.

As I moved across the pool, my aunt's face emerged through the steam. She was in earnest conversation with two men. One was one of her partners at cards: the sallow man whom I normally recognized by his distinctly shabby clothes. The other was Captain Mould, looking greyer and more sinister than ever through the swirling steam, beads of moisture collecting on his moustaches. He was talking fast, his face expressing no emotion at all, while my aunt and the other man listened intently. My aunt saw me approaching and nudged Captain Mould significantly. He stopped speaking at once and turned to me, his face growing even blanker as his eyes met mine. 'Why, Miss Williams,' he said expressionlessly. 'What a delight to see you here. I hope your decision to take the waters is not due to any ailment?'

I disclaimed, and did my best to withdraw from the conversation, but was not permitted to do so. 'You manage to make the costume of the baths positively fetching, Miss Williams,' Captain Mould remarked tonelessly. 'The flush from the steam has given you roses.'

I didn't believe a word he said. I wasn't sure he intended me to. Even in the heat and steam of the water, his presence sent chills down my spine. I was relieved when at last I was allowed to leave the water and shed the revolting canvas gown. I towelled myself dry, wishing I could rub the sulphur smell off my skin, and wrapped my morning gown about me once more. It's over now, I told myself.

I was wrong about my ordeal being over. From the baths, my aunt led me into the pump room. A great crowd of bathers was gathered there, inelegantly clad in morning robes, all of them with that steamy, scorched look the hot waters gave. A distinct aroma of sulphur clung to them still. My aunt led me to the pump, where she purchased a glass of the spa waters for each of us. I stared at the cloudy liquid in distaste. I could smell the rotten eggs without lifting it to my mouth.

'I've just been *bathing* in that,' I objected. 'And so have all those other people. I'm not *drinking* it!'

'You are under a misapprehension, Miss Williams,' said Captain Mould in his level voice. 'This water is taken from the spring, *before* it passes into the bath. It is quite clean, and remarkably beneficial, we are told.'

'By whom?' I asked suspiciously.

He smiled. At least I assumed it was a smile. He could equally have been baring his teeth at me. 'Our doctors themselves recommend it. Our good Queen Anne

162

once obtained the gift of good health from these waters. Long live her rightful heirs and the *true* King of England!'

My aunt frowned at him, but he responded with his usual bland look and took a pinch of snuff. He'd shown his politics very clearly; King George the First was *not* a descendant of Queen Anne, even I knew that much. I made a non-committal noise in my throat and made no move to drink from my glass. My aunt sipped at hers with a look of great concentration on her face. I thought of being forced to accompany her here every morning and my heart sank.

On our return home, Mr Charleton was just emerging from his own house across the street. Seeing me dressed for the baths, he gave a satisfied smile and tipped his hat to me. My aunt curtsied in return, but I pretended I hadn't seen him and went indoors in silence. It was the last glimpse I saw of him for some time. After this meeting, he seemed to vanish from the Bath altogether. Did that disappoint me? I was too angry with him to miss him at first, but gradually admitted to myself that the city was dull without him.

Meanwhile I found myself completely tied to my aunt's routine. When I finally managed to escape her supervision for half an hour one afternoon to run to the post office, Mr Allen was absent. 'Did you say your name was Sophia Williams?' asked Mr Allen's assistant, looking at me over her spectacles.

'That's right,' I agreed hopefully.

'Mr Allen asked me to give you this,' she said, putting a screw of paper into my hand with 'Miss S. Williams' scrawled across it in an unformed, semi-legible hand. She handed me a letter too, and to my great joy I recognized Jack's writing at long last. I handed over the payment to receive the letters and with a hurried word of thanks, I left the post office. I opened the note whilst walking swiftly back home.

'*Dear Miss Williams,*' it said. '*I can see it is not easy to get near you. Mr Allen has said he will give you this note and you can reach me through him. I should like to find my sister, but in the meantime, do not worry about me. I have got work here. Yours, Bill.*'

I folded the note up and stuffed it into my sleeve, arriving home breathlessly a bare five minutes before Aunt Amelia came downstairs from a rare afternoon nap. I was sitting with my stitching in my hand and a book of sermons open before me when she came into the room. She gave me an approving look and I bent my head over my work to hide a smile.

Although I was relieved to hear from Bill, I had no idea when I'd be able to contact him. I also needed to find Jenny and ask her whether she was willing to meet him. I had no wish to incur her anger again.

It wasn't until bedtime that I had an opportunity to read Jack's letter. It was brief: a scrawled account of army life which was obviously suiting him. He'd signed it 'your loving cousin, Jack', and I treasured his words, glad for his sake that he was so happy.

* * *

The days passed without another opportunity to leave the house alone. My aunt seemed tireless, not needing to rest during the day nor stirring from the house without me. Although she still spent her afternoons in play at Harrison's, I could no longer slip away from there either, as she now had a willing deputy-chaperone in the shape of Captain Mould, who watched me closely.

It was quite astonishing how fatiguing doing almost nothing could be. I'd been active and busy all my life without ever experiencing exhaustion. And yet the round of social nothings, the endless chatter, the trifling, insipid activities that made up daily life at the Bath, wore me out completely. I had nothing to live for, nothing to hope for and it drained my energy as exertion had never done.

'You're very quiet, Sophia,' remarked my aunt as we sat over dinner one evening. 'I do believe you are learning decorum at last.'

'Aunt, I fear you may be right,' I agreed wearily. 'I clearly misunderstood the word until now.'

CHAPTER NINETEEN

The weather grew hotter as the summer advanced. The city air was as thick as soup, with no movement or freshness in it. I found every breath an effort in my layers of restrictive clothing. The smells were intensified and the fashionables were carried through the streets with scented handkerchiefs to their noses. The sedan chairmen sweated profusely as they bore their passengers. I felt bad accepting a ride at all, but, as my aunt pointed out, if we walked to spare the men, they would starve.

A day came that was hotter than ever. I had little inclination to go out into the scorching streets. The early trip to the baths had been bad enough. Aunt Amelia insisted, however, and chairs were called at eleven o'clock. The bells had been ringing all morning until my head ached with their clamour, and as we passed by the abbey on the way to Harrison's I could scarcely think for the noise. They always rang for new arrivals and for services, of course, but this was something else. This was an excited, prolonged peal.

As we alighted from our sedan chairs outside Harrison's, the opportunity I'd been longing for came at last. Mr Allen was walking past. I scrabbled frantically in my pocket for the reply to Bill I'd been carrying with me.

'Mr Allen!' I cried, hurrying after him, catching his sleeve to get his attention. He turned in surprise and then smiled.

'Why, Miss Williams,' he exclaimed. 'It's been quite some time.'

He began to make his bow, but I prevented him, tugging on his sleeve and speaking quickly, knowing the clamour of the abbey bells would drown my voice and there was no way my aunt would hear a thing. 'I can't get out at present, Mr Allen,' I said hurriedly. 'But I have a letter here for Bill Smith.' So saying I reached out and shook his hand, passing the note and a coin as I did so. 'Will you make sure that he gets it?'

'Of course I will. You're well?' he asked courteously.

'Very well, thank you. Only somewhat hampered with chaperones,' I said with a wry smile. 'And you?'

'Oh yes, very well indeed, I thank you. There is plenty of work for me to do and I like to be busy.'

I smiled at him, pressed his hand and turned away. My aunt was already walking towards me, a frown upon her face. 'What *do* you think you are doing rushing up to a post office worker in the street and shaking his hand as though he were a gentleman?' she demanded, dragging me towards Harrison's. 'That is forward, hoydenish behaviour, Sophia! Men like Mr . . . whatever-he-calls-himself, should be invisible to you.'

'Yes, Aunt,' I said meekly. Her words made me angry; Mr Allen was in my opinion more of a true gentleman than many we mixed with at Harrison's. However, I was too pleased with the success of my stratagem to wish to provoke her by arguing.

In the tea room we found a number of people talking earnestly over the noise of the abbey bells. 'It's not right, I say,' insisted an elegantly-dressed lady in a pink damask gown and cream petticoats, 'to give such a welcome to Sir William Wyndham when he openly declares he's against our king!' She fluttered her fan in a way that clearly revealed her perturbation.

'Many loyal Britons question why the Stuart heir was passed over for such a distant connection, my lady,' said Captain Mould with a sneer.

'And a German at that,' scoffed Mr Wimpole with a flourish of a scented lace handkerchief. 'The Elector barely speaks English! Send him back to Hanover!'

'We've welcomed him and crowned him,' cried the lady with the fan. 'We cannot turn on him now. It would be treason!'

A silence fell. Across the way, the abbey bells continued to peal. My aunt shifted uncomfortably beside me, twisting her reticule in her hands, but remained silent. Captain Mould inhaled snuff and watched the scene unfold with every appearance of pleasure. 'Fie on you all!' cried the lady with the fan. She tossed her head angrily. 'I'm a loyal Englishwoman, true to my crowned king, and won't stand for it!'

A man was ushered into the rooms, looking flustered and trying to smooth his clothes to look smarter. 'Lady Carew?' he asked the lady in pink. 'You sent for me?' Lady Carew drew herself up to her full height and addressed him in a clear voice that carried throughout the tea room.

'You're in charge of the bells?' she asked. 'I understand they've been pealing all morning in honour of Sir

William Wyndham's arrival and for the Pretender?'

The man nodded. 'That's right, my lady,' he said nervously. 'Sir William is a freeman of the city and we wished to honour him. He, in turn, asked us to honour the Stuart heir.'

'When you have done welcoming and honouring whom you will, I wish you to ring the bells again,' said Lady Carew. 'This time announce that the peal is in honour of King George. I will pay you and the crier well for your trouble.'

The man looked deeply uncomfortable. His eyes darted here and there, trying to gauge the mood of the crowd. 'There's mixed company at the Bath, my lady,' said the bell ringer nervously. 'Some guests may be offended at our ringing the bells for . . . King George.'

'Offended?' cried Lady Carew, her cheeks growing hot with anger. 'How so? He's our king!'

I admired her courage, speaking out against so many hostile people, fighting so passionately for what she believed in. I understood little of the heated emotions around me, but I realized for perhaps the first time how high feelings ran over this matter. There were more mutters and someone murmured 'He's no king of mine!'

At that moment, a newcomer entered the room and sauntered up to the group. Lady Carew turned to him with relief. 'You'll support me, won't you, Mr Charleton?'

I hadn't seen Mr Charleton for weeks and had begun to think he might have left the Bath for good. But here he was, resplendent in a fine new coat of pale blue velvet, snow-white lace at his throat and wrists, his wig beautifully powdered and curled, a sword half-hidden in the skirts of his coat. I felt my heart give a bound of pleasure at the sight of him and repressed it sternly.

'Oh undoubtedly, Lady Carew,' said Mr Charleton lazily as he walked forward. 'I make it a point never to disagree with a lady. The more beautiful she is, the more eager I am to partake of her opinions.'

There was some scattered laughter and the tension began to ease. Mr Charleton bowed to Lady Carew with considerable elegance and kissed her hand. 'What am I agreeing to?' he asked, looking around him with a charming smile.

'For the bells to be rung for the king,' exclaimed Lady Carew, tapping his arm with her fan. Her voice shook a little. 'The bells should be pealed for His Majesty King George, don't you agree?'

'By all means,' said Mr Charleton promptly. 'They are rung for everyone else, why not for King George too? Does anyone disagree with the lady? Surely not!'

His tone was light and there was more laughter. The muttering had stopped. People were turning away, talking among themselves.

'That's typical of Charleton,' I heard one man say with a chuckle. 'Too taken up with the ladies to think about politics.'

I frowned, for I thought myself it was rather the other way around. Mr Charleton's flirtations were light and insincere, while his interest in politics seemed to run deep. And certainly he'd diffused the anger with his banter. It had been neatly done.

The bell ringer bowed stiffly to Lady Carew and finally accepted the guineas she was holding out to him. 'We'll carry out your wishes at once, my lady,' he said and hurried away. Mr Charleton offered Lady Carew his arm and the two of them strolled outside together. I saw Beau Nash clap Charleton briefly on the shoulder in passing and the two of them exchanged a look. Several people headed for the card tables and my aunt eyed them wistfully.

'Well, ladies, I do believe the excitement is over,' said Captain Mould. 'And really it's far too hot for arguments. Would either of you care for a walk in the gardens?'

'I really am finding it rather warm today,' sighed my aunt, fanning herself. 'You two go ahead without me. Go *on*, Sophia,' she said firmly, giving me a little shove when I hesitated. Her eyes strayed back towards the card room.

Most reluctantly, I placed my fingertips on the lizard's proffered arm and accompanied him down the steps and out into the gardens. I thought he'd talk about the scene in the tea room, but he didn't. At first he confined his remarks to the fineness of the weather and the splendid views of the surrounding hills. Then he began to pat my hand and look at me, licking his lips in a way that made me long to run away. 'Is your father returning to the Bath soon?' Captain Mould asked. 'I'm looking forward to making his acquaintance.'

'He's twice written to delay his return, sir,' I replied. 'But I imagine we'll see him soon.'

'I intend to ask him for your hand when he returns,' my unwelcome companion told me, shocking me into silence. 'You are just the sort of bride to suit me; pleasant enough to look at, docile, of good family.'

I fought a constriction in my throat; a surge of sheer panic. 'You do not ask whether I would welcome the match,' I managed to say at last.

Captain Mould raised his eyebrows very slightly. 'Why would I? It's your father's decision, not yours.'

'These days, sir, I believe it is customary to consult the bride's inclination as well as her father's,' I said in a stifled voice. I was having trouble breathing. The sun beat mercilessly down upon me and I felt trapped and desperate. 'You're old enough to be my father and I feel no love for you!'

'Love! What sentimental nonsense. You'll learn to love me as much as is necessary. I consider the disparity in our ages a blessing. It will allow me to form you as I wish. And all women need a man to take their decisions.'

It was too monstrous to discuss calmly. He was proposing not a union of two souls, but a complete subjugation. I was struck by a horrifying realization: my father might approve of this entirely. The thought stole my equanimity. I broke away from Captain Mould and fled to the far end of the gardens. Leaning over the wall, I looked down at the muddy Avon, winding its sluggish way towards Bristol and the sea. I was fighting nausea. My fear of my father and my fear of Captain Mould seemed to merge into one and I felt the old terrors threatening to overcome me. My heart was pounding and my hands were as cold as ice despite the hot sun scorching me. 'Breathe, just breathe,' I murmured to myself in a jerky, uncontrolled voice. 'Don't let them defeat you.'

I'd never been overcome like this in public. I needed

to recover myself before anyone noticed. I gripped my hands together and tried to slow my rapid heartbeat. A glance behind me showed that Captain Mould had seated himself upon a bench under a tree and was watching me, one knee crossed over the other, very much at his ease. I was determined not to return to him. But it was ironic: my persistent rudeness had rid me of all possible friends but him. He alone would not be deterred. My plan was in ruins. There was no one I could turn to, who would shield me from the snuff-taking lizard.

My heartbeat had slowed, but my hands and feet were still numb and chilled. I shivered despite the fierce heat. Footsteps approached me and I held myself quite still, dreading to hear Captain Mould's cold voice right behind me. It was a huge relief to hear quite a different tone: 'Miss Williams? It *is* you! You will burn out in the sun like this with no parasol!'

'Mr Charleton,' I gasped with relief. 'How glad I am to see you!' I grasped his arm as I spoke and then was ashamed. Whatever would he think of me? But before I could withdraw my hand, his own hand had closed upon it, holding it fast. 'Miss Williams, you're not well!' he exclaimed.

I assumed he was teasing me and gave a shaky laugh. 'Because I'm pleased to see you? Yes, I suppose that must seem strange.'

'Yes, but I wasn't thinking of that. You're standing in the hot sun and yet your hand is as cold as ice. You look as though you have seen a ghost.'

'I have in a way,' I admitted. 'Or perhaps a glimpse of the future.'

Mr Charleton looked puzzled, as well he might, and I shook my head. 'Take no notice of me, please. I do indeed feel ill and should dearly like to go home. Would you be so kind, sir, as to escort me to my aunt?'

At once, Mr Charleton offered me his arm. He led me past Captain Mould, who made no move to stop me, but merely gave me a smug smile. Mr Charleton found me a seat in the tea room and fetched me a dish of tea. 'Drink this,' he urged, 'while I look for your aunt.'

I accepted the tea reluctantly, sure that I could swallow nothing. I was wrong. It made me feel stronger. Mr Charleton was soon at my side again. 'Your aunt is in the middle of a game of ombre and judging by the stack of bills at her elbow she is winning,' he told me. 'Mine is therefore the pleasure of escorting you home.'

'She always wins,' I said. 'This is putting you to a great deal of trouble. I can walk myself.' It occurred to me that this was my first opportunity to go into the city unsupervised all week. I should make the most of it, no matter how unwell I felt. It was essential I purchased some practical clothing; a night-time expedition was urgently required to relieve today's shock.

'Absolutely not,' said Mr Charleton at once, taking my hand and drawing it through his arm. 'You are ill, and the city is becoming an increasingly unruly place.'

His manner was protective, and I couldn't be completely unmoved by his kindness. It was rare enough that anyone showed me any concern. I followed him meekly, not needing the support of his arm, but not rejecting it either. 'I'm feeling so much better now,' I assured him. 'What do you mean the city is becoming unruly?'

'I'm surprised you haven't noticed.' Mr Charleton hailed one of the line of sedan chairmen that were jostling for custom outside the rooms, and handed me into a chair. It was lifted and began to move. Mr Charleton walked beside me, conversing through the open window.

'I've noticed nothing,' I said, wrinkling my forehead, trying to think. 'But then, I've scarcely been in the city this past week, and have gone everywhere by chair and with my aunt. And that was entirely your doing, sir!'

'Do I detect resentment there?' asked Mr Charleton. 'It was partly for your own protection.'

'You detect fury, not resentment. How dared you betray me to my aunt like that? You don't understand . . . you have no idea!' I paused and then asked: 'What do you mean 'partly' for my own protection? What other reason did you have?'

'To protect others from your actions.'

I sat silent, my heart beating fast, shocked once again about how much he seemed to know about me. What was he going to do? Tell my father? Or worse: report me to the magistrates?

There was a press of traffic at the Grove, and the chair halted. 'You don't deny that the people of this city need protecting from you and your friends?' asked Mr Charleton. He sounded grave.

'You exaggerate, sir,' I said with an uncomfortable laugh. I would admit nothing. I bit my lip and looked away. As I did so, a display in a shop window caught my eye. An idea to change the subject and to solve my problems came to me. I turned back to my companion and said: 'Mr Charleton, could you lend me your assistance, do you think?'

'Of course,' Mr Charleton said in a polite but subdued voice. He sounded disappointed.

'It's my . . . Aunt Amelia's godson's birthday soon, and . . . his family, in Devon, are poor and we wanted to send him a new set of clothes. Something practical rather than formal. But we really need the help of someone who understands boys' clothing! My aunt and I have been in quite a puzzle to know exactly what to buy. But you will be able to advise me.'

I was very pleased with my story, invented as it had been, on the spur of the moment. I glanced sideways at Mr Charleton, hoping he would oblige me. 'You wish for my help and advice, Miss Williams?' He still sounded disappointed. Had he really expected me to admit anything to him?

'Indeed, I do.'

Mr Charleton called to the bearers to pull over and let me out so that we could enter the shop. Under his watchful eye, I lied glibly, explaining that the imaginary godson was 'near my own height, though perhaps a shade taller'. I couldn't tell whether or not he was suspicious of me as he helped me select breeches the boy might like, and recommended woollen stockings rather than worsted as they were less scratchy. 'And definitely not that shirt, Miss Williams!' he assured me. 'Trust me; the lad will prefer this one with the smaller collar. Much more *à la mode* and more manly too.'

I didn't argue, though I preferred my first choice. Instead, I added a cap to the growing pile, paid for the items and waited patiently while the shopkeeper made up a brown-paper parcel for me. Considering how ill and despairing I'd felt just a few moments before, I felt light and energized now. At last I had a means of escape within my grasp. My trammelled existence would once more be broken up with freedom and excitement. And tricking Mr Charleton into helping me was simply delightful.

When we reached home, Mr Charleton handed me out of the chair. He kept hold of my parcel, however, while he paid off the chairmen, thus foiling my plan to escape into the house and avoid further questioning. When they'd left, he bowed over my hand. Retaining hold of it, he looked closely at me. 'You seem much better,' he said.

'I am. It must have been a momentary faintness,' I agreed. 'I feel quite restored now. Thank you for bringing me home, though. I'm very grateful. And of course I'm grateful for your advice too,' I added kindly, repressing a grin.

'I'm happy to see you so much restored. But, Miss Williams, please, please, promise me you won't go out into the city alone. It isn't wise.'

'I'm so confined by my aunt, sir, there's little chance of that,' I replied, determined to promise nothing. I moved to pull the doorbell to be let in, but Mr Charleton caught my hand again.

'Not so confined that you can't get out of the house. I *know* what you have been up to,' he said softly.

I looked down at his hand on mine. I felt sick; he knew things about me he had no right to know. Gathering my courage, I looked up at him. 'Know what?' I said unsteadily, dreading what I might hear.

'I recognized those chairmen, when we rescued you from them. That was a dangerous game. Come, Miss Williams. Confess you bribed them to tip Sir Oswald out.'

I laughed shakily, weak with relief that he knew no worse. 'You're sorely mistaken, sir,' I told him lightly. 'I had nothing more to do with his accident than that I was guilty of enjoying the spectacle. The rest is coincidence.' I disengaged my hand and pulled the doorbell. As the peal rang through the house, I curtseyed to Mr Charleton. 'You'll forgive me if I leave you now, sir? The sun is making me feel unwell again. Thank you for your escort.'

CHAPTER TWENTY

I could hardly wait for darkness to fall that night. The prospect lightened my mood so much that I was even able to be civil to my aunt. She too was in a good mood when she returned; relaxed and cheerful after her win at the tables that afternoon.

'We shan't be going to the baths in the morning, Sophia,' she told me over supper. She reached for some gravy and poured it over her mutton and potatoes. 'After the Sunday morning service at the abbey, we have a treat in store for you.'

I looked up. For one moment I thought it really might be something nice, and then my common sense reasserted itself. '*We?*' I asked suspiciously. 'What treat?'

'After you felt ill, Captain Mould was saying how very stifling the city has become in this heat wave. He suggested an afternoon outing in his carriage tomorrow, to get some fresh air: a trip to Lansdown to admire the views and see the ancient hill fort. There! Won't that be lovely?'

'I can hardly wait,' I said with heavy sarcasm.

'You're quite the most ungrateful girl I've ever met,' snapped my aunt, putting down her cutlery with a clatter and glaring at me, her good mood gone.

'I dislike Captain Mould,' I told her. 'He frightens me. You don't like him either!'

'I . . . ? Nonsense! And it's not for you to have likes and dislikes!' exclaimed Aunt Amelia sharply. 'Goodness knows *you* haven't made yourself popular here. If you had scores of admirers, perhaps you could pick and choose. But you have not. You'd do well to remember that and make yourself a bit more generally agreeable.'

The night air was clammy, as though the city was exhaling its moist, steamy breath all over me. I shuddered slightly as I clambered over the sticky roof tiles and onto the parapet. I'd had to tie a scarf around my breasts before I put my shirt on. They'd definitely grown recently; I was developing a woman's figure. That had put me in a bad mood. I didn't want any signs of womanhood upon me, especially not any that limited my freedom.

I strolled through the streets, enjoying the freedom of my shirt and breeches, my long brown hair hidden under my boy's cap. The official night life of the city was over very early, but many people were still out drinking and gambling in the less select and glamorous surroundings of the city's inns and taverns.

On the corner of Cheap Street, I ran into Mr Charleton walking along in earnest conversation with Mr Allen. I didn't trouble to conceal myself. Sure of my disguise, I merely pulled my cap down a little lower over my face and walked by. Mr Charleton looked right at me, but no glimmer of recognition appeared in his face. I walked on feeling gleeful and triumphant.

The streets were busier than I'd seen them at night. Groups of men were walking together, entering and leaving inns or merely hanging about, rowdy with drink. I strolled up and down the High Street for more than an hour hoping to catch a glimpse of Jenny. She was nowhere to be seen. Eventually I gave up and bought myself a pie from a servant girl at the kitchen window of an inn.

Heading down to the river, I climbed over the wall into Harrison's gardens to eat in peace, settling down on a bench in the shadows. The gardens were closed and dark. It was peaceful. A soft breeze rustled the leaves of the trees and cooled me. I leant back, closed my eyes and felt temporarily at peace. The loud voices and drunken singing from the city reached me only faintly.

On the way home, I took a shortcut through the abbey courtyard, as I knew this was a likely spot for Jenny to be; plenty of fat pockets to pick. Unusually, a horse was tethered outside a lighted inn. There were few horses to be seen in the city at any hour, but this late at night it was surprising. A young lad was sitting on the ground next to him, but had fallen asleep at his post, his head tipped back until it rested on the wall behind him, his mouth open.

I walked on, looking closely at the ragged figures sitting or standing in the shadows. I'd only gone some thirty paces further, when an urchin in rags erupted out of an inn in front of me. The lad had already run halfway across the road before I'd recognized Jenny in boy's clothes. Before I could call after her, several men piled out of the door after her shouting 'Stop thief!' Two of them spotted Jenny, and took off after her at a run. She was drawing ahead of them until a burly man stepped around a corner and she cannoned into him, lost her balance and fell headlong onto the stones.

'Catch her!' yelled the men in front of me. The large man made a grab for Jenny, but his protruding belly prevented him from bending forward easily and she wriggled free. She stayed on the ground on all fours, however, fighting for breath as the men closed in on her. I realized she was winded from her fall. If they caught her, she would be hanged for sure. I had to do something, quickly.

I watched helplessly until I remembered the horse. Turning around, I sprinted back towards it. The reins were looped loosely over a post and I grabbed them, flinging them over the horse's head, startling him. The stable boy had been roused by the shouts but was still sitting on the ground, rubbing his eyes, groggy with sleep. By the time he'd scrambled to his feet, I was already mounted.

'Hey, you can't take that horse!' he shouted. I took no notice, kicking the animal straight towards Jenny. Nervous and confused by this strange turn of events, he clattered across the cobbles, head high. I forced him to barge right into the knot of men around Jenny. One was knocked to the ground, the rest scattered with shouts of shock and anger. I reached my hand down to the dirty, bruised girl in the gutter. She grabbed it without hesitation and swung herself up into the saddle behind me. Then we were away, Jenny's arms around my waist, into the narrow alleys of the city. We wound this way and that to lose pursuit.

'Left, left,' cried Jenny hoarsely behind me. I wheeled the horse sharply and we cantered down a narrow alley, terrifying a drunk, who staggered out of our way in the darkness, slipping in the rubbish. 'Now right,' gasped Jenny. We'd reached the city wall. 'Now over there,' said Jenny, tugging at my sleeve. I rode to a water trough placed against the wall, a tree overhanging it from the other side. Jenny slid down from the horse's back, placed a foot on the trough, grabbed the overhanging branches and swung herself up onto the wall. Balanced there, she turned and beckoned.

'But the horse . . . !' I said doubtfully.

'They'll find him,' she replied impatiently.

I knotted the horse's reins loosely over his neck, gave him a pat, and followed Jenny down onto the trough and then up into the tree. She grabbed my arm and helped pull me up. The horse, relieved of our weight, set off at a smart trot down the street.

'Quickly. Follow me!' whispered Jenny. She climbed through the tree and dropped into the grass on the other side of the wall. I jumped down after her. Jenny set off at a run, a shadowy figure in the darkness. I followed, wondering where we were going.

We ran across two meadows, pushed through a tangled copse in the pitch darkness and then skirted a cornfield. Jenny vaulted a gate at the far end of the field; a boy's trick. I copied her and saw her teeth flash white in a brief, approving grin as I landed, and then she was off again, running lightly between a huddle of cottages. They cast their dense shadows over us as we followed the narrow cart-track between them. Lights shone from an inn, the other houses were in darkness at this late hour, their inhabitants slumbering.

At the end of the village street was a narrow lane. Jenny made for a tumbled-down hovel at the end, pushed open the creaking door and disappeared into the gloom. A few seconds later, light glowed from a candle thrust into the embers of a small fire. I could see enough to step inside.

It was a small, low-ceilinged room with a smoke-blackened fireplace and dingy walls. The furniture was shabby: a crooked table, some battered chairs and a dresser with untidy shelves. The smell of the tallow candle was strong; an earthy, animal scent that made me cough. Jenny was peeling off her jacket to peer at her bruised upper arm.

'You're hurt!' I exclaimed, but she shrugged it off. 'It's nothing,' she said. She poured some water from a jug into an earthenware bowl and dipped a cloth into it. 'My knee hurts more.' She pulled up her breeches, revealing a graze that was oozing blood. She dabbed at it with the wet cloth and then looked up. 'I got to thank you,' she said, her eyes meeting mine. 'It was lucky you was there. I'd be in the lock-up now else. The man was less drunk than I thought.'

'You're welcome,' I told her. 'I was looking for you. I have news and I need your help.'

'What news?' asked Jenny, catching her breath as the water stung her graze.

'Your brother Bill is here. He's come to the Bath to find you.'

The graze was forgotten, the cloth thrown aside. 'Bill

184

here?' gasped Jenny, her face joyful. Then her expression changed, the sparkle of pleasure fading, to be replaced by one of pain and suspicion. 'You mustn't tell him where I live! Oh, why did I bring you here?' Jenny clenched her fists. She was glaring at me now. 'This were all a trick, weren't it? So you could find out where I lived and betray me!'

'Betray you?' I cried indignantly. 'He's your *brother*! He cares about you. I didn't ask you to bring me here and I wouldn't dream of telling him where you are unless you want me to.'

Jenny's suspicious eyes flashed at me in the flickering candlelight. 'Swear to me you won't give me away!' she insisted.

'I give you my word. I only want to help you.'

Gradually her fists unclenched and the fire died out of her eyes. She sat back down, still staring intently at me. 'You're the quickest-tempered, most suspicious person I've ever met,' I told her, exasperated. 'Why do you want to hide from him, anyway? A minute ago you were delighted to hear he was here.'

Jenny picked up the cloth. There was a flush in her face. 'Look how I live!' she muttered, indicating the unkempt, tatty room with disgust. 'You knows what I do fer a living! I don't want to shame him. He's got strict notions.'

'Won't you at least meet him?' I coaxed her gently. 'He's come all this way. You don't have to tell him how or where you live.'

'I could do that,' she agreed slowly. 'It'd be good to see him. As long as there's no following me home,' she added, casting me another frowning look.

'I'm your friend. Is it likely I'd betray you?'

'Friend,' snorted Jenny. 'You with your fancy clothes, grand house and la-di-da ways. You're only *friends* with the likes of me as long as it suits you.'

'I'm sorry you think that,' I said, stung by her harshness. 'I'll relieve you of my unwanted presence.' I got to my feet as I spoke.

Jenny laughed. 'Now who's quick-tempered?' she said.

'With good reason,' I said walking to the door. Jenny had hurt me. I'd really meant what I'd said about friendship.

'Oh, give over, do,' she said. 'I'll even say I'm sorry.'

I paused, staring at her resentfully. She laughed again and I grinned reluctantly in return. Walking back to my rickety chair, I said: 'I need your help.'

'The help of a common thief?' asked Jenny with a self-derisive snort.

'I would prefer to describe you as an out-of-the-ordinary thief,' I said.

'No, Miss La-di-da, there's dozens like me in every city.'

'I wish you will call me Sophia,' I said. 'Listen. An expedition has been arranged for tomorrow, after church. A Captain Mould is to take us out of the city for the day. We're driving up to Lansdown for a picnic.' I sighed. In different company it would be an agreeable change to life within the city walls.

'What do you need me for?' Jenny asked me curiously. The self-derisive note had gone from her voice.

'It would give me *so* much pleasure to see Captain

186

Mould robbed,' I said with a grin. 'You and your father can keep anything you take.' Jenny looked less than thrilled. 'Isn't that what you wanted?' I asked. 'To know when rich people are leaving the city?'

'A day trip,' said Jenny disparagingly. 'No one won't be carrying much in the way of money, and you'll be back before dusk. Me father won't risk holding up a chaise in broad daylight.'

'I see.' I paused, remembering how the chairmen had wanted to rob me of my gown. 'What about our clothing, and the men's swords and wigs?' I asked. 'Everyone will be finely dressed for an excursion.'

Jenny nodded slowly as she turned this over in her mind.

'Good. So then I need to find a way of delaying our return,' I said. 'Do you have any ideas?'

A sparkle appeared in Jenny's eyes as she considered this. 'The coach could be disabled,' she suggested. 'That would make you late back.'

'Tell me how,' I said. 'And I'll do it.'

CHAPTER TWENTY-ONE

I was weary when I finally hoisted myself up onto the roof of the stable. The sky was pink with the dawn, the short summer night already over. As I scrambled up the drainpipe from the stable roof, firm hands grasped me and pulled me up. I cried out in shock. 'For your own sake you should keep quiet,' said a familiar voice. 'I'm not going to hurt you.'

'Mr Charleton,' I gasped. 'What are you doing here?'

'Waiting for you, naturally. What a stupid question.'

I was astonished to be discovered and annoyed by his tone. 'Why? And how on earth did you know I'd climb up this way?'

Charleton leaned back against the side of the house. He looked quite at his ease on the rooftops, his immaculate clothes unwrinkled and not a hair of his wig out of place. He'd exchanged his smart boots for a less smart pair of pumps with flat heels. There was a particularly grim look on his face which made me uneasy.

'For goodness' sake, Sophia, did you think I wouldn't recognize the clothes I'd helped you buy? As to finding your route back into the house, it was obviously not going to be by the front door, was it? I've known about it since the night at the theatre.'

'I could have sworn you didn't see me tonight,' I exclaimed, annoyed. 'And did you follow me home from the theatre?'

'I don't always show the world what I notice,' said Mr Charleton. 'And yes, I did. What did you mean by lying to me about those clothes being for a godson?'

'I could hardly tell you the truth could I? It's really none of your business! Besides, no harm has come to me.'

Mr Charleton looked at me, his face inscrutable. 'It's not you I'm worried about. You are making it abundantly clear that you can look after yourself. Where have you been?'

'Again, that is absolutely nothing to do with you.'

Mr Charleton didn't get angry, as I half expected, instead he sighed. 'Come, Miss Williams, shall we be a little more frank with one another?'

I wondered what he expected me to tell him. I wasn't going to betray my friends or myself. I stood silent, waiting for a more definite accusation from him.

'Miss Williams, you heard the talk in the rooms, this afternoon!' he said at last. 'Let us be honest with each other at least. I know your family have Jacobite sympathies. You support the Pretender. I don't seek to change your mind or judge you. But, Sophia, take care what you are about!'

I opened my eyes wide in amazement. Even his use of my name passed almost unnoticed. 'But none of that is anything to do with me!' I cried, half-angry, half-relieved that he didn't know the truth. 'I don't give a tinker's pot what king is on the throne! I just want to go out.'

Mr Charleton looked sceptical. 'I'm more than willing to believe you are involved for the sake of the thrills alone. But listen to me a moment! Our country is in a state of unrest. We have a Hanoverian king on the throne, put there by parliament to prevent the succession falling into Catholic hands. Many, many people are unhappy with the choice. Treachery, uprisings, even full scale rebellion are afoot; we don't yet know the sum of it.'

He paused, waiting for a reaction. 'It sounds very exciting,' I said candidly.

'It's not exciting, it's dangerous. Have you any idea what an uprising on this scale would be like? Windows smashed, shops looted, buildings blown up, bloodshed in the streets. Possibly even a civil war. I've no wish to see such devastation.'

'Nor me,' I said taken aback. 'And, sir, truly, it's nothing to do with me! This is almost the first I've heard of any of it!'

'Oh, I'm certain you know all this,' he said impatiently. 'I'm giving you a chance to get clear, Sophia. I don't want you to get hurt. Because trust me, this rebellion or whatever is being planned here in the Bath is doomed to failure.'

'I repeat: none of this is anything to do with me. And anyway, why should you care about me?' I asked.

'I've asked myself the same question many times. You are a damned troublesome child, Sophia! If I'd dreamed you'd dress yourself in those boy's clothes, I'd have put you over my shoulder and carried you straight home before I helped you buy them! If what you say is true, then at least promise me you won't go out until this is over!'

'You have to be jesting!' I exclaimed. 'You have no right, no authority over me at all. I'll make you no such promise.'

'You may think this is a jest, Miss Williams. I don't. If you won't give me your word, I shall require those clothes from you,' said Mr Charleton. 'If I can't get you to understand how dangerous the situation is, then I must take steps to enforce your safety and the safety of the city!'

I made a move to escape, turning to flee up to my room, but Mr Charleton caught me around the waist and pulled me back to face him. He was suddenly very close, his dark eyes looking down into mine, a stern expression in them. I struggled frantically, heart hammering. 'Please, you don't understand, you have no idea!' I cried as I fought him. 'My life is unendurable. What do I care about politics? How can they matter to me compared to the life I'm condemned to lead? I'm confined and hemmed in, allowed to exercise neither my mind nor my body. I would go insane without some escape. This is all I have!'

'How can I trust your word? You've lied to me often enough.'

'I'm not lying now!' I said hotly. His closeness was affecting me; I could smell the sweetness of his breath and feel the warmth of his body against mine. I ceased struggling, hoping instead to reason with him.

'Then you do not need to go out at night! You say you are confined, but it's not true. You go out to the baths, to Harrison's, and to balls. You walk, you dance. Why is that not enough for you?'

191

'How should that be enough?' I asked, trying to keep my voice reasonable, but failing. 'No books except for religious ones, no learning at all. Embroidery and music, both of which I abominate! Dawdling along in a ridiculous gown at my aunt's side, exchanging nothings with people I don't care about. Waiting to be married to an old man like Captain Mould who will be as bad as my father. Being told what to do, even what to think! Would that be enough for you? To never be allowed more? To have no *hope*?'

I'd succeeded in startling Mr Charleton with my vehemence; his hold on me slackened. I twisted and leapt away from him. Slipping on the slate tiles, I scrambled up over the roof. I ran full-pelt along the parapet, ignoring the dizzying drop to my right, pretending it was safe to take the route at this speed. I could hear Mr Charleton behind me, but not close enough to catch me. I slid in through my open window and slammed it shut before he could reach me, closing the wooden shutters across the window so he couldn't look in. I could hear him tapping on the glass, but ignored him. I'd escaped this time, but the man was becoming a serious inconvenience.

CHAPTER TWENTY-TWO

I awoke after four hours' sleep to a hot, sultry day, the sun already burning down on the new houses. I wondered, not for the first time, at the gentry choosing to spend the hottest months of the year walled up in a crowded, humid city in the bottom of a river valley. They could scarcely have found a stuffier, more airless spot.

By the time we'd been to prayers and were climbing into Captain Mould's hired chaise outside our house at eleven o'clock, the heat was intolerable. Trim Street was like an oven. The chaise was crowded with the captain, one of his cronies and his wife, and the two of us, but it did at least have a hood that could be drawn down, so there would be fresh air around us. I was crushed onto a seat that was too small to accommodate three, between Aunt Amelia and Mrs Wicklow, a woman of dubious personal hygiene and a tendency to sweat profusely.

The day was intolerably dull. The fresher air and fine views were all ruined for me by the suffocating presence of Captain Mould, who stayed as close to me as my own shadow. I struggled to keep my temper, and began to wonder how I was to sabotage the coach unnoticed.

At noon, Captain Mould's servants laid out a picnic in the shade of some beech trees. Captain Mould leaned in towards me smiling his yellow-toothed smile, his thin cheeks stained brown from his snuff habit. 'Can I tempt you . . . with a little light luncheon, Miss Williams?' he leered into my face.

I shuddered. 'To luncheon you can, but to nothing else I assure you!'

'Sophia!' My aunt spoke sharply. 'You misunderstand the captain.'

I was silent, knowing I hadn't misunderstood. Captain Mould smirked.

After luncheon, which consisted of cold meats, freshly-baked bread, fruit and a light white wine, everyone fell quiet. The heat was oppressive and it seemed none of the adults had any inclination to leave the shade. My aunt fell asleep with her mouth open, and Mrs Wicklow soon followed her example, though she managed to be more discreet about it. The atmosphere grew somnolent. The steady hum of bees, flies, and other insects around us was hypnotic. I fought the lassitude, knowing this was my chance. Seeing the others sleeping, Captain Mould's eyes gleamed and he drew closer to me. I turned my back to him pointedly, lying down beside my aunt, feigning sleep.

Captain Mould must have given up on me, for I heard him suggest a walk to Mr Wicklow. I waited until they were out of sight before I got up and walked back across the field to the carriage. The sun was scorching, the ground baked hard. My skin burned and my petticoats stuck to me uncomfortably, but I was wide awake once more.

There were several other groups of day-trippers dotted here and there under the trees, enjoying luncheon or resting in the shade. I wondered if all their parties were as dull and ill-assorted as ours. A burst of distant laughter told me that at least one was merrier than us.

Our horses had been unharnessed and stood under the leafy canopy of a large beech tree, skin twitching, tails swishing to shoo away unwelcome insects. The chaise stood beside them, the hood pulled up now, ready for the drive home. I looked around for the coachman and groom. They were leaning over a gate further down the field, exchanging compliments with a group of farm girls who were probably taking a break from haymaking.

I went to the near carriage wheel and drew the small metal tool Jenny had given me out of my pocket. It had been knocking uncomfortably against my leg all morning. I unwrapped it from my pocket handkerchief and bent down by the wheel, searching quickly for the pegs Jenny had described to me. I found one, but I couldn't shift it, even with her tool, so I crawled under the carriage and tried the other wheel. Here I was luckier, able to loosen two pegs until they were ready to drop out. I left them loose, trusting my handiwork wouldn't be noticed.

As swiftly as I could in my cumbersome clothes, I crawled out from under the chaise and shook out my petticoats. I'd picked up a few smudges and grass stains. I rubbed ineffectually at them, hoping my aunt wouldn't notice. Then I hurried back across the sun-baked field, and rejoined the sleeping ladies.

The rest of the outing passed in a haze of heat and boredom. We walked, talked and then Captain Mould's servants poured lemonade for the ladies and wine for the gentlemen. The air cooled as the day mellowed and everyone grew livelier, but none of them had anything to say that interested me. At length the talk turned to returning to the city. 'There's a special service in the abbey tonight, and I should hate to miss it,' said Mrs Wicklow, fanning herself.

Well, I'm afraid you will, I thought gleefully to myself. And you're going to get robbed into the bargain, if the end of the day goes according to plan.

The chaise bounced and jolted promisingly as the horses pulled it along the narrow lane that led back to Lansdown Road. I held my breath, aware that every bump and lurch threatened the weakened wheel. The excitement made me feel alive again after the numbingly dull day.

I'd delayed our departure as long as possible by begging to go on a last walk to see the view down over Bristol. Captain Mould had accompanied me and had rendered it hideous with his talk of wedding plans. I returned angry and sickened, but had the consolation of seeing that the other day-trippers had all departed and that the brightness was fading from the sky.

Once more the carriage jolted into a pothole, and bounced out again unscathed. It was more unnerving than I'd expected, waiting for a crash. But by the time the chaise jerked back onto Lansdown Road, still intact, I began to grow anxious for quite a different cause. What if the wheel held after all? Then there would be no robbery and no humiliation for Captain Mould.

I was just wishing I'd removed the peg completely when we began the steep descent towards the city. Almost at once, we hit a pothole and the jolt took the wheel right off. The body of the carriage lurched forward and with a tremendous splintering of wood and smashing of glass, it crashed down to the ground, hurling us all forward.

The impact jarred every bone in my body. I hit my head on something so that it spun sickeningly for a moment. There was a silence, stillness, a suspension of every faculty except shock. And then Mrs Wicklow began to scream.

The ladies had all been pitched forward onto the men. Mrs Wicklow, finding herself sprawled full-length on top of Captain Mould, had gone into hysterics. My aunt was scarcely better placed, her limbs tangled with those of the respectable Mr Wicklow, and with only a few seconds' delay, her voice was raised in a screech to match Mrs Wicklow's. The racket made my ears ring.

Even in the undignified position in which I found myself, wedged face down in a press of struggling bodies, I had a strong inclination to burst out laughing. I suppressed it and struggled upright. I must have dug a foot or an elbow into someone in the process, as a male voice cried out. I grasped the strap at the side of the carriage, now dangling at an angle above my head and pulled myself up out of the confusion. I managed to haul myself out, one foot on the squabs to aid my ascent.

The upper half of my body emerged from the gloom of the carriage into golden evening light, and a scene of complete chaos met my eyes. I paused for a moment to survey the wreck of the chaise, the smashed glass, the splintered wood, the dazed coachman and the terrified, plunging horses.

It wasn't easy to scramble out of the carriage. My hoop hindered my escape, and made modesty quite impossible, I feared. I tried not to think about the view the occupants of the coach must have of me. I jumped lightly to the ground. My petticoats were torn, my hair coming unpinned, and I was becoming aware of minor hurts: I'd bitten my tongue, and bruised one knee rather badly.

I cast a swift, anxious glance at the coachman and groom, hoping they hadn't been injured. The groom was sitting by the side of the road, holding his head and looking dazed, while the coachman was clinging to his seat, now tilted at a steep angle, unable to let go for fear of slipping off, hanging onto the reins with one hand.

I stepped up to the horses' heads, catching the tangled reins and trying to soothe them one by one. Once they were calm, I checked them swiftly for injuries, relieved to find superficial hurts only.

Meanwhile, the hysteria inside the carriage was not abating at all. I grinned to myself at the chaos I'd caused. How furious Captain Mould must be. I had the pleasure of seeing his fury at first hand, just a few moments later, as his head appeared out of the carriage. He was straining to climb out, his face dark red, his wig askew and much dishevelled. Once out of the wrecked vehicle, he assisted Mr Wicklow, and between them they hauled out the two distraught, hysterical ladies.

My aunt sat sobbing noisily on the bank while Mrs Wicklow clung to her husband's arms and shrieked: 'Oh, I thought we'd all been killed! I'm sure every bone in my body is broken! Oh, what a terrible accident.'

Seeing Captain Mould's expression of revulsion, I thought I would add to his irritation. 'Oh, Captain!' I shrieked in a high-pitched voice, running forward to grasp his sleeve. 'Oh, I was so frightened! Whatever shall we do? Oh, oh, the poor carriage! It's all smashed, look! Look!'

Furious, he tried to pull his sleeve from my grasp, but I clung on tighter and began to sob more noisily than either of the other women. I hoped I was giving him a disgust of me. 'Leave me alone, you stupid, ignorant girl,' he said angrily, giving me a shove so that I fell backwards into the road. I cried noisily again, heaving pretend sobs into my pocket handkerchief as the captain twitched his coat straight and marched off towards the horses. I watched him under my lashes as he started haranguing the coachman for careless driving. 'You're a damned stupid fellow!' he shouted.

'It wasn't my fault, sir,' the poor coachman protested, still white-faced with shock. 'There was a pothole!'

'I don't want to hear your lame excuses. Stop sitting around, you lazy, good-for-nothing scoundrel and help me untangle these horses.' The captain began swearing under his breath as he fought to straighten out the mess of harness and frightened horses the accident had caused.

The sun had slipped below the horizon, the dusk creeping up on us. I thought it wouldn't be long before Jenny arrived to set the seal on this ill-fated expedition. I'd scarcely had the thought when the drumming of horses' hooves reached my ears. The others heard it too. Captain Mould straightened up, listening, and my aunt turned towards the sound and cried: 'Oh, help is at hand! What a relief!'

Their dismay when a pistol shot rang out over our heads and two masked horsemen appeared was a delight to see. The two horses pulled to a halt in a cloud of dust and noise, and in the confusion, I saw the larger man level a pistol at Captain Mould's head. 'Nobody move!' he ordered loudly. 'Now. One at a time, hand over your valuables to my partner. Any tricks and your friend here dies.'

The temptation was almost overwhelming, but I resisted it and stayed quietly where I was, hands folded in my lap, watching the scene.

'How *dare* you?' demanded Captain Mould in a shaking voice. 'I'll have the law on you for this!'

'You do that, old man,' recommended Jenny's father in his hoarse voice. We all knew he'd be far away without a trace before Captain Mould could go to the magistrates.

Meanwhile, Jenny was taking rings and a garnet necklace from my aunt, gold bracelets and a brooch from Mrs Wicklow, as well as a diamond pin and a snuffbox from Mr Wicklow. A purse was wrested from Captain Mould that looked worth stealing, plus a lace pocket handkerchief. 'And now your wig,' commanded Jenny's father.

'My wig? Damn, how dare you?' shouted Captain Mould, going red. 'You can't force me to undress on the public highway!'

A slow grin spread over the highwayman's face, revealing broken, discoloured teeth. 'But that's exactly what I be goin' do,' he said. He pulled a sack from his saddlebag and threw it to Jenny. 'Wigs, coats, cravats, and gowns,' he ordered.

'No!' objected the victims, with various degrees of vehemence. I said nothing, enjoying their discomfiture. I had no particular objection to walking back to town in my petticoats. It was almost dark after all. But I could see the prospect utterly humiliated the others.

The highwayman cocked his pistol with an ominous click, and held it closer to Captain Mould's head. The angry colour swiftly faded from the captain's face, to be replaced by an unhealthy pallor. 'Very well, you'll get what you want,' he stuttered. 'But get that damned pistol away from my head.'

His antagonist didn't move, and slowly, carefully, Mould removed his wig and dropped it into the sack the masked Jenny held out to him. His velvet coat and embroidered waistcoat followed, then his expensive lace ruffles and cravat.

He stood, much diminished, a small, grey, shaven-headed older man, sweating with fear and the closeness of the evening, while his companions also divested themselves of their outer garments, both ladies whimpering with shame and fear.

It was my turn. With the ghost of a grin at Jenny, I began to wriggle out of the most hated of my gowns, chosen specially with the hope I'd be robbed of it before the day was over. But before I was properly out of it, we were disturbed by the rumble of coach wheels and the sound of hooves from the Bristol direction.

'Quickly!' urged Jenny's father, snatching the sack from her and slinging it over his saddle. Jenny leapt onto her horse and they were both gone in a swirl of dust before the carriage drew into sight around the corner.

I stood foolishly half in, half out of my gown, while Captain Mould turned and waved to the coach, trying to attract its attention in the gloom. But the coachmen, seeing the smashed carriage and its passengers clearly robbed, simply whipped up the horses and passed us at a dangerously reckless pace on the steep hill.

'Why aren't they stopping?' wailed my aunt. 'Why would a coachman drive past us when we need help?'

'Because this is sometimes a ploy,' growled Mr Wicklow. 'Coach appears to be in distress, carriage stops to help, and gets robbed. They were frightened.'

There was a silence as we all took this in. 'Then what are we going to *do*?' quavered Aunt Amelia.

'Walk,' stated the captain harshly.

It was a sorry, footsore group that finally reached the city gate an hour later. There was a glow in the sky and a hubbub of noise from within the city walls.

A group of men stood in the archway, blocking our way. 'Where are you heading?' one asked as we approached. He and his companions stared in surprise at my companions' undress.

'Trim Street first,' Captain Mould replied. 'We've been robbed. Is there something wrong in the city?'

'It's engulfed in lawlessness. I'd advise avoiding the city itself and skirting the walls to Trim Street.'

'What do you mean by lawlessness?' asked my aunt sharply.

'There's a mob storming the Meeting House,' the man explained. 'I'm under orders to let none in. You can walk around the walls to Trim Street.'

My aunt and Captain Mould exchanged significant glances but said nothing until we were walking in the dark towards Trim Street. They then conducted a low-voiced conversation which I could hear nothing of.

Captain Mould and the Wicklows parted from us at our house and I knocked. The door was opened by our butler, whose usual calm appeared to have deserted him. It took only a moment for me to see the reason. Behind him, immaculately dressed as ever, but frowning heavily, stood my father.

CHAPTER TWENTY-THREE

Father contained his rage until we'd been ushered into the first floor drawing room, and the servant had been dismissed. 'I return after a long absence,' he began quietly, 'expecting to find my daughter carefully chaperoned; respectably occupied by the activities of the city. I even hoped she may be on the point of contracting an advantageous engagement. That was, after all, the point of my return to this country and our costly sojourn in this city.' He left a long silence, staring contemptuously at both me and my aunt. 'Instead of which, what do I find?'

Neither of us ventured a reply. He didn't want one.

'I find you've both left the city in the company of some half-pay officer, returning long after dark without most of your clothes! If this gets out—and it will!—Sophia's reputation will be in ruins! It's a scandal!' He gave vent to his fury by turning on my aunt, grasping her by the shoulders and shaking her roughly. I could swear I heard her teeth rattle. She whimpered in pain and fright and began to sob.

'Oh, be silent, woman!' shouted her brother. 'Go to your bedchambers both of you. I want you out of my sight!'

I fled thankfully to my chamber, but not to bed. As soon as I reached my room, I threw off my outer clothes and scrambled out onto the roof where I pulled on my breeches and shoes. It was a risk to leave the house so early; my absence could be discovered. But I had to see what was going on in the city.

From the roof, I could see the flicker of a fire burning somewhere in the city centre. I scrambled down the drainpipe, bruising my knee in my haste. Soon I was racing swiftly along the dark streets towards the disturbance.

A huge crowd was assembled in the square behind the abbey. There were shouts, loud voices chanting and the sound of things breaking. A bonfire burned brightly on one side of the square, lighting the scene. I stopped, lingering in the shadows, getting my bearings.

Most of the crowd seemed to be gathered around the Quakers' Meeting House at the bottom of the square. They were throwing missiles: as I watched, a glass bottle smashed against the stone wall of the house, spraying glass and liquid everywhere. The crowd surged forward excitedly, and men started hammering on the large front doors of the meeting house.

'Come out, you dissenter scum!' voices were shouting. 'Or we'll burn the building down!'

A chant of 'Long live the High Church!' was taken up in the square. For a few moments every voice was in unison, and then the voices disintegrated into a formless mass of shouting and abuse once more. I realized this was a riot like the ones I'd read about in the papers. The unrest had spread to Bath just as Mr Charleton had warned.

Looking up at the windows of the building, I saw a face pressed against the window. It was a young face, just a child, full of fear. A shout went up as others in the square saw it. The face disappeared quickly and only a moment later, there was another smash, and the window where it had been shattered under a rain of bricks and stones.

I shuddered. What had only a moment before been an exciting scene, was now an ugly confrontation. It seemed likely that innocent people were going to be hurt. The crowd were battering at the door, throwing their weight against it. Someone smashed a downstairs window and tried to climb in, but was repulsed fiercely from inside the building. He fell back into the crowd clutching his shoulder.

There was an angry surge in the crowd and a volley of missiles and abuse in response to this. I watched the crowd, convinced there was someone I knew beside the injured man. I stared hard. It was difficult to recognize anyone in the flickering torch and firelight that lit the square, but that hair, that set of shoulders . . . surely that was Bill? What was he doing in the riot?

I began to push forward, trying to reach him. The mood of the crowd was vicious now. Shouting and chanting, they were piling firewood and broken furniture in front of the door. A man stood over it with a flaming torch, ready to set light to it. I pushed harder, trying to slip through the tightly-packed mass of protesters. I was jostled, pushed this way and that, my feet trodden on and my jacket pulled. Someone barged me from one side so hard I nearly went down, clutching at someone's arm, desperately trying to stay upright. The man shook me off, but I was up again and moving slowly forward.

The fire at the door was crackling now, the smoke from the wood curling up the stone front of the building. 'Bill!' I yelled. My voice was lost in the shouts of the mob. A small gap opened to my right, and I bent and wriggled through. Now I could see it was indeed Bill. He was no longer shouting and jeering with the rest of the crowd. Instead he was kneeling as it surged and shouted around him, trying to tend the man who had been wounded. I reached his side at last and grasped his arm. At first he didn't notice me in the press. 'Bill,' I shouted into his ear, shaking his arm. He started and looked round at me.

'It's me, Sophia!' I said in his ear. His look of puzzlement quickly turned to surprise and then relief.

'Help me!' he pleaded. 'They've all gone mad!'

Between us, we helped the injured man to his feet, trying not to hurt his bleeding shoulder. We supported him as Bill tried to push through the crowd, to escape the press of excited, enraged bodies that surrounded us. Once they realized we were moving away from the action, they parted to let us through, surging in to fill the space we left as we passed.

We struggled on, the weight of the man leaning on us growing heavier with every step, until we reached the south wall of the abbey. Then Bill stopped, lowered the man to the ground and pulled aside his coat to look at the injury. The shirt beneath the coat was soaked with bright, wet blood. The man was barely conscious, his head lolling. 'He needs a hospital,' I said at once.

'I got no money,' said Bill. 'Neither does he.'

'Is he a friend of yours?' I asked, scowling. 'What sort of company have you got into that you thought it was a good idea to attack a church?'

'He's Tom. He works with me is all,' said Bill defensively, pulling his own coat off, stripping off his shirt and folding it to a pad so that he could press it to the wound. 'And there was no plan to attack the church. Just to protest. It got out of hand.'

'You're telling me,' I said. The ugly scene continued behind us; the racket almost drowning our voices. 'Let's get him to the hospital before he dies,' I shouted. 'I can pay.' Bill looked doubtfully at me and then nodded. He knew my family were wealthy. He didn't need to know I only had access to that money because I'd stolen it. I had a feeling he wouldn't approve of my behaviour, nor of Jenny's part in the robbery.

'I thought of you as strict and law-abiding,' I told him as we bent to pick up the injured man once more. 'What on earth were you doing as part of a Jacobite mob?'

'It's people like them in there that took the throne from the rightful king!' Bill said. 'I support the Stuart heir. I never meant no harm though.'

'I don't know anything about kings and rightful heirs, and I don't care,' I said. 'But just look at them! Howling and beating at the Meeting House, their humanity entirely gone! If they get that child, they'll tear him limb from limb.'

I wasn't sure what made me suddenly so passionate, unless it was the immediate danger, the naked hate in the voices and faces of the mob. Perhaps also the memory of Mr Charleton's warnings of blood in the streets: the violence of the mob had brought the truth of his words home to me.

'I can see that,' said Bill, throwing an uncomfortable glance at the crowd. 'But just because some of 'em behaved bad, don't make the cause wrong.'

I had no chance to reply. A crowd of official-looking men came pouring into the abbey square. We were pushed aside in the sudden rush and had trouble keeping Tom from being knocked to the ground.

'Magistrates and constables,' yelled Bill to me. Shouts for order were rising above the yells and jeers. The men pushed forward to the door, the crowd scattering around them, and raked the fire away from it. The flames were beaten out with sacks, and a group of officials began remonstrating with the ringleaders. There were angry shouts, protests, and some skirmishes, as the rougher element of the mob tried to continue the riot. A fight broke out and one of the magistrates was knocked to the ground. There was a cheer from the crowd, but it was short-lived. The man responsible was quickly overcome. Other men were arrested too. The crowd began to melt away, breaking up and resolving slowly into human beings again.

With Tom hanging, a dead weight, between us, we walked away from the scene. As we struggled along, I saw Mr Charleton. At the same moment he caught sight of me and our eyes locked. There was no friendly acknowledgement from him, no greeting. I realized what he was thinking: here I was, in the thick of a riot, helping a young man who'd been involved. Mr Charleton's eyes were hard and he looked disappointed. He turned away without coming close enough for me to explain.

It shouldn't have mattered to me in the least what he thought of me. Why should I care? I knew the truth. But somehow it mattered a great deal. I wanted to run after him and tell him the riot had none of my support. But Tom's weight on my shoulders, the blood still oozing from the wound in his shoulder prevented me. I staggered on, feeling as though my arm was being wrenched from my shoulder.

The hospital was noisy and crowded with the sick. A few had been hurt in the riot, most had other complaints. I left Bill with Tom in a long queue, waiting to see a doctor and ran home through the streets to fetch enough money to pay for whatever treatment was needed. The coins jingling in my pocket, I ran back to the hospital, an idea forming in my mind. I found Bill slumped on a bench in a hallway, looking exhausted. 'Tom's being tended,' he said when he saw me. I nodded and handed over some coins. 'Thank you,' said Bill uncomfortably.

'There's something I have to do,' I said. 'I can't tell you what in case it doesn't work out. Will you wait here for me? I might be a little while.'

It wasn't far to the inns and taverns near the abbey where Jenny had her patch. A few determined drinkers and gamblers lingered, but the disturbance had driven most inhabitants to the safety of their lodgings. I decided Jenny must have called it a night too; the atmosphere in the city was sullen and edgy. Reluctantly, I made for the city walls, climbed over and set out for Jenny's cottage. Clouds had come up, making the darkness dense. I wasted time losing my way in the woods and coming out at the wrong place. I had to cast about to find Jenny's village, locating it at last by the glimmer of lamps through the alehouse window.

I approached the cottage cautiously, afraid of running into Jenny's father. But luck favoured me. The door was ajar, and candlelight showed me Jenny at the table. When I whispered her name, she jumped and hurriedly swept coins from the table into her hand. 'What do you want?' she demanded fiercely once she'd seen who it was. 'You shouldn't come here.'

'I know. But Bill is at the hospital. I thought you might want to see him.'

Jenny clutched at my coat sleeve in alarm. 'He's hurt?' she cried.

'No! I'm sorry to have frightened you,' I reassured her at once. 'A friend of his is hurt. I just thought . . . it would be neutral ground. It will be so complicated to set up a meeting, so I came to fetch you now while Bill is waiting.'

'Give me a moment,' said Jenny. She vanished into the darkness of the cottage a few minutes later. She had combed her hair and exchanged her coat and breeches for a plain gown, less shabby than any I'd seen her in up to now. Without another word, Jenny led the way back to the city, over the wall and across the city to the hospital. When we reached the entrance, she hung back, suddenly nervous, letting me take the lead.

Bill stood awkwardly in the entrance hall waiting for me, his eyes drooping with tiredness. When he saw his sister by my side, he gasped. 'Jenny?' he asked dazed.

In a second they were in each other's arms. Bill wept unashamedly and clung to his sister. Jenny pretended not to cry, wiping her eyes when she thought we weren't looking, her voice gruff as she replied to the flood of jumbled questions Bill asked her.

I stood a little to one side, moved by their reunion. Then I went quietly into the hospital, to enquire after the well-being of the patient.

CHAPTER TWENTY-FOUR

I was tired as we left morning prayers the following day. It had been a long night, and I'd had too little sleep even for me. My father, Aunt Amelia, and I walked the short distance to the Grove to join the promenade. Outwardly we were in harmony; a happy family reunited after my father's absence. Below the surface, bad feeling, anger, and resentment seethed.

Father was furious with my aunt. He'd condemned her inability to chaperone me adequately. She'd thrown the blame on me, complaining of my lack of conduct. The only thing that had calmed my father somewhat, the only mitigating circumstance in his eyes, was my aunt's assurance that Mr Charleton still showed a decided partiality for me. 'He's danced with her at every ball,' she'd cried tearfully. 'He's walked with her in the gardens and even escorted her home!'

'Do you think his intentions are serious?' my father had asked, still frowning. 'Does he have money for marriage?'

'I dare not say! He cannot address himself to me or to her, you know. But perhaps now that you have returned . . . '

I knew that far from proposing for my hand, Mr Charleton was likely to cut me entirely after last night.

What would my father say then? Would he finally give this scheme up? I tried to tell myself that if falling out with Mr Charleton allowed me to go home, then it was a price worth paying. But he'd been kind to me, and often surprisingly perceptive. His ill-opinion troubled me and had kept me awake during the few hours I'd spent in my bed last night.

The Grove was crowded; excited chatter all around us. The talk was all about the riot in the city. Everyone had seen the smashed windows and blackened doors of the Meeting House and many had heard the disturbance. As I walked beside my father, I heard snatches of conversation from all sides: 'A regular mob . . . the High Church . . . show that imposter . . . damned false king . . . ' My head spun with it and the memory of the scenes of the night before. It was being treated as a topic for gossip. It was being discussed eagerly; almost gleefully. *That's not how it was*, I wanted to shout. *I was there. It was brutal, ugly. Vicious.*

I closed my eyes briefly. When I opened them, Mr Charleton was right in front of me. His face showed no emotion, either pleasure or otherwise, at the sight of me. I caught my breath, wanting to explain what had happened last night. But there were no words to convince him that I was innocent of any involvement. Besides, my father was beside me, watching us both.

Mr Charleton gave me a cold, formal bow and passed on without a word. I sensed my father's eyes on me and quaked inwardly. My father took hold of my elbow and gripped it so hard that I couldn't forbear a squeak of pain. 'Be silent, Sophia, we are in public,' he hissed in my ear.

'Tell me why the supposedly enamoured Mr Charleton will barely acknowledge you?'

'I . . . I don't know, Father. He was still friendly only yesterday.'

'What have you done?' my father's voice grew so soft in his anger that I could scarcely catch the words.

'Nothing, that I know of,' I lied, ashamed to hear the pleading in my voice. To tell him the truth was unthinkable.

At Harrison's, Captain Mould awaited us, bowing over my hand and my aunt's, and waiting for an introduction to my father. If I'd hoped he'd be repulsed, I was mistaken. My father shook his hand, and fell into conversation with him. I moved away, sickened and restless. Only a few minutes later, I saw him sitting down to play at cards with the captain. My heart sank still further. The afternoon seemed painfully long without even the hope of Mr Charleton's company to while away the time. It was deeply uncomfortable to have quarrelled with him.

I expected my father to be angry with me that evening, perhaps even punish me. But, strangely, he said not a word. He was even, in his way, cheerful. He discussed the recent riot at length with my aunt and gave moderate praise of the captain. He looked at me meaningfully as he did so. I felt my throat close with horror.

I needed to get out of the house, away from his abominable presence. As soon as I was sent to bed, I wriggled out of my gown, petticoats, and hoop, and clambered up onto the roof in my shift and bare feet. It was a warm night, but there was a pleasant breeze up on the rooftops; it stirred my damp hair and caressed my over-heated skin. I would go to Jenny, I decided, and hear how she'd got on with her brother. It would be good to see a friendly face.

I lifted the tile to retrieve my breeches and shoes and reached my hand into the roof-space. My hand closed on empty air. Certain that I was mistaken, I reached in again and groped around. My fingers met only timbers. My heart started to thump. Where were my clothes? Not to mention the large sum of money that I'd wrapped in them. Had my father somehow discovered my hiding place? I tried to calm my quickened breathing and to think straight. Surely he wouldn't have been able to contain his anger if he'd discovered I'd been sneaking out? No, it couldn't be him. But then who? My thoughts jumped instantly to the only person who knew about the hiding place: Jenny.

As I had the thought, there was a soft clatter of roof tiles behind me. I whipped around to see a small slight figure illuminated by the moonlight. 'Jenny!' I exclaimed. 'I thought for a moment . . . that you'd betrayed me. Tell me you only hid them for a jest!' My relief was so great that I could have laughed heartily over such a decep-tion. But instead of smiling and confessing, Jenny looked confused.

'Hid what?' she asked.

'My clothes and money,' I said, trying to stem the ris-ing tide of panic inside me. 'They're gone.'

'Not me,' she said with a shrug. 'You sure you looked properly?'

'You're the only one who knew!' I said, forgetting to keep my voice quiet. When she looked blank, I launched myself at her. With surprise on my side, I succeeded in knocking her over and pinning her onto the roof. I knelt on her chest, holding her arms down, and hissed into her face: 'Where are they? What have you done with my money?'

Jenny looked up at me, fury glinting in her eyes. Then she twisted ferociously beneath me, knocking me sideways with ease. Before I knew what had happened, I was sprawling with my face shoved into the slate tiles and my arm burning as Jenny twisted it. 'Is it likely I'd come up here for a chat if I'd prigged your stash?' she demanded, her voice vibrant with anger. 'I ain't got the slightest idea where it is. You bin careless, I daresay.'

'I haven't,' I answered, gasping with the pain in my arm, the slates grazing my face as I struggled to escape her grip.

'Well, it wasn't me! You said we was friends and I *almost* believed you. I come here to thank you for taking me to see me brother yesterday. And now you're accusing me! Say you're sorry!' Jenny demanded.

'I'm sorry!' I gasped. 'If you say it wasn't you, I believe you.'

The grip loosened a little. 'No more attacking me then!' Jenny said.

'Much good it would do me,' I muttered resentfully.

She released me and stood over me, daring me to break my word. I sat up and rubbed my sore arm. 'There was no need to hurt me,' I said crossly.

'Who started it?' asked Jenny. Then she began to laugh. 'Fighting like a couple of cats on the rooftops,' she said.

I only managed a faint smile. The loss of my possessions was too serious for laughter. I crawled over to the hiding place, and lifted the tile again allowing the moonlight to shine into the gap. There was only gaping blackness. Carefully I reached in one more time, and explored the roof space. Unexpectedly my fingers closed on a slim package. It wasn't my breeches, nor yet the leather of my father's purse. Puzzled I pulled it out and turned it over. It was a hard rectangle wrapped in brown paper.

'What's that then?' asked Jenny.

'I've never seen it before,' I replied, unwrapping it. Inside the paper was a slim volume. I could just make out the gold lettering. *The Rape of the Lock* by Alexander Pope. A small piece of paper fluttered out of the package and down onto the tiles. I turned it this way and that, trying to make it out in the moonlight. It was just one word. *Sorry*. 'Sorry,' I repeated out loud. '*Sorry!* How dare he?'

Jenny raised her brows in a question.

'Mr Charleton,' I said bitterly. 'It must be. He's the only one besides you who knows this is my route out of the house. And he knows I want to read this book. He's preventing me from getting out of the house, and leaving me poetry as compensation. If it had been my father, it would have been a book of sermons I found here. Or a birch cane for a beating.'

Jenny squatted down beside me and rocked on her heels. 'So,' she said. 'Why?'

I poured out my tangled story of friendship mixed up with hostility and suspicion. How he'd followed me onto the roof, tried to prevent me going out at night and suspected me of involvement in last night's riot. Jenny listened silently, then drew a die out of her own pocket and tossed it casually, catching it deftly again. 'Do you care for him?' she asked, off-handed.

'Not a jot,' I assured her swiftly. I was glad of the darkness to hide my traitorous flush. The truth was I had confused feelings towards Mr Charleton. I didn't understand them myself.

'So you don't think you should do like he says?'

'Absolutely not,' I said, this time with complete truth. 'He has no right to interfere with my activities! I told him so.'

Jenny grinned, her teeth gleaming in the moonlight. 'Well then,' she said. 'Here's a plan. I get you more clothes. You help me out with a little job I needs doing tomorrow night.'

'Anything you like,' I said promptly, without pausing to consider what I might be required to do. 'I'll go insane if I have another spell of being tied to the house.' Privately, I considered it served Mr Charleton right if I got into mischief after he had behaved so treacherously. A very small voice whispered that it could have been worse. He could have gone to my father and told him what I was doing. I stifled the voice and refused to be grateful. He had no right to interfere.

'I'll meet you here tomorrow night then,' Jenny said with a grin.

'Aren't you going to tell me what we'll be doing?'

'It'll be a surprise,' replied Jenny, vanishing silently into the darkness.

I crept back into my room, frustrated to be deprived of the outing I'd looked forward to all day. I hated to admit it, even to myself, but the poetry did sweeten the disappointment. Though not as much as the prospect of an adventure tomorrow night.

Overnight, a new subject for gossip succeeded the riot. From one moment to the next, it seemed forgotten, and all the talk was of costumes. Beau Nash had announced a grand masked ball to close the Bath season. Precedence was to be set aside in favour of disguise, and there was to be a classical theme.

I couldn't care less how I spent the final ball of the season. A masquerade didn't excite me in the least. I listened all the next day to the excited chatter about Helen of Troy, Zeus and Paris, and yawned, biding time until nightfall. My only disappointment was the absence of Mr Charleton from the round of daily activities. I had a few choice words stored up to say to him.

CHAPTER TWENTY-FIVE

Jenny was true to her word, arriving with a bundle of boy's clothes, a cap and shoes at dusk. She herself was in a ragged gown. I followed her as she made her way by dark alleys through the city and across the wall. From there we made our way to a tumbledown stable in a field where two horses awaited us ready saddled and bridled.

'So what is it we're doing?' I asked at last. Jenny was stripping off her gown, stuffing it into her saddlebag and pulling on breeches, shirt, and black coat. Once the transformation was complete, we swung ourselves up onto the horses' backs and made our way at a brisk trot across the field.

'Holding up a coach, o' course,' she said with a grin. 'There's two loaded pistols in your saddlebag. And a mask.'

I felt a slight lurch in my stomach. 'I told you I didn't want to rob,' I said.

'Well, we ain't after his valuables so much as his papers,' said Jenny. 'So that's all right, ain't it?' She led the way through a gate into a lane. The shadows were deep here, and I could see little as the horses walked briskly up the hill. When I didn't reply to her question,

Jenny admitted, 'Though they said to nick his purse as well, to make it look less suspicious.'

'Who are you doing this for?' I asked curiously. 'And what's it about?'

'Dunno who they are or why, but they're paying me five guineas and I can keep any valuables I take,' said Jenny with a grin. 'They said as how this was important. I'll go halves with you. The clothes I've give you are for free.' She grinned wickedly in the moonlight.

'And why isn't your father helping you instead of me?'

Jenny frowned suddenly. 'He was supposed to be. This was his job. But he got took,' she said shortly. 'He's in gaol.'

We reached the brow of a hill and left the lane, pushing into a wood. 'He got taken, and you want me to take his place?' I asked incredulously. 'And what if *we* get caught?'

'Oh, not on the highway,' Jenny assured me. 'He was taken in the rumpus in the city the other night.'

'He was rioting?' I asked, remembering the violence of that night.

'Not exactly,' she said evasively.

'What then?'

'He was more using the fuss to his advantage, like. Oh, all right, he was picking the pockets of them that was. But he got arrested for all that.'

'Can you manage without him?' I asked concerned for her.

'I'd do a sight better without him,' said Jenny caustically. 'If only he hadn't left me with never a penny, his drinking debts and the rent unpaid the past two months. I got to have money. That's what tonight's for.'

'Can't Bill help you?' I asked.

'Lord love you, he ain't got no money. Spent it all getting here, didn't he? I can look after meself.'

I stifled my misgivings and resolved to hear her out at least.

'Listen,' said Jenny, 'this man who's comin' along, he'll be armed. This ain't goin' to be an easy plucking. I thought we should rope the road to be safe. Then we can hide in the trees and jump out at 'em.'

'Rope the road?' I asked incredulously. 'Do you mean tie a rope to bring down the horses?'

'We're outnumbered and they're stronger than us. There ain't no other way.'

'I'm having nothing to do with that,' I said firmly. 'Chances are the horses would have to be shot. They don't deserve that.'

The wood opened out into a field, the moonlight was bright, and Jenny pushed her horse into a canter down the slope. 'If you're going to be soft about it . . . ' she said derisively over her shoulder.

'Not soft, just humane,' I said urging my mount after hers. 'How long do we have?'

Jenny shrugged. 'After dark was all they said, on the road back from Bristol. Driving a curricle with his own pair o' horses. So that's unusual enough that we'll not mistake it this time o' night.'

'A curricle,' I echoed. 'So there'll only be space for one groom. That makes it easier. But . . . we need more people, surely? If this is important, as you say it is, we can't afford to muff it. We need a lookout to tell us it's the right carriage; we can't afford to rob a wrong one first in case they alert the magistrate.'

The more I thought about this the more anxious I became. We slowed to a walk, and emerged onto a tree-lined road. 'Why is this being entrusted to two girls?' I asked. Jenny looked away and didn't reply. 'Jenny?'

'All right, so they don't know I'm a girl. And this was entrusted to me dad and his cronies, not to me. But now he's not here and some of them are in prison and all. The rest is gone to ground; can't find 'em. There was no one but you. And I need the money.'

I silently cursed Mr Charleton for taking my own stash of money. If I'd still had it, I'd have given Jenny what she needed and called this dangerous robbery off. Should I ask Mr Charleton? Tell him the trouble a friend of mine was in and ask for my money back? No, he'd never believe me now.

Jenny pulled up and I reined in beside her. The night was very still without the thud of our horses' hooves or the creak of leather. 'This is the spot I picked,' she told me.

'Very well,' I said reluctantly. 'I'll help you just this once if we try a decoy.' The incident of the carriage crash on Lansdown was fresh in my mind. Drivers were suspicious of decoys, yes, but what if it was one they *had* to stop for?

'Hold on a moment,' said Jenny belligerently. 'Are *you* telling *me* how we're going to do this? Or am I hearing wrong?'

'No, you're hearing right,' I retorted.

'And how many carriages have you held up so far? In your long, experienced career on the High Toby?' she demanded sarcastically.

'Just the one, as you well know, but . . . '

'Whereas I bin playing this game since you was still wetting your napkins, so let me decide how we'll do it.'

'Firstly, you're not much older than me, so let's not compare pot-training,' I said. 'Secondly, if you've got an idea that doesn't involve crippling two horses and risking us getting shot, I'm happy to hear it.'

A long silence hung between us. I was the first to break it: 'Will you at least hear my idea? There's less danger if we stop the wrong carriage, for they won't see the pistols. And if we're caught, there have been no horses killed, so it's a less serious crime.'

'Don't fool yourself,' said Jenny bitterly. 'This is a hanging matter either way.' She sighed. 'Go on then. Spit it out.'

I started to strip off my coat, and then my shirt. 'Put your gown back on, and get your pistol out,' I said, handing her my shirt and pulling my coat on again, buttoning it up. 'Wrap that up to look like a baby. You're going to be a damsel in distress.'

When I'd explained my plan to her, Jenny sniffed disapprovingly. 'I don't see why I should be the one in petticoats, nor with a babby,' she said. 'Why can't you do that bit?'

'You're the one with a gown,' I retorted. I'd barely persuaded her to play her part as I wanted, when we heard the distant sounds of a carriage. Jenny hurried to lie in the road clutching her white linen bundle, and I concealed myself in the trees. I buttoned my black coat and pulled my mask down over my head with some distaste. It was fashioned from an old, smelly stocking, with holes cut into it to see through. To my mind, a proper mask would be required to give highway robbery the romance and flair it was generally credited with. I adjusted the unsatisfactory mask, and tucked my pistol into my coat. It was loaded, as Jenny had told me, but not cocked.

A few moments later, I saw Jenny get up from the road and melt into the trees. I frowned, wondering what she was playing at. The carriage would be upon us at any moment and we'd miss it. Sure enough, only a few moments later, it swept around the corner. I relaxed. It was a post-chaise drawn by four horses, a coachman handling the reins, an ostler riding one of the lead horses and a groom on the box seat nursing a large, heavy weapon.

As it passed me, I breathed a sigh of relief that we hadn't tried to meddle with it. Jenny was beside me in the darkness, a shadow under the trees, her white bundle the only thing that was visible. 'You get an ear for whether it's two horses or four,' she said in my ear. 'With experience, that is.'

Her tone was mocking; before I could retort she'd vanished again. A solitary rider passed us, but otherwise the night was still for nearly an hour before we heard the sound of another vehicle. It was a warm night, but I was growing chilled standing so still, and my nerves were on edge with the tension. I could see Jenny at some distance from me, listening carefully. All at once, she stepped quite deliberately out into the road and lay down. I guessed the carriage we wanted was on its way. I wiped my hand on my breeches and gripped my pistol.

Everything happened very fast. The curricle came round the corner at a slapping pace, and Jenny began to cry out and wave a grubby pocket handkerchief frantically at the driver. 'Help me!' she cried. 'Please help!'

I held my breath. For one appalling instant I thought the curricle wasn't going to stop in time. But the driver saw Jenny and pulled up his pair at the last moment, with Jenny almost under their feet. At the same time, whilst both men's attention was on Jenny, I left the tree-line and dropped down behind the curricle, hiding in its shadow.

'See if she's all right, will you, Baines,' said a heart-stoppingly familiar voice. I froze in horror and crouched lower.

'Sir, this could be a trap,' I heard the second man urge.

'Then take your pistol, but we can't drive over the girl,' pointed out the first voice reasonably. 'There are laws against that sort of thing.'

The servant stood up. As he did so, I caught hold of the back of the curricle with one hand. I paused, holding my breath until the moment when the servant Baines climbed down clumsily into the road. At exactly the same time, I hoisted myself up behind them, hoping that my own weight on the curricle would go unnoticed. Baines seemed to be an older man, not very agile, which gave Jenny an easier task than I was going to have.

I was experiencing a heady mix of horror and exhila-ration. A part of me wished I could call to Jenny and stop this robbery in its tracks. But it was too late. So I threw myself into it, revelling in the danger and the reckless adventure. After all, there was a wonderful irony in robbing Mr Charleton in revenge for stealing my things. For it was his voice; I was almost certain of it.

The servant was bending over Jenny now, pistol in hand, asking her if she was hurt. She was weeping loudly, covering any sounds I might make, and crying out her concern for her poor sick 'babby' and how she'd sprained her ankle.

That was when Baines made his mistake. With one last glance around him, he tucked his pistol into his waistband and bent to scoop Jenny up in his arms and move her from the roadway. Knowing what was coming, I eased my own pistol out of my coat and pressed its cold nose into Mr Charleton's neck.

'Don't move,' I whispered in his ear. I felt his sharp intake of breath, the tension in his body in front of mine. He knew now what was happening, but was powerless to shout a warning to his servant. Baines too had frozen, the muzzle of Jenny's pistol appearing instead of a baby as she unwrapped her bundle.

'Arms up, very slowly,' I whispered to Mr Charleton. He sat quite still, not moving.

'This is a mistake,' he said. 'You'll regret this.'

I saw his hand stealing towards his coat and knew I had to convince him. Reluctantly, I drew back the safety catch on my pistol until it clicked. I was now pointing a loaded, primed weapon straight at Mr Charleton's throat. The thought that the gun could go off in my hand made me shake, but I did my best to put my fear aside.

Mr Charleton was taking me seriously now. His hands

were moving slowly into the air, his lace ruffles falling back from his wrists. Taking great care not to put any pressure on the trigger I held, I reached around him slipping my hand inside his coat. My fingers met the cold iron of a pistol and I withdrew it carefully, dropping it into the road.

I felt inside his coat again. I couldn't find the papers. Then I noticed that his waistcoat was unyielding under my fingers and guessed they were inside it. I slid my hand inside his waistcoat and there they were; a bundle of folded sheets.

I could feel Mr Charleton's heart beating strongly through the thin layer of his shirt and somehow that unnerved me more than anything else had done so far. I quickly drew the packet of papers from his waistcoat. My mind started noticing strange things, like the fact that they were still warm from the heat of his body.

'I don't want papers,' I growled softly, trying to make my voice gruff and hoarse and as unlike my own as possible. 'Where's yer purse?'

'If you don't want papers, then give them back to me and I'll tell you where my money is,' Mr Charleton replied, remarkably calmly for a man with a gun at his neck.

'Give us the money and I'll think about it,' I said, sliding the papers swiftly into my own coat behind his back.

I heard Mr Charleton catch his breath, and bit my lip, hoping my voice had not given me away. How could he possibly guess who I was? He thought me at home, safely tucked in bed, not out on the king's highway with pistols and an accomplice.

His next words made me even more suspicious that he'd guessed my identity: 'I fear I've hidden my purse in my breeches,' he said lazily.

I stood quite still, balanced on the back of the curricle. Mr Charleton was playing a game with me and this was check. I wasn't about to explore his breeches and he knew it. I blushed hot at the very thought.

'At the front, on the right-hand side,' he added helpfully.

Still I made no move. I was torn between calling his bluff and sheer embarrassment, my free hand clenched indecisively at his shoulder. 'Would you like me to get it out for you?' he asked, his voice mocking me.

'You keep your hands where I can see 'em,' I said as gruffly as I could.

'I make no such requirement of you, you see,' replied Mr Charleton, not moving. 'Please, help yourself.'

I didn't know what to do. Every second we delayed put us in greater danger. I decided to give up on the purse. Reluctant as I was to steal any personal possessions from him, I was forced to do so to make the robbery look real. From his left hand, I drew a gold signet ring. Then I reached into the lace of his cravat, seeking the pin I knew he always wore there and drew it out. These would have to suffice.

'I've got you covered,' I whispered. 'A man is pointing another gun straight at your head from the side of the road. If you move in the next few minutes he'll shoot you dead.'

I prepared to jump back down into the road, but Mr Charleton's voice made me pause. 'For pity's sake,

Sophia, if it really is you,' he said softly. 'Don't take those papers. You cannot possibly understand the consequences if you do. I'll give you what money I have on me. And yours too.'

I hesitated. Would it be better for Jenny to have whatever sum of money Charleton carried about him, or the five guineas she'd been promised? I decided the risk of exchanging more words with Charleton and the insuperable barrier of those breeches outweighed the possible benefits to my friend.

'I dunno what you're talkin' about. Don't move,' I repeated and dropped into the road. I ran into the trees at a crouch. Seeing me go, Jenny left Baines and vanished into the shadows. Both men sat still and silent in their places for a moment. But as I reached the trees and turned, I saw Mr Charleton jump down into the road, groping for his pistol. I waited until he straightened up, the moonlight gleaming on his gun. Then I took very careful aim and shot his hat off his head. The horses startled and plunged and Baines cried out in shock. Only Mr Charleton remained quite still in the darkness. Side by side, Jenny and I flung ourselves onto our horses and made off swiftly into the night.

There was no delighted exhilaration following this robbery as there had been after we waylaid my father. The situation was too dangerous for laughter. 'He recognized me,' I cried low-voiced to Jenny as we cantered across the moonlit fields. 'I *have* to get home before him, or I'll be in such trouble.'

Jenny nodded, tight-faced, and instead of taking me back to the stables, she led the way at a swift trot through villages and across fields until we reached the city walls. 'Give me the stuff and go,' she said, riding close to the wall where a tree grew up against it. I stuffed the papers, jewellery and pistols into the saddlebag, and kicked my feet out of the stirrups.

'Watch yourself,' I told her earnestly. 'Hide everything where it can't be connected to you. I think we may have done something more serious than we realized tonight.'

'Don't worry about me,' said Jenny brusquely. 'Jest get yerself home.'

She caught the bridle of my horse and held him, while I stood up on his back, and from there swung myself into the branches of the tree. 'Go!' I called as I crawled onto the city wall.

Jenny nodded her farewell, and led my horse away at a brisk pace, fading into the darkness as I dropped down into the street on the inside of the wall. I was back in the city, but I still had some distance to go to reach my room. By the time I crawled back through my window, I was panting, fighting for breath, my toes and hands scratched from clinging to the stonework. My biggest problem had been what to do with my clothes, for they would be my greatest risk of betrayal. I'd hidden them between the straw bales in the loft of the stable yard and climbed up onto the roof in my shift and bare feet.

As soon as I dropped into my room, I could hear voices. My father's was raised in anger. What must he think to be roused in the middle of the night? I shut down the sash window behind me. Dragging my nightgown on over my sweaty shift, I dived between the sheets. Already heavy feet were mounting the stairs. At any minute they would be with me. I lay still, trying to regulate my breathing, trying desperately to quiet my heartbeat, but not succeeding. The door of my room burst open, and my father marched in, holding an oil lamp aloft.

'There you see my daughter, gentlemen. In bed, as I assured you. What trouble could she possibly be in at this time of night?'

I looked at the men, wincing in the light, feigning sleepiness and confusion. I was aware my cheeks were hot from running and my hair tangled, and so I groaned softly. 'Father,' I murmured. 'I have such a pain in my stomach.'

He bent over me, resting one cool hand on my brow. 'You're burning, child,' he said pretending unusual fatherly solicitude. 'You have a fever!'

'I've been lying here . . . too ill to call out,' I whispered, playing along.

I was aware of the men taking an involuntary step back from me, fear of contagion in their faces. 'I shall call a physician at once,' my father promised. He turned back to the men. 'As you can see, my daughter is ill. That should satisfy you. Now I wish you to leave.'

'We had very reliable information,' replied the man in charge. 'We're going to search the premises before we go.'

My father bowed his reluctant assent. 'Very well, but we're law-abiding citizens and you'll find nothing,' he said. 'Besides, the front door has been locked and bolted these several hours.'

The men turned my entire room upside down. Clothes were pulled out of drawers, shoes and gowns out of my closet. My hairbrushes and creams were pushed aside and the floorboards checked for hiding places. The men even climbed out onto the roof to check the tiles with lanterns. That made me certain, not that I needed proof, that Mr Charleton was behind this search.

Of course they found nothing. No clothes, no papers, no jewellery. But their search made me think frantically about the stolen papers. What was so important and so valuable that Mr Charleton could command a magistrate and his men to get out of bed in the middle of the night? Clearly something momentous, and I feared something legal and above board too. Dear God, what had we done?

I lay moaning, clutching my belly. I was convincing, for beads of sweat stood out on my forehead with the fear that the men might search as far as the stables and find my discarded clothes. Fortunately for me, they didn't.

They left, making only curt apologies to my father. I barely had time to breathe a sigh of relief before the doctor arrived. He poked and prodded at my belly while I pretended it hurt. Finally he left, leaving behind him a prescription for a purge. 'She's in no immediate danger that I can see,' he told my father. 'But you cannot be too careful with these conditions. Call me back if the fever should recur.'

My father forced me to drink the doctor's vile medicine. My plan to empty it out was thwarted by him standing over me and watching until every last drop had been drunk. I coughed and gagged, but kept it down. I prefer not to think about the consequences it had upon my digestive system afterwards. I lay in bed feeling genuinely weak and ill.

My mind revolved around Jenny and Mr Charleton all that long day as I lay in bed. I needed to do something. Get a message to Jenny somehow; find out what was in those papers. Perhaps prevent her from selling them on. But I was trapped once again. I had no way of contacting her.

As for Mr Charleton, I wanted above all to avoid him. My fake illness allowed me to do that at least. Memories of the encounter the previous night haunted me as I lay staring restlessly at my ceiling. I recalled the warmth of his body as I searched him for the papers; the way he had sat so still when I had pressed the pistol against his neck, and the moment when I was sure he'd recognized me. How he had taunted me. My face flushed even at the memory. I would blush again when I saw him, I knew, and betray myself. It was good if some time passed before we came face to face.

I itched to escape the house at nightfall, but my father prevented that too. 'You shall share your aunt's bedchamber from now on, Sophia,' he ordered me that evening. 'That way there can be no more questions about your night-time whereabouts. That will no doubt reassure you as it does me.'

'Yes, father,' I said meekly, eyes lowered, feigning obedience while my heart beat fast in horror. How was I going to contact Jenny now?

CHAPTER TWENTY-SIX

As soon as I was 'back on my feet', as my father put it, a few days later, my aunt escorted me to the dressmaker's. 'It will be touch and go whether she can even have costumes ready for us now,' she complained as we got into sedan chairs outside the house. 'Every lady of fashion at the Bath has been there before us, thanks to your indisposition.'

I tried to recollect what it was we needed costumes for, but failed. There had been some event or other, I was sure, but the adventure of the robbery had wiped it from my memory. It was my aunt's instructions that recalled the occasion to my mind.

'For the masquerade,' she was saying to the dressmaker. 'Sophia is to be Persephone.'

'Persephone?' I exclaimed, horrified. 'No one asked me about that! I don't wish to be Persephone. She gets trapped in the underworld for six months a year and has to marry Hades!' I shuddered.

'It's all arranged, Sophia,' my aunt said, her voice slightly higher pitched than usual. 'Your father and I agreed it whilst you were unwell.' She turned back to the dressmaker. 'I'm to be Demeter and plan to carry a wheat sheaf. It's the perfect time of year, after all. So a costume to set that off would be perfect.'

The following two hours consisted of fabrics, patterns, drawings, tape measures and pins. I fidgeted and wandered impatiently around the shop while I waited. It was impossible to take an interest in fancy-dress costumes while Jenny was out in the city somewhere with dangerous papers in her charge. Although by now, I reflected dismally, she had almost certainly sold them on. It was too late to undo whatever we'd done and Mr Charlcton would never forgive me.

That thought shouldn't upset me as much as it did. But the memory of the walks, talks, and dances together, and even the night at the theatre, insisted on rising in my mind and refusing to be banished. I'd alienated almost everyone in the city and now I'd driven him away too.

When we arrived home from the dressmaker's, a chaise-and-four was waiting outside the house. I got down from the sedan chair in some confusion. 'A few days in the country are called for,' my father said curtly, appearing in the front door of the house, clad in his travelling wig and cloak, his hat under one arm. 'In you get, Sophia. Dawes has packed what you need.'

It was pointless to argue. Bemused, I entered the chaise. Aunt Amelia sat beside me looking unsurprised, so I gathered this plan had been made with her consent. 'But I don't wish to leave the city,' I said to her, low-voiced, so that my father didn't overhear.

'Nor I indeed,' she said casting me a resentful look. 'This is deeply inconvenient for me. But your father feels the city needs a few days to forget the gossip about you. And no doubt he feels his own finances and health will benefit from a break from Harrison's,' she added spitefully.

'Cards?' I asked.

'Cards, the fool,' she agreed sourly.

'You play too,' I pointed out.

'I have the sense to win,' she replied. 'And I certainly wouldn't play with the captain . . . ' She stopped abruptly to look out of the window as my father joined us in the chaise.

I looked covertly at him as the chaise rumbled forward over the cobbles. It was true he didn't look well. I'd been too caught up in my own affairs to notice. But now that I looked more closely, I could see he had a yellow tinge to his cheeks, shadows under his eyes and a look of strain hung about him. I also noticed something else I hadn't spotted before: his watch and chain were missing from his waistcoat. How deep and recklessly had he been playing these past weeks?

We stayed at an inn in a village some ten miles outside Bath. My father took long walks, ate well and slowly regained his health. I spent the long days in the inn garden. It was fortunate for me that Dawes had packed the large volume of sermons from my room, inside which I'd secreted *The Rape of the Lock*. I secretly read and reread the slim volume until I knew it almost by heart. It was the only thing that kept me sane.

My aunt was restless. She found it difficult to sit still, jumped at sudden noises, and tossed and turned in her bed at night. I lay locked into the bedchamber with her, also wakeful, unused to so much time to sleep, wondering if Jenny was safe and well and wishing I had some way to reach her. But six interminable days passed before we were on the road back to Bath.

Our costumes had been sent home in our absence ready for the ball in a week's time. Meanwhile there was to be a Tuesday ball at the Guildhall. My father gave me a lecture beforehand: 'We've almost reached the end of the season, Sophia, and still I haven't received one tempting offer of marriage for you. If you don't exert yourself to please some gentleman in this next week, I shall be forced to consider other options for your future. They will not be appealing alternatives.'

'Father, *anything* would be more appealing to me than marriage,' I assured him earnestly.

'You're gravely mistaken,' he said abruptly. A swift glance showed me his face had reverted to its usual impenetrable mixture of dislike and inflexibility.

'But, no, father, indeed, I should like to work . . . I should like . . . '

'There is no work for such as you that would not disgrace our family name!' he said. 'No! Women of family do not work.'

His voice dropped and became silky with menace: 'There are other ways of being rid of unwanted and unmarriageable daughters that you can scarcely imagine, girl. I suggest you think long and hard about that.' His voice grew still softer: 'I have lived in dark corners of the world where English law doesn't reach; where no one knows nor cares what becomes of an insignificant girl. It is not only Africans that can be sold, Sophia. You would fetch a good price. But you wouldn't find that life congenial.'

I managed to force a whisper from my suddenly dry mouth: 'You would not . . . you could not . . . '

He walked to the door, paused and turned to look at me. 'Believe that I would. Remember, Sophia. You have one more week. I will not be answerable for the consequences otherwise.'

The door closed behind him. I looked down at my hands where they rested in my lap and saw they were trembling. When I tried to rise, my legs wouldn't carry me, and I had to sit back down. I knew of the miserable cruelty with which African slaves were treated. I remembered the years my father had lived in the West Indies and imagined the tortures he no doubt enjoyed inflicting on his own slaves. I felt sick. I didn't think he was bluffing. There was no doubt in my mind he meant what he said or that he would be capable of going to any lengths.

This battle between us was no longer a game. Perhaps it never had been. It was something far darker than I had ever understood. No less than a deadly duel of wits and courage with my own survival at stake.

The ball at the Guildhall was the usual mix of bright lights, sparkling, rich costumes, and empty gossip. It felt false and unnatural to me next to my possible future. But, for tonight, I myself was a part of the glitter and glamour of the ballroom in a pale blue gown over a profusion of white petticoats. My hair had been dressed and powdered, with a few curls allowed to fall down over my shoulders.

My aunt stayed close by my side, until Mr Nash presented me to some elderly gentleman for the minuet.

In the country dances she insisted I take Captain Mould as my partner. My heart sank, but he didn't trouble me greatly. He seemed preoccupied, and spoke little to me, bowing after the second dance and turning away. I breathed a sigh of relief, turned to look for my aunt, and stopped dead as I found Mr Charleton before me, as immaculately dressed as ever, this evening in crimson and cream. 'Good . . . good evening, sir,' I said as calmly as I could. 'I hadn't seen that you were here tonight.'

'I've only just arrived. Will you give me the pleasure of the next dance?' His voice was cold. A slight shiver ran through me. I had enemies every way I turned.

'I'm afraid I'm tired, sir,' I told him, 'I don't wish to dance.'

'You're mistaken, Sophia,' I heard my father's voice say behind me. 'You have no wish to give offence to Mr Charleton.'

I was forced to lay my hand on Mr Charleton's arm and suffer myself to be led into the next country dance. 'You've been out of town,' remarked Mr Charleton curtly as we took our first steps.

'Yes, my father wished to take us out of the city for a spell . . . for his . . . for our health,' I stammered, uncomfortably aware of my father's watchful eyes on me from the side of the room. Mr Charleton cast a glance at my father.

'I'm sure he did,' he said drily. 'It won't surprise you to know that I've been looking for you?'

'It would surprise me greatly,' I said, slowly regaining some command over myself. 'I would have thought you'd have far better things to do with your time.' Mr Charleton swung me roughly into a turn and I nearly lost my balance. 'Please, have a care, sir,' I said indignantly.

'I *do* have many better things to do,' he said, his voice curt with anger. 'Unfortunately, you've intruded upon my business in a most serious manner.'

This was a direct accusation. The dance swept me away from him for a spell, as I took a turn with another gentleman. I had time to compose my features before Mr Charleton took my hand again. 'You don't answer me, Miss Williams.'

'I don't understand you, Mr Charleton. I haven't seen you for a week. In what way could I possibly have troubled you now?'

Mr Charleton completed the final steps of the dance in tight-lipped silence. The minute the music stopped, he took my hand and led me swiftly to a window where there were fewer people. There he swung me to face him, took my chin in his hand and compelled me to look into his eyes.

'Was that or was that not you who held me up on the road back from Bristol?' he demanded. His voice was low to avoid anyone overhearing his words, but it was vibrant with anger.

'You're ridiculous, sir,' I countered him, staring back as boldly as I could. Silence reigned between us for a moment. From the corner of my eye, I caught sight of my father staring at us. 'We're being watched,' I told him. 'My father is walking towards us; he will ask you what you mean by accosting me in this way.' I tried to pull away.

'Your father will do no such thing,' Mr Charleton replied. 'He's too desperate to get you a husband to come between us during such a promising conversation.' He let go of my face, instead catching my hand and lifting it to his lips. 'He will hope I'm proposing to you,' he said, pressing a kiss upon it.

A shock went through me at the touch of his lips. I tried to pull my hand away. 'I believe I've complained before of your arrogance,' I told him in a furious, but not quite steady, voice.

'Whatever can you mean, Miss Williams? I'm apparently desperately in love,' said Mr Charleton. He kissed my hand again, looking into my eyes, though his look was anything but amorous. I was embarrassed, angry, hurt and my heart beat fast.

'You hate me. Please, let me go,' I begged him. 'People are watching.'

'Let them,' he said. 'Did you or did you not hold up my coach and steal papers from me?'

'Do I look like the kind of girl who would do such a thing?' I demanded desperately.

'No, Miss Williams, in this guise, you look both innocent and adorable, but we both know that there is another side to you.' He held my hand in a grip of iron so that I couldn't pull it away.

'I should like to hit you,' I told him, keeping my voice as low as his.

'I daresay, or even hold a pistol to my throat.'

'Yes, that would appeal to me,' I retorted. Despite his vice-like grip on me, I felt I was winning. He couldn't force me to admit anything.

'Or search my breeches for a purse?' enquired Mr Charleton.

It was utterly unexpected, and I felt a flush flooding my face, betraying me.

'I . . . no . . .'

'That recalls the incident to your mind, doesn't it, Miss Williams?' said Mr Charleton. 'Where are those papers? This is no game. This concerns the security of this city; perhaps even of the nation!'

'I don't know,' I gasped, trying to back away from him, appalled by his words and by the anger in his face. 'I never had them. I don't know where they are.'

My back was against the wall. Mr Charleton closed in on me and leaned one hand against the wall, bending towards me. He was clever, I couldn't deny it. He must look like a lover to the rest of the room, whilst he tormented me with his questions. I turned my face aside, made wretched by the difference between what this looked like and what it really was. 'Who were your conspirators? Who helped you?' Mr Charleton demanded. 'Who fired that shot?'

I shut my lips tightly and shook my head. I had given myself away, but not for the world would I betray Jenny. I hoped that at least she was safe somewhere and had been paid for what we'd done. 'You have no idea of the harm you may have caused,' said Mr Charleton sternly. He didn't say it as a threat, but as a reproach.

'What harm?' I asked. I felt dreadful. Mr Charleton simply shook his head at me. 'I'm sorry,' I whispered, ashamed.

'It's too bad we are on opposing sides,' said Mr Charleton. 'I would have preferred to have worked with you than against you.'

'I'm not on a side . . . ' I cried. 'This has all been a stupid mistake! I wish I could undo what I've done.'

Mr Charleton looked sceptical. 'The only way you could do that would be to retrieve those papers unread,' he said. 'You can't do that, can you?'

I shook my head miserably. 'I don't think so. If only you hadn't taken my money, there would have been no need . . . '

'Money?' interrupted Mr Charleton. 'But this was never about money was it? Money I can give you if you need it, for God's sake. There are far bigger issues at stake. What about the notes that your aunt passes on, Sophia? What hand do you have in that?' He broke off abruptly. 'Here comes your father,' he said, taking a step back and bowing over my hand. 'You may pretend to him I've been whispering words of love to you, to which you've refused to listen. You've told me there is no hope for me.' A ghost of a smile crossed his face as he spoke.

I gripped his hand in sudden fear. 'No, I can't tell him any such thing,' I gasped. 'He'll kill me.'

Mr Charleton kissed my hand lightly and looked at me, a smile briefly replacing the strained look in his eyes. 'You exaggerate, Sophia,' he replied.

His use of my name and the softening of his tone caught me by surprise. That and the fear of my father's reaction combined to make unfamiliar tears start into my eyes.

'I don't,' I said simply, blinking them back. 'You have no idea.'

Mr Charleton frowned, but then turned to meet my father with a bland smile. 'How do you do, Sir Edward?' he said pleasantly. 'I've just been telling your daughter how very beautiful she looks this evening.'

My heart gave a bound of relief, and I was aware I was trembling. There was nothing my father could take exception to in this, surely? He was smiling back, clearly pleased. Mr Charleton turned back to me. 'I hope you'll reserve a dance for me next week at the masquerade?' he asked. Waiting only for my nod of consent, he bowed and left us.

'Good, Sophia,' said my father approvingly. 'Did he hint at marriage at all?'

'No, father,' I said meekly, watching Mr Charleton wretchedly as he slipped out of the ballroom.

'But he came only to dance with you by the look of it,' said my father complacently. 'He's gone again now. So perhaps next week he will propose. That's a connection that would bring honour to the family.'

I knew that Mr Charleton wouldn't propose, but was grateful to him for delaying my father's fury.

That night, I stole the key and sneaked out of my aunt's bedchamber, determined to escape through my room and find Jenny. Wild plans of recovering the documents and running away buzzed in my head. I hated Mr Charleton to think so badly of me. Especially as even after everything I'd done, he'd still shielded me from my father's wrath. And I had to escape my father. I didn't know what sort of life would await me if I was forced to fend for myself, but it couldn't be worse than the fate implied by my father's threats.

I succeeded in leaving the room without waking my aunt, but when I reached my bedchamber on the third floor, the door was locked against me. Desperate, I crept downstairs. The front door was bolted and chained. Once I had cautiously freed up all these barriers, I found that it had been locked too. The back door was similarly barred and all the windows now had locks on them. No doubt this had been done whilst we were away.

I slid down to the cold flagstones of the kitchen floor and half sat, half lay against the wall. I was utterly trapped. The situation was too serious for either tears or tantrums, and I sat there quiet and still, breathing hard, my mind working furiously. I had to find a way of escaping during the day. There was no other possibility.

CHAPTER TWENTY-SEVEN

Mr Charleton wasn't at either the Grove or Harrison's the following day. I didn't know whether to be relieved or disappointed. My aunt stayed by my side while my father played lansquenet for high stakes in the card room, drinking glass after glass of burgundy. We walked in the garden. The heat of the summer had faded now, and it was a cool day with a brisk breeze; just the sort of weather to be climbing the hills around the city, not meandering pointlessly in a garden. When we went in for tea, we were joined by Captain Mould. 'Good day, ladies,' he said, giving us a stiff, military-style bow, so different from Mr Charleton's distinguished elegance. 'I hope I find you well?'

'Quite well, thank you,' said my aunt, looking flustered. She turned to me, 'Sophia, would you get me some more tea, please?'

Aware that she wanted to be rid of me, I accepted the dish she held out to me and walked slowly across to get it refilled. Something made me pause and glance back halfway across the room, and I saw a slight movement between them, so swift I barely followed it, but I was almost sure it was the handing over of a letter or note. How many times had I seen that earlier in our stay at the Bath? Was it really love-letters, as I'd imagined? Mr Charleton had said something about notes at the ball last night; I hadn't thought about it after my father had interrupted us. But now I wondered.

While my aunt drank her tea, she cast longing glances at the card room. Captain Mould suggested she went to play, and offered to walk with me in the gardens. Aunt Amelia got up at once. She wasn't supposed to leave me, but my father was far too engrossed in his game by now to notice, and the lizard was a chaperone of sorts.

Unwillingly, I accepted his escort out into the gardens, withdrawing my hand from his arm at the earliest opportunity. My mind was occupied with wondering where he might have secreted the paper my aunt had handed to him, and whether it would be possible to abstract it. If I gave it to Mr Charleton, might he believe that I wasn't working for the rebels? I'd stopped telling myself I didn't care what he thought of me. I cared deeply. I knew I'd put myself in the wrong.

'So, Captain,' I asked provocatively. 'Do you think we have seen the last of the riots in the streets? It's been several weeks now.'

'This is hardly a fit subject for a young lady,' replied the captain, and as he spoke, he passed his right hand inside the rim of the hat that he carried under his left arm. *So that is where the note is*, I thought. *Concealed in the hat.* 'Should we not rather talk of the forthcoming masquerade? You must be excited.'

'I find I can contain my excitement, sir,' I replied. 'It is after all, only a ball with masks.'

'True, but you ladies find such events irresistible, you

know,' said the captain with an air of condescension. 'I'm looking forward to the evening with every expectation of pleasure. I hope you will keep dances for me.'

I looked down at my feet, unwilling to commit myself, but knowing there was unlikely to be any escape. No one else would ask me. Even Mr Charleton's request I discounted. 'Indeed, I hope that you will very soon do more than dance with me,' continued Captain Mould. 'I intend to speak to your father again today about our union.'

'My father doesn't favour you, Captain,' I replied, trying and failing to keep my voice steady. 'Perhaps you aren't sufficiently wealthy or high-born. He's a proud man.'

The captain laughed softly and stopped walking. We were at the far end of the garden, overlooking the river. To avoid looking at him, I leaned over the parapet and looked down into the murky brown water of the river. It hadn't rained for a while, and the water level was low, an unpleasant tang arising from its muddy depths.

The captain's hand was on my arm, caressing me. 'I think he will favour me very shortly,' he told me. 'You see, I've won rather a large sum of money from him. These things can make it so very difficult to say no. Pride becomes a luxury.'

My skin shrank from his touch, but I forced myself to stand still and not flinch away. His hand slid slowly up my arm to my shoulder. Still I didn't move. 'Miss Williams, we could deal well together,' said the captain. 'If only you would be guided by me! I'm certain your father won't stand in the way of your happiness.'

How little you know, you vile lizard, I thought bitterly. My father would oppose my happiness with his
dying breath. And in any case, there would be no happiness to be found in marriage to you. Was that to be my
choice? Marriage to Captain Mould or some dark fate
threatened by my father? Either was a death sentence. I
would run away. Destitution couldn't be worse than the
choice of fates before me. But before I went, I would try
and redeem myself in Mr Charleton's eyes. I half-turned
to Captain Mould.

'My father would be very pleased to see me married,'
I admitted.

'There, I knew it,' he said, a note of triumph in his
thin, nasal voice. 'And you, my dear?'

'Does not every girl secretly dream of matrimony?'
I asked with a simper, nauseated at my own falseness.
Captain Mould stared down at me triumphantly. He ran
his lizard tongue over his lips and smoothed his great
moustaches. Then he cast a swift glance around him,
drew me behind a tall bush where we were unobserved
and slid one arm around my waist.

I wanted to be sick. I hated the smell of him, and
loathed having him so close, but I stood quite still. Any
minute now he was going to try and kiss me, and I didn't
think I could bear it, but it would give me an opportunity
to try and take the note from him.

The captain drew me into his arms, whispering that
we would soon be married and that he had known all
along I would learn to love him. Amazed at his gullibil-
ity, I ran my hand along his arm as though in caress, but
reaching cautiously for his hat. As the captain bent his

head, however, I lost my courage and turned my face aside. I simply couldn't make myself kiss him; it would be too vile. I remembered Hellena's words of disgust on the subject of kissing an old man in *The Rover*: 'Nuzzle through his beard and find his lips,' she had said. I shuddered.

Captain Mould didn't seem to notice. He kissed my cheek instead, and then dropped a wet kiss on my neck. I had my hand on his hat now. Revolted to have his whiskers on my skin, but forcing myself to remain passive, I slipped my hand inside the hat brim and felt along the lining until my fingers met the slight bulge of paper. It was the work of a moment to grasp and withdraw it.

I pulled away quickly, not needing to feign the hot blush of embarrassment. 'Please, sir!' I exclaimed. 'You presume too much!'

'I shall speak to your father,' said Captain Mould, almost panting in his eagerness. He caught at my hand, dropped a lizard-kiss onto it, so very different from Mr Charleton's kisses the previous night, and hurried away.

I leaned back over the parapet, gulping the air, trying to calm myself. I shivered uncontrollably for a moment and then began to regain my calm. I wanted to wash everywhere the lizard had touched me, and I wanted to run and shout to blot out the memory of those horrible moments. But the note was clutched tightly in my hand. I'd done it. If it was a love letter, I would scream with disappointment, but I was certain it wasn't. Swiftly glancing around me to check I was still alone, I unfolded the slip of paper. It meant nothing at all to me; it was scribbles and gibberish. After an initial lurch of disappointment, I realized it could be code.

I had to get it to Mr Charleton. He might know what to make of it, though I did not. Having searched the tea room and the card room fruitlessly, I stood irresolute, at a loss what to do next. As I hesitated, I saw the captain approach my father at his card table, only to be entreated to join him. To my relief, he did so, taking a seat, being dealt a hand, and poured a glass of wine. If he was to play he would have no opportunity to speak to my father immediately.

My aunt was seated three tables away with a party of ladies, but had her back to me. I was unsupervised, and none of them realized it. This was the moment I'd been waiting for. I left Harrison's, my mind running on whether to seek Jenny or Mr Charleton first. As I walked along the street, my heavy, cumbersome petticoats swaying and my high heels threatening to twist my ankles, I realized that finding Jenny in these clothes would be completely impracticable. I'd never make it to the village where she lived, nor be sure of finding her there even if I did.

Instead I hurried to Trim Street, making my way past my own front door towards number two where Mr Charleton resided. The butler who opened the door informed me that his master wasn't at home. 'Can you tell me where I might find him?' I begged. 'It's extremely urgent. I know he would want to get this message.'

'Sorry, Miss, I've no idea,' replied the butler, his face blank and his voice expressionless. I imagined he was shocked by a young lady calling unaccompanied on a gentleman, but was too well-trained to show it. 'Would you like to wait for him?'

I stood on the doorstep, irresolute. He could be out for hours. 'No, thank you,' I said and turned away. What should I do now? I couldn't walk into the busy stable yard to retrieve my boy's clothes in the day time. I had no money for a chair and no idea what to do next. I turned and walked slowly back along Trim Street, trying to decide whether I should search the city for my quarry or return to Harrison's before I was missed and hope to see him later in the day.

I'd almost decided to go back when a low whistle from the roof of the stable caught my attention. I looked up and saw a grubby face framed by tangled brown hair peering down at me. 'Jenny!' I cried with relief, but she shushed me urgently. Glancing around her, she disappeared from sight for a moment and then reappeared on the wall. She was still in her boy's garb, but looking thin, dishevelled and dirty. She dropped down beside me. 'I've been waitin' here, tryin' to speak to you for days,' she said.

'I'm so sorry. I've been locked in. I was recognized, you know, that night. I've run away now and I won't go back. Not ever.'

'You're goin' to run away?' asked Jenny doubtfully. 'In that get-up?' She looked at my brocade gown with its tight bodice over quantities of lace petticoats. I looked down at it too, and had to laugh.

'I've got breeches hidden in the yard. I'll sell this.'
'Where will you go?'
'To Windsor to look for my cousin,' I said. Jack was the best friend I had in the world, and I was sure he

would help me if only I could get to him.

'Windsor's a long way,' began Jenny, and then she gasped and pulled me into a doorway, using me to shield herself from sight. Voices were approaching behind us.

'What's wrong?' I asked. 'Who's looking for you?'

The men passed and Jenny grabbed my hand, led me along Trim Street away from the city out into the open fields beyond. I lifted my petticoats out of the mud and took care how I placed my feet. Jenny stopped behind a clump of trees and turned to face me.

'I've been hiding,' she said. 'All the time you've been away. I can't risk being seen, I can't go home and I've spent me last farthing. I'm so hungry!'

'What happened?' I asked horrified.

'They cheated me, didn't they? Took the papers off me and didn't give me a penny. Jest this . . . '

She turned her left cheek towards me and I saw it was discoloured with a fading bruise and a nasty cut. I caught my breath. 'So we did all that for nothing?' I asked despairingly. 'We robbed Mr Charleton, those papers have fallen into the wrong hands, and you haven't even been paid . . . This is dreadful. They . . . they were important papers, apparently, Jenny. I think we did a very wrong thing in taking them.' I rubbed my hand over my face and groaned.

'What are they about?' asked Jenny.

'I don't know. But they're something to do with preventing those riots.'

'So the gentleman we took 'em off might pay to get 'em back?' asked Jenny hopefully.

'He would if we had them,' I replied. 'A minor point, but an important one.' I sank down on the grassy bank, heedless of my clothes, my petticoats billowing about me. Jenny knelt beside me.

'I've got them, but I didn't know what to do with them,' replied Jenny. 'They're hidden up in the stable yard.'

I stared at her blankly. 'But you said . . . '

'I know what I said. Only I nicked 'em back, didn't I? I wasn't being cheated like that. So I followed 'em and picked their pockets. They ain't even been opened. Thing was though, I didn't know what to do next. I couldn't even get to the fence to flog the jewellery; nearly got caught goin' there. I bin hidin' on the rooftops ever since, terrified they'd find me.'

I caught her hands delightedly. 'Jenny, you're a wonder!' I cried. 'Maybe it won't be too late to return them. Only . . . Mr Charleton isn't at home, and I don't know where to find him.'

I sat quite still, wondering what to do. 'Perhaps I should return to Harrison's after all,' I said reluctantly. 'It's my best chance of finding him. It's the masquerade in a few days and he said he'd see me there.'

'A few days . . . !' groaned Jenny. I looked at her. Her face looked pinched and pale with want. She couldn't sleep out on the rooftops indefinitely. I had no money to give her, not so much as a penny. An idea struck me.

'Mr Allen,' I said, jumping to my feet. 'He'll help us, I know he will.'

'Who?' asked Jenny.

'He's the postmaster and a friend of Mr Charleton's.

I'm quite certain he can be trusted. He's kept letters for me before; from your brother. Can you get the papers and meet me on the far side of Trim Bridge?'

We made our way swiftly along Trim Street, parted there, and I walked back into the city. I kept my eyes open for my family, hoping they wouldn't yet be looking for me. Jenny, when she rejoined me with her jacket bulging, was as jumpy as I was, looking about us as we walked.

I was deeply thankful to find Mr Allen behind the post office counter. 'Mr Allen,' I said keeping my voice low, though there were no customers but us. 'We have important papers for Mr Charleton. Can we trust you to get them to him safely? As soon as possible?'

With a surprised glance at me and a curious one at Jenny, Mr Allen swiftly called for his assistant to take over the counter and led us both behind it and into a small back parlour. A low table was laid with an untouched jug of ale and a plate of bread and butter.

'Sit down, both of you, please,' he said courteously. 'You can trust me completely. I'm in close communication with Charleton on a number of matters, and in his complete confidence. What is this about?'

By way of reply, I handed him the sheaf of papers Jenny had retrieved along with the ring and tie pin I'd stolen. Mr Allen looked questioningly at me. 'We need you to get these back to Mr Charleton,' I begged. 'They haven't been opened.'

Mr Allen caught his breath and looked searchingly at me. I blushed, ashamed of the part I'd played. 'There's more,' I told him. 'I took this from Captain Mould today. I have no idea what it says, or if it's important.'

Mr Allen took the crumpled note, smoothed it out and frowned over it. 'A code, but not one I've seen before,' he admitted. 'Who gave him this?'

My eyes dropped. 'My aunt,' I confessed. 'I didn't see who she got it from.'

'Your aunt? Yes, we've had our eye on her since you arrived,' he said, surprising me. A dozen questions ran through my head. Who was *we* and why were they watching my aunt? But I didn't get a chance to ask. Mr Allen was already speaking again: 'I need to get this to Charleton now,' he said. He grabbed his coat from a hook, and on his way back across the room, he took my hand and shook it, and then shook Jenny's grubby hand with equal respect. 'Before I go, are you in any danger for taking these?' he asked us both.

I shook my head. 'Not me. I may be in trouble for escaping from Harrison's, but that's all. In any case, I don't intend to go back. I'm going to run away. But Jenny is in some fear of reprisals.'

'In that case, Jenny, please stay here until I get back,' said Allen. 'I promise you'll be quite safe here. Please help yourself to this food and ale; you look as though you need it. Miss Williams, I'd like you to rethink your plan of running away.'

'I can't go back,' I said instantly. 'My father, he plans to . . . no, I can't.'

Mr Allen took both my hands in his. 'Please. If you would be willing to be eyes and ears for us within your family . . . I know it's a great deal to ask, but it could save lives. I've suspected all along Charleton was mistaken to believe you were part of the conspiracy. I can't say any more right now, it wouldn't be safe. But we need your help. You've done well today. Will you try and do more?'

I hesitated, unsure what I was agreeing to or why. I dreaded the thought of returning to the imprisonment of my father's house. 'Just for a few days,' added Mr Allen persuasively.

'Very well,' I agreed reluctantly. 'What am I looking for?'

'Any communication between your aunt, Captain Mould, and others. Do not take risks; they are dangerous people. But watch them. Either Charleton or I will be in touch to hear what, if anything, you've discovered. Do you understand?'

I nodded dumbly. Mr Allen released me, and almost ran from the room. I turned to Jenny. 'I don't know what any of this is about, but if I'm going back, it had better be right away,' I said. Jenny looked at me, her eyes large in her pale face. 'Eat something!' I recommended, indicating the bread on the table. She nodded, looking forlorn. 'He's a kind man,' I told her. Feeling bad about leaving her, I gave her a hug. She clung to me, her thin frame feeling as light as a bird's. Then I hurried back through the city, knowing it was too much to hope that my absence would have gone unnoticed.

CHAPTER TWENTY-EIGHT

I was kept locked in the house for three days after my escape from the Assembly Rooms. My copy of Pope's poem was found and confiscated and I had nothing to do but sew and read sermons. I grew so bored that even those occupations were eventually better than nothing. I neither heard nor saw anything that I could relate to Mr Charleton, and bitterly regretted ever having been foolish enough to return home. When I thought that I could be halfway to Windsor now, I wanted to scream in frustration. My only consolation was that nothing at all was said of Captain Mould and his proposing for me.

My aunt, forced by my father to keep me company, was moody and silent. My father returned home late at night, drunken and ill-tempered. He shouted at us both and then shut himself in his study. At the breakfast table, he was surly, his face etched with deep shadows.

The night of the masquerade arrived. At first I assumed I wouldn't be permitted to go to any, just as I'd been forbidden to attend any of the other events during the past days. But to my surprise, after we'd dined at four o'clock, I was sent to get changed. Dawes helped me bathe and wash my hair. When I got out of the bath, my costume was laid out on my bed.

My gown was purest, virginal white. Once I was dressed in the crisp petticoats and gown, I looked like a frost maiden. A profusion of lace was pinned around my neck and at my wrists, as though a waterfall had frozen in the act of tumbling over a precipice. I stared in the mirror, stunned by the vision the dressmaker had created for me. I was Persephone; unwilling child-bride, trapped by Hades in the underworld whilst winter reigned on Earth.

Dawes powdered my hair and my face, whitening my complexion to match my gown. Only my blue eyes and red lips had colour now. Then she tied a golden sash around my waist and a golden mask over my face. I surveyed myself once more.

'It's almost a pity to wear the gold,' I mused, surprised at my own degree of interest in my costume. 'It spoils the effect.'

'Well, you won't be wearing the sash in the morning, Miss, just the gown,' said Dawes briskly.

'In the morning?' I asked, looking sharply at her. 'Why should I wear such a fine gown in the morning?'

'Oh, no, Miss, my mistake,' said Dawes hurriedly. Her hands shook under my gaze and the powder pot she was holding slipped out of her hand, spilling powder onto the carpet. 'Oh, dear me, how clumsy I am!' she cried.

'Dawes,' I said sternly as she scrabbled to clear up the mess, 'why will I need this gown in the morning?'

She shook her head at me, and flushed deeper red. 'Tell me now,' I said, 'or I shall tell my father you've been helping me escape from the house at night.'

'Oh, no, Miss, I never did . . . you wouldn't!' she gasped. 'I'd lose my place!'

Tears started to her eyes, but I told myself she was keeping things secret from me and hardened my heart. 'Your wed-wedding, Miss,' stuttered Dawes. 'It's your wedding in the morning, b-but your father made me swear not to tell you. You're to wear this as your bride gown!' She pulled a pocket handkerchief out and dabbed at her eyes. I turned from her. I felt nothing. I was numb. When she handed me the last part of my costume, I stared dully at it.

'A pomegranate,' I said flatly, weighing the fruit in my hand. 'The very fruit Hades used to trap Persephone in the underworld.' I descended the stairs, allowed the footman to wrap my white cloak around my shoulders and left the house as though in a dream. Or perhaps a nightmare would be more appropriate. I was halfway to the Guildhall before I came to my senses. I needed to get away tonight, before it was too late. It was my last chance. I imagined riding away from the Bath, free at last, and my heart leapt. I would find an opportunity, I was certain of it.

It wasn't until we climbed out of the sedan chairs into the crush of arrivals at the masquerade that I saw my father's costume. He was clad entirely in green, the stiffly whale-boned skirts of his new brocade coat standing out fashionably from his body. His waistcoat was embroidered with greens and blues to portray seaweed, and his mask had been fashioned to match. Only the lace at his throat and wrists was foaming white like the crests of waves. In his hand he carried the three-pronged fork of Poseidon. It was a fitting costume: the dark and brooding brother of Zeus, banished to rule the murky depths of the ocean.

My aunt was attired in cream and gold, as Demeter, a sheaf of wheat carried in her arms. It was a beautiful gown, though a deal fewer buttered rolls during our stay at the Bath would have allowed it to fall on slenderer lines.

Hades, wreathed in black with a mask to match, approached us as soon as we entered the ballroom. I didn't need to hear his voice to know it was Captain Mould. He was my doom. But for me, unlike the real Persephone, there would be no six-month reprieve each year to enjoy the summer. I would be condemned to spend my whole life in the underworld.

The ballroom of the Guildhall was a sea of costumes; the identity of people known to me all summer by sight at least, hidden by hundreds of masks. If my mood had been different, I should have thought it exciting. As it was, I found it strangely intimidating.

I had no choice but to accept Hades as my partner for the first dance. I went through the steps in silence, keeping as much distance from him as possible. He didn't observe a like silence, however. 'What a very elegant gown, Miss Williams,' he said with meaning. 'I look forward to seeing it again soon.'

My stomach lurched as he spoke, remembering what Dawes had told me. It was true then. When had my father planned to let me know? When I woke up tomorrow perhaps?

'Ah yes, tomorrow will be a great day, Miss Williams,' continued the captain. His eyes glittered eerily behind his mask, making him appear more sinister than ever. 'A new beginning in more ways than one. You will awake to a new world; a cleansed world. It will be a new start.'

I stared, wondering what he meant. His words seemed to imply more than just our marriage. What did he mean by cleansing? I frowned, trying to read his expression, but it was hidden behind his mask.

At the end of the dance, Captain Mould kissed my hand and requested another. But before I could either accept or refuse, another masked man approached, dressed all in black and gold.

'Ah no, Hades, you shall not have the beautiful Persephone all to yourself!' he said, his voice mocking. 'That is not how it works. You have her only for a season and then must let her go.' He bowed to me and offered his arm. 'Will the daughter of Demeter dance with the winged messenger?'

He indicated his shoes: they bore the gold wings of the messenger of the gods. I curtsied, smiling. 'Persephone would be honoured, Hermes,' I replied.

Captain Mould gripped my elbow, and spoke low to Hermes. 'Just remember, my friend: you may borrow her, but she is bound for all eternity to return to me.'

Neither of us said anything to this. Hermes merely bowed slightly before leading me away. I felt sick. 'Are you engaged to be married?' asked Hermes as soon as we were out of earshot.

I bit my lip. 'I've not been informed of it, Mr Charleton,' I replied, for I'd known his voice at once. 'But my maid let something slip earlier. I believe I'm to be married in the morning.'

'It's outrageous!' he said quietly, his voice full of

anger. 'Damn, you're just a child, and he's an old stick. A retired captain. Those costumes are some kind of a sick joke; Hades capturing Persephone! What is your father thinking of?'

'Simply of getting me off his hands,' I replied. 'By any means possible.'

Mr Charleton pressed my hand comfortingly as he led me into the dance. 'The rumour is your father's been playing deep and is in debt to our friend Hades. Is that correct?'

'I believe so,' I told him honestly. 'But I know very little. I've been locked in the house for days.'

He nodded. 'I know.'

We couldn't speak again for several moments. When we turned at the bottom of the room, he took my hand and whisked me away from the other dancing couples to where the tables were laid out behind screens for supper later. I followed him behind the end screen where he took both my hands in his and leaned close.

'Thank you, Sophia,' he said. 'For the papers. You did the right thing.'

'I hope so,' I told him. His face looked strange, half-concealed behind the dark mask. 'It was my friend Jenny who retrieved them.'

'I know. I've been able to thank her in person.'

'Is she safe?' I asked eagerly.

He nodded. 'She's with Allen. His housekeeper's taking good care of her. Now, have you heard anything new, managed to intercept any notes since then?'

I shook my head sadly. 'I've been locked in, watched, and my aunt has been my chaperone,' I told him.

'Whatever is going on, she's not had a chance to do anything in the last days. Sir, what *is* going on?'

Mr Charleton leaned forward and whispered in my ear: 'A rebellion is being planned, Sophia. You could even call it a revolution. Beginning right here in the west; in the Bath. Something major, for we have intercepted letters about movement of arms and soldiers from France. The city is as full as it can hold of rebels, horses and weapons, and all the leaders are assembled here. The aim is to overthrow the government, depose the king and crown the Pretender in his place. But that can't be achieved by peaceful means.'

I could feel my heart beating fast with excitement at this news. So much at stake, and I'd had a hand in it, however clumsy and mistaken. 'How do you know all this?' I asked breathlessly, aware we might be interrupted at any moment, and I would lose my chance to hear more. 'What part do you play?'

Mr Charleton moved back from me, covertly watching the ballroom from the edge of the screen. 'I work secretly for the king and government,' he said softly.

'Like Aphra Behn!' I whispered. 'You're a spy!'

Mr Charleton was looking around the edge of the screen, and suddenly caught his breath. 'Sophia, our friend Hades has just given your aunt a note. I need to know what it says. As soon as possible. She's putting it . . . in her reticule.'

I nodded, my eyes lighting with excitement behind my mask. Then I remembered the captain's words: 'Mr Charleton, could they be planning something for tonight? He said . . . ' I frowned trying to remember the words. 'He said something like tomorrow will be *a new beginning in more ways than one. You will awake to a new world; a cleansed world. It will be a new start.*'

Mr Charleton's eyes were on me, though his expression was hidden behind that enigmatic black-and-gold mask. 'Sophia, go,' he said urgently. 'Get that note for me, but make sure you're not detected. I'll come and find you when you have it.'

'Do you have a piece of paper I can have?' I asked him. Understanding a part of my plan at once, he pulled a tablet from his coat pocket, tore a sheet from it and gave it to me.

I stepped out into the ballroom again and began threading my way through the crowd towards Aunt Amelia. The edges of the ballroom were tightly packed with people chatting and watching the dancers. It was slow work to get through them. To my surprise, several gentlemen stopped me and asked me to dance with them. My costume was clearly a success. And clearly also a good disguise, since most of the men now asking would normally not come near me. I smiled to myself, refused them all politely and finally reached my aunt's side, holding the folded paper in the palm of my hand. My heart was beating fast with the thrill of the task I'd been given: I was a real spy, like the famous Aphra Behn herself.

'Sophia, where have you been?' my aunt asked. 'The captain is looking for you.'

'I'm sorry,' I said, holding my hand to my head and feigning dizziness. 'But I don't seem to be feeling very well. In fact, I . . . ' I collapsed. As I did so, I hooked one finger into the drawstring of her reticule at her wrist.

There is no way to fall either elegantly or modestly wearing a hoop. I fear quite a number of the gentlemen in the room caught a glimpse of my stockings and possibly more. But I succeeded in both my aims: firstly the drawstring of my aunt's reticule snapped and it fell off her wrist, scattering its contents onto the ballroom floor. Secondly my aunt was so shocked and humiliated by my making such a spectacle of myself that she shrieked, cast her wheat sheaf aside and attempted to tug me to my feet rather than gathering her things. I made myself limp and lay like a dead weight on the floor.

'Wake up, Sophia!' she cried, bending over me. Peeping under my lashes, I saw her grab her smelling salts. Uncorking them, she thrust the phial under my nose. I choked and feigned waking, confused. As I sat up, I rested my hand on top of the slip of paper that had fallen from her reticule. It was almost done. I just needed a momentary distraction to make my aunt look away from me. Mr Charleton provided it: 'Is Persephone quite well?' enquired his calm voice somewhere above me.

Aunt Amelia looked up at him, and I caught the piece of folded paper up in my hand and dropped the other onto the floor in its place. It was the work of an instant. By the time my aunt looked back at me, I was already attempting to rise.

'Allow me,' said Mr Charleton, taking one of my hands in his, and slipping his free arm about my waist. He lifted me easily to my feet, and supported me there a moment. I leaned against him as though still faint, and felt him take the paper unobtrusively from me. He then took my fan from my wrist and began to fan me gently. 'It's very crowded and overheated in here, Persephone,' he was saying. 'I'm not surprised you were overcome. You'll be better directly.'

My aunt was picking up the contents of her reticule, stuffing them back in; the note was the first thing she retrieved. With luck she would pass it on without noticing it was now a blank piece of paper.

Mr Charleton found me a chair by the wall and handed me into it. 'You seem better now,' he said. 'I'll leave you to the care of your aunt.'

He left my side, and was soon lost in the crowd. I didn't see where he disappeared to, for my aunt was fussing about the dust on my white gown. 'Look! Just look at this mark!' she wailed. I twisted about and looked obediently. 'Oh, Aunt,' I sighed. 'It's nothing that won't come out with a little brushing.'

'Fainting on the floor of the ballroom!' she exclaimed tearfully. 'You will always be doing something shocking, Sophia! It's lucky for you your father wasn't here to witness your behaviour!'

'But indeed, I couldn't help feeling ill!' I exclaimed. 'Where *is* father?' I asked, looking around for him.

'In the card room playing at ombre with the captain,' said my aunt with a frown. 'I've warned him, but he won't listen to me.'

'Warned him about what, Aunt?' I asked, thinking it was ironic if my aunt had warned my father against playing at cards when she did little else herself.

'Against playing with the captain,' said my aunt, unusually forthcoming. 'Like Beau Nash, it's how he supports himself. You don't think he lives in such style on his army pension, do you? Only, unlike the Beau, he has no kindness in him. He does not hesitate to ruin fools who would game away their fortune.'

She stopped abruptly as Beau Nash himself arrived to enquire how I did after being taken ill. Aunt Amelia, greatly discomposed at having almost been caught speaking disrespectfully of the great man, blushed. I rose and curtseyed, however, and assured Mr Nash that I was very well now.

'Please do not risk dancing again tonight, Miss Williams,' the Beau begged. 'It will not do to have young ladies fainting away at the Bath balls.'

'I promise you I won't, sir,' I assured him. He bowed and turned to my aunt, engaging her in polite conversation. I took the opportunity to slip away and searched for Mr Charleton. But among all the bright and exotic costumes in the ballroom, I could no longer see the black and gold mask, nor the gold-winged shoes. My aunt was still talking, and my father and the captain apparently still busy gambling. It was time for me to go.

I would like to have found out what was in the note. I should like to have spoken to Mr Charleton one more time. But it was not to be. I walked quietly from the room, went down the grand staircase, collected my cloak and left the building. No one tried to stop me, no one appeared even to notice that I was leaving. I couldn't believe my good fortune.

The air was cool outside. The summer was definitely drawing to a close. I pulled off my mask, wrapped my cloak about me, and tried not to think about how I would fare alone with winter coming on. Nothing could be worse than what my father planned for me. And I had a feeling I would be able to look after myself.

My first destination was the pawnshop, open at all hours for the desperate and destitute. I needed to part with my beautiful gown. I couldn't repress a smile when I imagined how furious my father and Captain Mould would be if they discovered what I'd done with my costly wedding gown.

I'd barely taken ten steps when I saw Mr Charleton ahead of me. He was standing quietly at the corner of the Guildhall, watching something around the corner. The gold wings had disappeared from his shoes and he had wrapped a plain black cloak over his gold laced coat. His mask dangled from one hand.

I paused and then walked hesitantly towards him. But before I could reach him, he vanished around the corner. He was walking like someone who didn't wish to be observed. My curiosity aroused, I followed him, stepping up to the corner of the building as he had done, and peeping round it. At first the street appeared empty, but then I caught a flash of movement, and spotted a dark shadow with a hint of gold disappearing down some steps into what looked like a basement of the Guildhall. He paused for a few moments at the door, bent over the keyhole, and then went inside.

This time I hesitated longer before following. Perhaps he was on some secret business, and I'd be in the way. But my curiosity and my wish to see him one last time won. I stepped around the corner and ran lightly down the steps after him.

The door opened easily and silently. I slipped inside with a rustling of petticoats and closed it softly behind me. It was almost dark, only the flicker of a torch shining in through a small window. I descended the staircase and followed the silent corridor.

A heavy wooden door barred my way and creaked when I opened it. A stale, musty blast of air hit me in the face; the dank smell of the Bath basements, tinged with the rotten-egg stink that was characteristic of the city.

The corridor divided here. I stood still, uncertain which way to go. A door stood ajar just to my right, so I stepped inside, trying to make out the room in the gloom. I'd only just seen the shape of barrels piled up together when I was grasped from behind, a strong arm wrapped tightly around me and a hand clamped over my mouth so that I could scarcely breathe.

'Sophia, what the *devil* are you doing down here?' Mr Charleton breathed in my ear.

I sagged with relief, sighing as he released me. 'I followed you . . . ' I began, but he clapped his hand over my mouth again.

'Whisper,' he said. 'I don't know who else is down here.'

'I was looking for you to say goodbye,' I whispered obediently. 'And to ask what was in the note.'

He released me, clicking his tongue with annoyance. 'You have no sense of danger!' he exclaimed. 'And next time you want to creep up on someone, don't wear so many petticoats! The note contained information that led me down here. And just as well, by the look of it.'

He went across to the barrels, forced one open and appeared to be examining the contents. I wasn't sure how he could see a thing in this gloom and was about to say so when he exclaimed under his breath: 'Great God!' He returned to my side. 'Sophia, I'm glad you're here after all. I'm going to need your help.'

His words sent a surge of excitement through me. My flight from the city and the pawnbroker were both forgotten in an instant. I was a spy once more. 'What do I need to do?' I asked eagerly.

'Take a chair straight to Mr Allen's lodgings,' he said. 'He's at number seven Lilliput Alley.' He reached into his coat pocket for his purse. 'Here's a shilling to cover the fare. Listen carefully now; this is important. He must instantly send a message to General Wade that he's to move into the city *at once*. Not wait until later, as we agreed earlier. Tell him there's a quantity of gunpowder and fuses beneath the Guildhall, and that I shall stay here and guard it until he gets to me. He must come here first, and deal with the cache at Slippery Lane afterwards. Do you understand me? Can you repeat it?'

Reeling with shock at the seriousness of both the message and the threat to the city, I repeated everything back to him. 'Should all the people at the masquerade upstairs be warned?' I asked in a shaking voice.

'I think not,' said Charleton. 'They can't possibly be intending to blow the place up with so many people inside; a number of them loyal supporters. Our sources suggest that the main attack is planned for tomorrow. Now go!'

I nodded, only partly reassured, and turned away,

clutching the shilling. Mr Charleton was drawing his sword and stationing himself by the door. 'Please take care,' I whispered. I was afraid for him down here in the dark with all that gunpowder right next to him.

'*Go!*'

Embarrassed, I turned and fled back down the dark corridors towards the stairs. I was halfway up them when I heard the sounds of voices on the other side of the door. I froze in horror, and saw the handle turning. As quietly as I could, I whisked myself through a doorway and hid behind it; I stood completely still, trying to quiet my breathing. Any movement at all would set my petticoats rustling again.

The door at the top of the stairs opened and several pairs of feet descended. Male voices spoke in urgent but hushed tones. The only words I caught were 'left it open, you idiot'. A faint grating sound followed.

I thought I recognized Captain Mould's voice and felt sick. The men were heading straight for where Mr Charleton was waiting. I had no way to warn him. I peeped out after they'd passed me but could make out only a group of shadowy figures in the gloom. There was nothing I could do to help, I realized, except carry the message to Mr Allen as fast as I could. Accordingly, I lifted my voluminous petticoats and ran softly out of the room, and up the stairs. When I reached the door and turned the handle, however, it wouldn't budge. I tried again, convinced I must be mistaken. It still didn't open. Panic rising, I twisted it this way and that, pulling, pushing, and shaking it. It was locked.

CHAPTER TWENTY-NINE

The sounds of shouting and raised voices reached me from the room where the gunpowder lay. I turned, feeling blind in the darkness and utterly helpless. Mr Charleton was relying on me to carry his message, and I was trapped. I heard a clash of steel and knew that they were fighting.

Hurriedly, I searched the other rooms to see if any of them had a door that led outside, but it was pointless. I remembered perfectly well that the outside of the building only had one doorway. There were no windows, only a grille high above my head that opened onto the street above. I couldn't shout for help however, for the rebels would certainly hear me before anybody outside did.

I was at a loss. What could I do? There must be something. The sound of footsteps running back towards me made me realize my main task: to remain undiscovered. If I was caught, too, there was no chance of doing anything to help. To conceal myself, I pushed behind an old cabinet that had been deposited down here to rot, one of its doors hanging off the hinges. There were spiders' webs, dust and dirt, but I ignored them, crouching a little, for the cabinet was barely taller than I was. I wished my hair hadn't been dressed so high and that my gown and cloak were not so brilliantly white; it was a bad colour for hiding in the dark.

The footsteps came right into the room where I was and paused. I held my breath. There was such a long silence that I could hear the blood pounding in my ears. But then the door banged shut and the footsteps moved on. I heard a voice call: 'There's no one else down here!'

I let out my breath in a long sigh of relief, but remained motionless, listening. A spider crawled onto my neck, tickling it, and I brushed it away with a shudder. Still I didn't move from my hiding place. There were footsteps running backwards and forwards, and the clatter of something heavy. Once I heard someone cry out, and my heart jumped into my mouth, for I was sure it was Mr Charleton. The thought that they might hurt him, or even kill him, made me feel desperate.

It was some time before the pairs of feet went back past my room towards the cellar steps. The sound of running followed them and a shouted warning. The men left the cellar and banged the door behind them. This time I clearly heard the key grate in the lock. Their footsteps and voices came to me once more as they passed swiftly along the street above me and faded.

Had they all gone, or had they left someone down here? Had they taken Mr Charleton with them, leaving me alone? I had to find out at once. I wriggled out of my hiding place, and crept from the room. All was quiet except for a soft hissing sound in the distance. I paused a moment listening, but it wasn't a sound I recognized. I walked cautiously down the corridor. I was hampered by my petticoats that hushed and rustled as I walked, swaying and brushing the walls of the narrow passage-way. I cursed the ill-chance that had set me on this adventure in such unsuitable clothing.

I turned the corner and thought there was an acrid smell of burning in the air. It was faint, but definitely there. Thinking of all that gunpowder, I quickened my pace. The door to the room where I'd left Mr Charleton was open, and a thread of ash led into it. I paused, afraid I might be running into a trap. There was a sort of glimmering, sparkling light coming from the room.

I walked in to see Mr Charleton tied to a chair and gagged. He convulsed frantically at the sight of me, fighting his bonds, and rolling his eyes. I ran to him at once, but he shook his head desperately, making unintelligible sounds and looking at something to my left.

I turned to look, and my heart stopped in horror. The sparkling light was moving swiftly across the floor towards the barrels. I stood staring at it, trying to make sense of what I was seeing. One part of my mind was telling me stupidly what a pretty light it was, like a small firework. Another was screaming at me that it was a fuse. It would cause a much bigger firework in a few moments; one that would blow half this building to pieces, and I was in a room with it.

I tried to run towards it with an indefinite idea of putting it out. But it was as if I was in a nightmare. My limbs were heavy and unresponsive. I was running through water. My mind was frozen in shock while the fuse moved at an appalling speed away from me towards the heaped barrels. It was not even the thought of my own death that paralysed me, though that passed through my mind. It was all those hundreds of people above me, dancing, talking and playing cards, completely unsuspecting. And the knowledge that Mr Charleton was tied up behind me, as helpless as I was to escape our fate.

Something freed up inside me, and I was moving, running, picking up my petticoats and stamping my fashionable white shoe down onto that brightly burning fuse. The spark escaped from under my foot and kept burning. I stamped again. It faltered, but then brightened again. The gunpowder was very close now and my heart was in my throat.

The third time, I ground my shoe onto the spark and kept it there, holding all my weight down on that foot. I could feel the heat through my sole. The hissing stopped and the silence seemed loud around me. Slowly, carefully, dreading what I might see, I lifted my foot from the fuse. There was nothing there but a smoky pile of ash. We were in semi-darkness once more.

To be safe, I picked up the fuse and pulled it away from the gunpowder. It came free in my hand, a frighteningly short piece, and I threw it out of the room into the corridor beyond. I was dizzy with relief.

I turned back to Mr Charleton who sat slumped in his chair. I hurried to his back to free his hands. The knots were pulled so tight that I couldn't loosen them, no matter how hard I tugged and dug my nails into the fibre of the rope. I stood up to untie the gag instead. It too was tied cruelly tight and I had to tug and work at it to loosen it, but at last it came free.

'Are you all right?' I asked him at once, but only a strangled, muffled groan came from him, and I realized the men had stuffed a cloth into his mouth. I pulled at it and the fabric came free, leaving him retching and choking. I applied myself once more to the bonds at his wrists.

'Thank you,' he managed to gasp at last, his voice hoarse. 'Thank God you didn't get out of the cellar! Mr Allen could not have . . . ' he stopped to cough and gasp for breath.

'Could not have reached you in time,' I agreed soberly. 'The whole Guildhall would have gone up. All those people . . . ' I suddenly felt faint, and had to lean against his chair for a moment, breathing deeply, trying to recover myself.

'I don't think . . . such an atrocity was ever the intention of the leaders of this rebellion,' said Mr Charleton. 'That would set public opinion against them. Something went wrong somewhere. Can't you free my hands?'

I returned to the bonds, having got my momentary weakness under control. 'I'm trying, but the knots are so tight,' I said breathlessly. Part of my difficulty was that my hands were shaking, but I didn't like to admit it. 'Did you say there was an arms cache in Slippery Lane?' I asked as I tugged at the knots.

'I did, but please strive to forget the details. They are most secret.'

'I just wondered . . . was that the business you and Mr Allen had there? The morning I had that unfortunate encounter with the chairmen?'

'It was indeed. Do you not have scissors or something equally useful in your reticule, Sophia?' Mr Charleton asked me.

'No, I don't carry a reticule. I've nothing to keep in one; no smelling salts, no money.'

'How very remiss of you. You'll know better in future,' he remarked.

'If you are in a mood to be jesting,' I remarked, 'you cannot be as badly hurt as I feared. And I believe I've had to speak to you before about using my name, sir.'

'We are a little past the formalities at present, wouldn't you say?' Mr Charleton's voice was still hoarse but it was growing stronger. His knots however still wouldn't budge. In frustration, I tried to grip them with my teeth but only succeeded in hurting myself. 'Are you biting me or untying me?' demanded Mr Charleton. I laughed shakily and tugged uselessly at the knots.

'If scissors are so useful, why do you not carry some?' I demanded.

'I had a number of tools and a sword with me. Unfortunately, no matter how competent a swordsman I may consider myself, I was no match for five men. They took everything from me. I suppose it's too much to hope that they left the door unlocked behind them this time?'

'I haven't checked, but I heard the key . . . ah! It's loosening now!' and sure enough, as I spoke, the first knot came undone. I untied the rest and the rope fell to the floor. Mr Charleton was rubbing his wrists and wriggling his fingers to help the blood begin to circulate again. I knelt at his feet and started to tug at the knots around his ankles.

'Your gown will be quite ruined,' Mr Charleton observed.

I laughed at the irony of it. 'What a trivial matter to

concern yourself with. Besides if it is so ruined that it can never be worn again, I'll be pleased. I rather think it was to have served as my wedding gown tomorrow.' I shuddered at the thought.

'In that case, let us by all means sacrifice it,' agreed Mr Charleton.

The knots around his ankles were not so tight, and quickly came free. We both stood up, looking awkwardly at one another. 'So now what?' I asked.

'We find a way out,' Mr Charleton replied. 'As quickly as possible, for I imagine those men may soon be back to see what went wrong with their little firework display.'

'I've looked,' I said dubiously. 'There's no other door. But let's by all means look again.'

We made a quick search of the cellar. There was nothing. Mr Charleton attempted to climb onto the cabinet to reach the grille to the street, but one of its legs was rotten and gave way beneath him, collapsing onto the floor. He jumped clear, unhurt, and swore.

'That grille is our only hope, as far as I can see,' said Mr Charleton. 'It's a link with the outer world, even if it's not an escape route. We can't shout, because the conspirators may be watching and listening. But if we could attract someone's attention more discreetly, they may be able to fetch help. The soldiers should be in the city soon, but Allen won't know where to find me. I should have sent him a message after you intercepted the note.'

'Did I not do a great job, getting the note for you?' I asked, hopeful of praise.

'Appalling,' replied Charleton crushingly. 'You drew far too much attention to yourself, and if your aunt had not been a complete amateur at intrigue, she would have guessed what you were after at once.'

There was a silence. Mr Charleton laughed and pinched my chin gently. 'Don't look so crestfallen,' he told me. 'You did very well for a first attempt. The way you exchanged it for a blank paper and passed the note on to me was particularly neat. I'm sure Aphra Behn would have said you had promise. If you want praise, you can have it for your marksmanship. Jenny assures me it was you that shot the hat from my head the night you held me up. Now are we going to try and get out of here?'

Only slightly mollified by his words, I looked up at the opening and put my mind to our difficulty. I knew the High Street ran past overhead, and that there might be any number of people out there. 'If I could stand on your shoulders, I might be able to reach up there,' I said.

Mr Charleton looked startled. His eyes swept over my gown and a slight smile crept into his eyes. 'It was really very thoughtless of you to embark on this adventure in that attire, Miss Williams,' he said. 'Did you not realize that breeches would be more appropriate tonight?'

'My friends *will* keep confiscating them,' I retorted. 'I struggle to hold on to a pair for more than a week or so at a time. Turn away, would you?'

Mr Charleton did so. 'Are you really going to undress?' he asked amused.

'Certainly not,' I replied. 'That would be immodest. I'm merely going to climb out of the costly cage I'm trapped in.'

I shed my cloak, laying it over a mouldering chair, and then stripped off my gown, and threw it on top. Layers of lace petticoats followed, and finally I undid the tapes of my hoop and stepped out of it. I stood in my white linen shift and stockings, and although that may not be conventional public wear for a young lady of family and fashion, it was a perfectly adequate covering. Lastly, I kicked off my high-heeled shoes. The stone floor was cold on my stockinged feet and the air of the basement was damp. I shivered a little.

'I'm ready,' I said. To my relief, Mr Charleton neither stared nor made any remark, but merely enquired how it would be easiest to climb up. In discussing this, I lost any embarrassment I felt for appearing in my underwear. In the end, Mr Charleton shed his tightly-fitting coat, I climbed onto a chair and from there to sit on his shoulders. Standing up was trickier than I'd expected. There was a lot of wobbling and a few near falls involved.

'Ouch! That's my ear, Sophia,' exclaimed Mr Charleton as I knelt on his shoulder and almost lost my balance again. 'If you feel tearing it off would benefit our enterprise, please do go ahead, but I should prefer to keep it.'

I couldn't help laughing; perhaps the danger we were in had robbed me of sense. 'Sophia,' Mr Charleton chided me: 'We're locked into a cellar with some twelve barrels of gunpowder and the desperate rebels who placed them here might return any minute to see why they haven't yet gone off, but please don't let me hurry you!'

This sobered me. I managed to kneel on one of his shoulders while he steadied me as best he could by holding onto one hand and one leg. By stretching precariously, I just managed to catch hold of the bar of the grille above me, and then it was an easy matter to stand. Once I was upright, Mr Charleton steadying me with a firm hold on my ankles, I could see a portion of the street.

A pair of boots walked by. 'Hello!' I called quietly to them, but although they slowed, they didn't stop. Another pair came near; shoes this time. 'Help! Help us!' I called. The pace of the shoes quickened as their owner hurried away from us.

'They don't want to stop,' I called down to Mr Charleton.

'Keep trying,' he replied. He sounded breathless, as though he were gritting his teeth. It occurred to me that slight as I was, I was perhaps no lightweight to have standing on his shoulders for any length of time. I addressed several more pairs of feet through the grille before one approached.

'Help!' I called to whoever it was. 'Please help! We're trapped in the cellar and need to get a message to our friends!'

'Would that be to Mr Allen?' asked Jenny's voice, and I almost wept with relief, reaching my hand through the bars. She gripped my fingers tightly.

'We bin lookin' everywhere for you! We only knew you was supposed to be at the Guildhall. Is Mr Charleton there? How do we get you out?' she asked me.

'He's here, and would be grateful if you hurried!' called Mr Charleton, his voice muffled.

'The door's over to our left, but it's locked!' I told Jenny. 'And please hurry! There's gunpowder down here, and they've already tried to set it alight once! They may come back!'

'I doubt it,' said Jenny. 'The city's crawlin' with soldiers. That general bloke's arrived, and no one'll be trying nothing now. We'll be with you as quick as we can, but I'll have to find Mr Allen.'

She disappeared and I looked down at Mr Charleton. 'How do I get down?' I asked uncertainly. It was a long drop.

'Can you hold your own weight on the grille a moment? Then if you let go, I could catch you,' he replied.

I gripped the grille tightly in both hands: 'Yes, let me go,' I called. He moved away, and I swung free for a moment until he gave the word. Then, taking a deep breath I let go. I fell in a rush, convinced I would hit the stone floor and injure myself. Mr Charlcton caught hold of my waist, broke my fall, and then overbalanced backwards and we both fell in a tangled heap onto the dirty floor.

'Are you all right?' I cried, realizing that by landing on him, I'd had the easiest fall. I hurriedly pulled myself off him as I spoke, glad of the darkness to hide my blushes, and he sat up slowly, rubbing his elbow.

'Nothing broken, just bruised,' he said ruefully. He stood up and held his hands down to me. I put my own into them and he pulled me to my feet but didn't let me go. 'I think that's the end of our adventure,' he said looking down at me. 'Are you sorry?'

'Yes, of course,' I replied. 'It was all over very quickly.'

'For you, perhaps. I've been working on preventing this for many months. We should have worked together from the beginning.'

'If you'd told me what you were doing, we could have done,' I replied.

'I couldn't risk it. I knew your aunt was involved in the plot, I suspected your father too. How could I guess you were not?'

I felt awkward that he was still holding my hands and tried to pull them away, but he wouldn't let me. Instead, he drew me closer, sliding his arms about me. I protested faintly and not very convincingly. 'One kiss, Sophia?' he begged. 'I may never see you again.'

I could see no harm in a farewell kiss, and so offered him my cheek. But that, it seemed, was not what he had in mind at all. Instead, he drew me against him in a close embrace, bent his head and pressed his lips to mine.

I could have pulled away; perhaps I should have done. But to start with I was too astonished to move. No one had ever kissed me before. By the time I could think again, I realized I didn't want to. I may even have put my arm around his neck and kissed him back, but I have no clear recollection.

A hammering on the basement door made us break apart. 'Put your gown back on,' Mr Charleton whispered to me. 'You might prefer not to be stared at when they free us.' He took my face between his hands and kissed me softly one more time. Then he let me go and left the room. I could hear him calling through the locked door as I began the tedious task of buckling on my hoop and putting on my petticoats. My hands were clumsy. The memory of the unexpected kiss lingered strangely in my mind, making it hard for me to concentrate on tapes and buttons.

They must have found someone in the Guildhall with a key, for suddenly the basement was full of soldiers. I'd just managed to dress myself when they burst in on me. As I left the room, I spotted Mr Charleton's mask lying on the floor next to where my gown had been. Something made me pick it up and take it with me. Jenny was waiting for me outside, and we hugged each other in relief.

The next hour was a blur of strange faces, questions and a flurry of activity as the gunpowder was removed from the building and carried away. The whole city was, as Jenny had said, full of soldiers, smart in their gleaming uniforms and polished boots. The streets echoed with the sound of shouted orders and the tramp of marching boots. I didn't see either Mr Allen or Mr Charleton again.

'It's time for me to go,' I whispered to Jenny.

'Go?' she asked in astonishment. 'Go where?'

'I'm going to run away.'

'Now, in the middle o' the night?'

'Yes. It's the best time. If I stay, I'll be married to that odious lizard first thing in the morning. I need to fetch my breeches, and then I hoped you might help me get out of the city and . . . steal a horse,' I confessed.

Jenny grinned, her eyes lighting up. 'I know where the rebels kept a load o' their horses,' she said. 'It was me told Mr Allen and Mr Charleton all that. It won't even be real stealing, cos their owners is all goin' to prison.'

Unnoticed in the commotion, we slipped away from the crowd outside the Guildhall. We were stopped at Trim Bridge, for all the city gates were under guard. However, having given our names and addresses, we were allowed to pass. I retrieved my breeches from the hay bales and hurriedly exchanged my costume for their inexpressible comfort.

'Jenny,' I said softly. 'I think I should fetch some of my trinkets and clothes from the house before I go. Will you wait for me?'

Jenny caught hold of my sleeve. 'Don't you get yourself caught, whatever you do,' she said.

'I won't.' I was certain it would be safe. I was only going to creep into my room through the window, pick up a few things and disappear again.

The upstairs of the house was in darkness when I reached it. Most of the servants would be asleep and my father and aunt were probably still out, though they must have noticed my absence by now. I pushed the window open, relieved to find it unlocked. Then I dropped into the room, and stole softly across to my jewel-box. I'd barely put my hand upon it when the door was flung open behind me and light poured into the room. I froze, my heart jumping into my mouth in shock.

'You!' exclaimed Aunt Amelia, an oil lamp held aloft in one hand. 'What are you doing in here? And in those clothes! What have you done with your gown?'

I didn't reply, frantically trying to fabricate some story that would account for my disappearance. Bitterly I regretted I'd not gone with Jenny at once. What would it have mattered that I had no money, if only I could have been away from the city and free?

My aunt didn't wait for me to answer. The light of

her lamp fell on my trinket box and she pounced on it, snatching it from me. 'Aunt?' I cried astonished. 'What are you doing?'

'What am I doing? I'm trying to save myself from the wreck of this family's fortunes,' she cried. Her voice was different to usual. More decisive, entirely lacking her usual foolishness. 'You may as well know now, for you will certainly hear it in the morning: your father has gambled away everything he possesses. I warned him over and over again, but he wouldn't listen. Captain Mould ruined my husband, and now he's ruined my brother too. There's nothing left. And your father can find nothing better to do than to head for the taverns to drown his sorrows in liquor!'

I felt the shock of this news burn through me. It was so utterly unexpected that I could barely take it in. 'But you . . . you were working with him . . . ' I stammered, puzzled. 'Why?'

'The cause is greater than personal likes and dislikes,' she said.

'Do you mean the cause of the Pretender?' I asked. Aunt Amelia laughed in a way that made me shiver.

'Yes, that cause. But there was a greater one. Earning myself an independence while I was here.'

I didn't understand her. All I could think of was that my father had lost all his money. 'What are we going to do?' I asked numbly.

'*We?*' demanded my aunt, with a mocking laugh. 'What do you mean *we*? I'm leaving. You're nothing to me, Sophia. Do you really think I wish for the company of a spoiled, badly-behaved girl like you? I only persuaded your father to bring us here for the opportunities the place offered. I could never have afforded to come here and set myself up in such style alone after my fool of a husband lost everything. This time at least, I've made the money I need.' Her tone was spiteful and triumphant. She cared nothing for my father or me.

'You've been playing a part,' I said. 'You've been using us.'

'You are so naïve, Sophia,' she said scornfully. 'People like you are so easy to prey on. Luckily the Bath is full of such gullible fools, willing to believe that a foolish matron of good family who plays cards is honest. Only the captain knew better. He was the only one I feared. But he couldn't well expose me without exposing himself.'

'You've been *cheating*?' I whispered aghast. 'And the captain too?' I was shocked. Amazed. It had never occurred to me that her astonishing luck was anything other than just that. She'd deceived me completely. With an effort, I turned my mind from her betrayal to my own situation. 'I suppose we'll go home now,' I said. Sudden relief filled me at the prospect. I didn't need to run away after all. I didn't care about being poor as long as I was at home. I was used to it. 'Perhaps Father will go back to the West Indies.'

My aunt stared at me. 'Did you not hear what I said, or are you merely too stupid to comprehend it?' she snapped. 'I told you your father has lost *everything*. Not content with gambling away his fortune, he staked his estates and even his plantations. It's all gone, Sophia. You are penniless.'

And then she was gone, my mother's jewellery in her

hand, the door slamming shut behind her. I sat still for a few moments sick and shaking with shock, unable to frame my thoughts, unsure what to do. My home, I kept thinking. My beautiful, beloved home. I'll never see it again.

Rousing myself from my frozen, horrified state with a huge effort, I grabbed a cloak from my wardrobe and wrapped some essentials into it: a comb, a hairbrush, some clean underwear and a few of my more portable items that I could sell such as handkerchiefs, gloves and lace. Then I climbed through the window again, heart hammering at the thought that my father could return home at any minute, drunk and furious.

Jenny was waiting for me anxiously and led me out of the city to the stables. Together we crept into the deserted stable yard and I selected the most beautiful glossy black mare with a white star on her forehead and one white forelock.

We sneaked into the tack room to find a saddle and bridle. 'The grooms here is as lazy as can be,' Jenny whispered to me. 'They never guard the horses at night, and the catch on the stable yard gate is broke, so there's nothing to stop us getting out.'

I picked up a bridle and a saddle and turned to leave, only to see Jenny choosing one too. 'What are you doing?' I whispered.

'Going with you,' she replied, leading the way back to the stalls.

'But what about Bill? What about your father?'

'My father drinks up every penny I get,' said Jenny impatiently. 'And he beats on me too. And Bill . . . he's a good lad, my brother. I love him. Really I do. But he's soft in the head. He wants me to go with him to be a chambermaid in an inn. Can you see me stickin' at that more than half a day?'

I smothered a laugh and lifted the saddle onto the black mare. She nickered softly at the prospect of a night-time outing and lipped at my hands. I tightened the girth, stroked her soft nose and she let me put the bridle on her. 'We're off for an adventure,' I promised her. Then I turned back to Jenny. 'Are you sure?' I asked her. 'We've no place to go, and no money. I'm going to find my cousin in the hope he'll help me out, but it's a vague plan.'

Jenny grinned, her teeth white in the darkness. 'I know,' she said. 'It sounds better than sticking around here or cleaning out chamber pots.'

'Won't Bill be upset?' I asked.

'Yes. But I've promised him I'll stay in touch. You can help me write the letters.'

'I'll do better than that. I'll teach you to read and write yourself.'

Jenny grinned and pointed at the black and gold mask I'd looped around my wrist. 'I can see you've got a plan for getting money too,' she said and winked at me.

I grinned back at her. 'Do you happen to know where the grooms keep their pistols?' I asked.

CHAPTER THIRTY

The following weeks were some of the most uncomfortable but also some of the most exciting of my life. Jenny and I rode by day and slept in haystacks and barns by night. When we could find nowhere suitable, or when the need to wash overcame us, we took a night in a cheap inn somewhere. Usually these places were so full of bedbugs and men who thought that girls travelling alone must be easy of virtue that we were pleased to sleep rough again the following night. A snug nest in a haystack and a peaceful sleep was to be preferred to grubby sheets and a pistol ready under the pillow.

I sold my Persephone costume at the first market town we passed through. It fetched a good price and that should have kept us going for some time. But we had bad luck. My mare, whom I'd named Mayfly, threw a shoe and we needed to pay a smith for a new one. She went lame meanwhile, and we couldn't travel on for several days. Then the girth on Jenny's saddle broke and we had to replace it. The money was soon gone.

When it ran short, we quarrelled about how to replenish it. Jenny was all for holding up coaches, but I pointed out that it was immoral to rob merely for our own enrichment. 'That didn't stop you holding up Mr Charleton,' she pointed out.

'I did that for you!'

'This will be for me and all. I don't want to go hungry,' she said. 'Anyhow, what did you bring a pistol for if not for that?'

'It's wrong though. It's their money. What right have we to take it?'

'If they can afford to travel in a chaise, they can spare us a bit of change. See it as charity,' said Jenny.

'Charity is given freely, not taken at pistol point. Easy to hear you haven't been taught any morals.'

'Easy to hear you've never been faced with starvation while the rich dines off silver plate,' retorted Jenny. 'How much d'you think they'd pay me to wash out piss-pots like my brother wanted me to do? I could work my whole life and never afford a gown like that one you sold at Bradford-on-Avon. Show me a job girls can do what pays a decent wage and I'll do it.'

I turned my back on her and we didn't speak till morning. I spent a sleepless night thinking hard about what she'd said. It was the truth. It didn't make robbery right; nothing could do that. But things weren't fair.

Unable to think of an honest plan to get money, and faced with starvation if we did nothing, I finally gave in. But we agreed that we would take only cash from the travellers we robbed. 'No large sums and no personal possessions,' I stipulated. Jenny rolled her eyes and agreed.

After that we held up several coaches and took enough to keep us. I confess the exhilaration and the danger of the robberies meant more to me than the sums we made, though they were needed too. But the excitement of donning Mr Charleton's mask, and galloping towards an unsuspecting coach on a moonless night, not knowing whether we faced swords or pistols, quickened the blood in my veins and thrilled me to my very core.

After a robbery, Jenny and I would lie awake in the darkness, reliving it. We went over what we had done well, what mistakes we had made and how we'd felt as we rode at the coach; that dangerous moment when we didn't yet know if the groom was about to take a pot-shot at us. I would hold my mask in my hand as we talked, running my fingers over the smooth black fabric sewn with gold thread. One night Jenny reached out and touched the mask. 'That was his, wasn't it? He wore it at that party.'

'Yes,' I agreed. 'I found it on the floor and picked it up.'

'Do you miss him?'

I remembered the kiss in the cellars of the Guildhall and felt a tingle run over my skin. I recalled all the times we'd spoken together and he'd joked with me, and sometimes understood me. But I also remembered that he'd bid me farewell and hadn't seemed to sorrow. I must learn to forget him. 'No,' I said. 'I never think about him.'

'Liar,' said Jenny amicably.

The weather grew colder and the days shortened as autumn approached. We stopped lingering on the road, stopped making detours, and hastened our steps towards

Windsor. But when we finally reached the barracks, bad news awaited us. Jack's regiment had left for the continent many weeks before.

I sat dazed and lost in the coffee room of an inn that Jenny had taken me to. 'I don't know what to do,' I said in a voice that sounded as though it came from a long way away. 'I've thought for so long that Jack would be here and we'd work out what to do together. Now I don't know. I just don't know.'

Jenny took my hand and squeezed it comfortingly. 'We'll manage,' she said. 'We done all right so far, ain't we?'

'Yes, but that's different,' I said, and then stopped. How could I explain to Jenny that this had been an exciting adventure, a temporary existence? It had been a means to an end. I couldn't envisage living like this for ever; drifting, homeless and making our living by robbing others. Despite the excitement, the danger and the fact that I enjoyed Jenny's company, I wanted something more. 'I need some aim or purpose in my life,' I said, unsure if it made any sense.

Jenny shrugged. 'Gettin' enough coins together for a hot meal seems like a good enough purpose to me,' she said with a grin.

We moved on. Three nights later, somewhere between Windsor and London, we ran out of money again. We found no coaches to rob for several nights and became hungry and desperate. Which is how I found myself one night on the edge of a lonely heath on the main pike road to Reading. Waiting for a suitable coach in the dark and the wind had never seemed less like fun.

I was astride Mayfly, hiding in the shelter of some overhanging trees. Jenny was up in the trees, waiting to drop down onto the coach from a branch. It was a method we'd found effective once or twice.

'I'm freezing,' I complained as a bitter gust of wind swept over us.

'Me too,' said Jenny from the tree, her teeth chattering. 'At least you got the horse to warm you. This tree's like an icicle.'

'Shall we give up for tonight?' I asked her, trying to ignore the ache of hunger in my belly. The words had barely left my mouth when we heard the rumble of a carriage.

'As soon as we've robbed this geezer,' said Jenny with a laugh.

I pulled my mask on and backed Mayfly up. She arched her neck and pawed the ground impatiently. She might have been born to be a highwayman's horse; she had a fine instinct for the work, knowing just when to keep quiet and when to make herself as fierce and imposing as possible. When the coach was almost upon us, I urged her out of the trees and she leapt forward into the middle of the road, rearing up, pawing the air and neighing a challenge. I sat her easily, reins in one hand, pistol in the other and shouted: 'Halt or I blow your head off your shoulders!'

I'd left it a few seconds too late and the coach no longer had room to stop. To avoid running into me, the coachman wrenched his team to one side so that Jenny, dropping from the trees onto him, missed, banged painfully into the side of the chaise and then fell into the muddy road. I heard her swear colourfully, and to cover the sound, I shouted: 'Halt, I say! Stand and deliver, if you value your life!'

The coach lurched to a stop. With my pistol pointing directly at the coachman, he dared do nothing else. Jenny dragged herself painfully to her feet, pulled her own pistol out of her waistband and took over covering the driver. Meanwhile I rode up to the chaise door and pulled it open. I expected cowering passengers, begging not to be harmed. Instead, I found my arm grasped in a terrifyingly strong grip, and knocked hard against the doorframe. I cried out, my wrist went numb and I dropped the pistol. It hit the ground and exploded at Mayfly's feet. She reared and screamed with fright, and I was pulled out of the saddle by the relentless grip on my arm. Fear flooded me, and for the first time, the vision of the hangman's noose passed before my eyes. I'd been careless, and we'd been caught.

'Let her go, or I'll shoot!' shouted Jenny, trying to cover both the coachman and the occupant of the chaise, and succeeding only in waving her own pistol about uselessly. She never was any good with a gun.

The man stepped out of the chaise in a leisurely manner, twisted my maltreated arm behind my back, holding me in front of him, his free hand at my throat.

'Shoot me, my lad, and you'll kill your friend,' he said to Jenny. Then he looked at me in the moonlight, caught his breath and twitched off my mask. 'What do you mean by holding me up again, and this time wearing my own mask to do it, Sophia?'

CHAPTER THIRTY-ONE

'Mr . . . Mr Charleton?' asked Jenny uncertainly. 'What are you doin' here?'

'Searching for you two, of course. What a stupid question. Put the gun down, Jenny.'

Jenny lowered her gun. Mr Charleton released me and I sank to my knees, nursing my throbbing wrist. He knelt beside me, and ran his fingers over it, making me cry out in pain. 'It's not broken,' he said. 'But it will hurt for a while. I won't apologize; I was defending myself.'

I nodded, not feeling able to speak yet.

'Let's not linger here in this freezing spot,' suggested Mr Charleton. 'There's a pleasant inn a few miles on. Shall we head there for a chat?'

I was reeling with shock. I found myself helped into the chaise, while Jenny rode beside it leading my horse. The vehicle was soon in motion. I sat stunned, still nursing my wrist. It seemed a quite impossible coincidence that of all the coaches in the whole country to choose from, we had managed to hit on Mr Charleton's.

'Coincidence?' said Mr Charleton indignantly when I ventured to say as much. 'I've been hunting for you for weeks. Reports of two slight young lads holding up coaches in this area led me to drive up and down these blasted roads at night in the hope of being robbed. I thought you'd never find me.'

'But why would you be looking for us?' I asked him.

'All in good time,' he replied. 'Sophia, I'm sorry to tell you, you smell like a cow byre. How does that come about?'

'Oh,' I said, embarrassed. 'Jenny and I slept in one last night.'

'That would explain it. Was there any particular reason? Some attraction of a cow byre over an inn that I know nothing about?'

'Yes, it's free,' I said defiantly.

'Possibly,' he remarked, shaking out a scented pocket handkerchief and holding it to his nose. 'But it brings with it a very pungent odour.'

Cautiously I sniffed at the sleeve of my coat. 'Is it so very bad?' I asked apologetically. 'I can't smell it.'

'Which just goes to show how very far you have strayed from fashionable life at the Bath,' he remarked.

I said nothing more, but watched him as the chaise swayed and lurched over the uneven road. What did I feel about seeing him again? It was utterly unexpected. Almost unreal. But a part of me was pleased.

Our arrival at the inn caused a bustle. Ostlers met the coach and unharnessed the horses. Jenny handed over our own two horses to their care as well, and the landlord bowed us all into his inn, casting a disapproving eye over Jenny and me. I could see at a glance it was quite a different class of inn to those we'd been staying in; it was beautifully clean, wax candles were in use rather than tallow and the furniture was smart and cared for.

'A private parlour, please,' Mr Charleton said. 'And bring some hot milk for the ladies. I'll need a bedchamber for myself, another for the ladies, and, er . . . they will need a bath.'

'Yes, sir,' agreed the landlord wholeheartedly.

'Hot milk?' demanded Jenny in disgust when the landlord had bowed us into the parlour, had some candles lit and then withdrawn again. 'If you're goin' to lay out your ready on drinks, can't we have ale or a glass o' porter?'

'Hot milk will do you so much more good,' replied Mr Charleton firmly.

Jenny sat down and crossed her arms in a huff.

'Well,' Mr Charleton began, looking at us both. 'I was right then. All I had to do was drive around at night and wait for you to rob me.'

Neither of us replied. I felt a tingle of shame burning on my neck and ears. Or was that merely the effect of coming in from the cold? A servant came in to light the fire. It smoked a little, and then began to crackle. I found myself cheered by the sight of it. The arrival of the hot milk lifted my spirits further. I wrapped my hands around the mug and sipped. The creamy, sugared drink warmed me right through. I noticed that Jenny was drinking hers too, despite her protests. A sense of well-being began to spread through me.

'Do you not want to hear the news from the Bath?' asked Mr Charleton. 'You both played your part in the events there, after all.'

When I stayed silent, Jenny said: 'I s'pose you're going to tell us anyway.'

'I am. The rebellion was defeated almost before it had begun. The troops the rebels expected never arrived from France or Ireland. No lives were lost in fighting. Some ringleaders fled back to France, but there were many arrests. Sir William Wyndham, among others, is safely in the Tower of London now. And there was a tremendous celebration last week. The Corporation wanted to distance itself from the losing side, and so put on a great show of support for king and government. There were processions, cannon salutes and everyone there did a magnificent job of showing the world they had been loyal subjects of King George all along.'

He looked at us both, as though expecting a response. But our preoccupations had been so very different in the past weeks. We'd been concerned with the all-consuming task of getting enough food to eat and finding shelter at night. The events at the Bath, dramatic as they had been, seemed very far away. I tried to rouse myself to take an interest.

'That's good,' I said, and it sounded lame, even to me. Sleepiness was beginning to steal over me.

'You both disappeared in the midst of all the excitement,' Mr Charleton continued. 'If you'd only stayed, you would have seen everything resolved.'

'I wasn't staying to be married off to the lizard,' I retorted. 'I had no choice but to flee.'

'In fact, there was no danger of your being married at all. You couldn't know it, of course, but the captain was one of the rebellion's ringleaders. The Bath became too hot for him, and he fled. I pursued him as far as the coast where I lost track of him.'

'Gone?' I echoed blankly. For a moment I imagined that I might have stayed after all, but then I recollected that it would have been impossible. 'He was not my only reason for running away. My father had even worse plans for me if he did not succeed in marrying me off. I did the right thing.'

At that moment, a maid entered to inform us our baths were ready. Mr Charleton got to his feet. 'I can see how tired you both are,' he said. 'Have a wash, sleep and we'll talk more in the morning. Good night.'

It was good to immerse myself in the tub of warm water and scrub the weeks of accumulated dirt from my body. It was even better to sleep in a clean, comfortable bed. But I woke early, wondering what on earth was to become of me. I suspected Mr Charleton wouldn't agree to let us continue our robberies. It occurred to me he might even try and force me to return to my father. Unable to lie still any longer with that hideous possibility in my mind, I got up. I found my breeches and shirt had been washed for me overnight. I dressed quietly, so as not to wake Jenny, and went downstairs. The sun was shining brightly outside, sending rays of autumn sunlight slanting in through the windows of the inn. It crossed my mind that it might be best simply to run away now. I could be out in that sunshine in a matter of minutes, riding away from here. But the temptation of seeing Mr Charleton was stronger than my instinct to flee.

Mr Charleton, an early riser apparently, was in the parlour writing letters. I was strangely glad to see his tall, elegant figure seated at the table. I'd missed him more than I'd realized these past weeks. When he looked up and smiled at me, I found myself smiling back.

Mr Charleton put down his pen, got up to bow to me, and offered me a seat on the settle by the fire. When I sat down, he sat next to me. I expected him to speak, but he said nothing, merely staring abstractedly into the fire. At last after a long silence, he looked at me, his expression very grave. 'Sophia,' he said, and then paused as though unsure how to continue.

'What is it?' I asked him, alarmed, for he looked so serious.

'I have some news which is going to upset you.'

'Tell me,' I begged fearfully.

'Your father . . . '

I interrupted him. 'My father has gambled all his fortune away. I know that.'

'You know it? How?' asked Mr Charleton, startled.

'I saw my aunt,' I said. 'I went back to fetch some things and she was there . . . stealing my jewellery.'

'So it will be no surprise to you to hear that she fled the Bath?'

'None at all. Good riddance,' I replied. 'Though I'd rather she'd been arrested.'

Mr Charleton shook his head. 'That was never likely. She was a go-between; a mere messenger. With so many conspirators to deal with, she was of too little interest. And although we're sure that both she and the captain were card sharps, we couldn't prove it.'

'Do you mean she cheated?' I asked. 'You're quite right. She admitted as much to me.'

'That was foolish of her. Though it's good to know my suspicions were correct. But, Sophia, that is not the main thing I have to tell you. There is worse: I'm afraid your father is dead.'

I froze, trying to take in what he had said. 'That's not . . . possible,' I faltered at last. 'How can he be dead?'

All my life I'd stood in my father's shade. Even from the other side of the Atlantic, his shadow had reached me. And now he was gone? I couldn't believe it.

'It's true.'

'But how . . . ?' I asked and then before he could answer, a thought struck me. 'His pride would never stand the disgrace of the ruin he'd brought upon himself. Did he take his own life?'

Mr Charleton shook his head. 'No. He got into a quarrel over cards in a tavern, it's believed. He took part in a duel at dawn the day after the failed rebellion. He was shot through the heart; his body found in the fields. I'm so sorry, Sophia,' Mr Charleton said. 'It's an ending I've seen all too often when cards or dice take control of a man.'

'So I'm free?' I asked, hardly daring to believe it. 'I don't have to go back to him?'

'I beg your pardon?' asked Mr Charleton sounding startled. 'I thought you would be upset.'

'I am. Shocked too. But most of all I'm relieved. You can't even begin to understand what a tyrant he was. And I don't believe,' I said, musing, 'that he ever showed me even one bit of love. Not ever.'

'What will you do?' asked Mr Charleton. 'We don't know where your aunt has gone.'

'She doesn't want me. I don't know,' I said soberly. 'I really don't know. I thought the free life of the highway would suit me. I love the excitement and the uncertainty. But there's no *point*. I'm robbing people, doing wrong, without any justification at all. I want to do something that has a purpose. Oh, dear. It's hard to explain. But do you understand what I mean?'

'I do understand.' Mr Charleton's voice was kind.

'I need work. A task to do. A reason for living. And I have nothing.'

'I can see that. I've given the matter some thought. I do have an offer of sorts for the two of you. It's seemed to me that you would relish a more active life than you have led up to now, even if it meant stepping out of your class. Mr Allen is willing and able to offer you and Jenny work within the post office. He promises to take care of you, to help you find somewhere suitable to live. He's a very kind and trustworthy man, and has been rewarded largely for his key role in intercepting mail and quelling the rebellion. As you can perhaps imagine, a man in his position was invaluable to us. I predict he will make his fortune.'

'In rebuilding the city of Bath? I'm so glad!'

'Perhaps,' admitted Mr Charleton. 'But I think he plans to reform the Post Office first.'

'I'm happy for him. But . . . work in the *post office*?' I asked astonished. I thought about it and laughed a little. 'Well, I might be able to do such work. It's certainly a kind offer. But sir, do you see that suiting Jenny? We would be robbing the posts or running away within the month.'

Mr Charleton looked a little pained. 'And you, Sophia?' he asked. 'Could you be content with such a life?'

'I don't know. I wish to be useful and active, yes. But . . . ' I hesitated. Then emboldened by the kind understanding in his eyes I continued in a rush: 'I do long so for danger and excitement. More than I can say. Is that wrong of me?'

He laughed quietly and shook his head a little. 'How can I tell you it's wrong, when it's what I live and breathe myself? I turned down a career in the Church for this life, to my father's undying disgust. But I don't think you should be seeking your thrills in law-breaking. Quite apart from issues of right and wrong (and I never think they should be ignored) you will end on the scaffold that way.'

'I know. I don't wish to continue it. I wish . . . '

I paused, not knowing how to tell him what I wished. How could I explain that the weeks we'd spent apart had been unbearably empty? I blushed even to think of doing so. But something had to be said. In the end the words came out in a rush: 'I wish so much that we could go with you. We might be able to help you again!'

Mr Charleton was looking directly at me as I spoke and so I saw the changing expressions flit over his face. First his eyes flashed, and for an instant, I thought he was going to say yes, then they clouded and he looked down at his clasped hands. To my surprise, a little colour crept into his cheeks.

'Sophia,' he said, his voice hesitant and low. 'It was wrong of me. Very wrong.' He looked up, making an effort to meet my eyes, it seemed. 'That kiss. I'm more sorry than I can say. It was the excitement, the relief of that moment that betrayed me into indiscretion.'

This was a shock far greater than when he'd told me my father was dead. As bad as when I'd heard my cousin had gone. All this time, he'd regretted that kiss whilst I had treasured the memory. He didn't want me. While I sat soaked in hurt and humiliation, Mr Charleton took my hand in his and clasped it warmly.

'You see, Sophia, no matter what I may feel for you, no matter how I may wish things were different, I'm not in a position to be able to marry. I couldn't support a wife. You may see a wealthy man when you look at me, but it's an illusion; a smokescreen, to allow me to mingle with the people I spy on. Every penny my father has, and he's not wealthy, despite his title, will go to my elder brother. I have my own way to make in the world. Besides, I'm never in the same place for long. I move about, I disguise myself. You see . . . it is quite impossible. I'm sorry.'

His words were sorrowful, but my own heart had been lifting as he spoke. I smiled up at him, feeling as though the sunshine had come out from behind the clouds.

'But I don't want to be married!' I assured him. 'I wasn't begging for a husband! There's nothing I want less. Why do you think I fled the Bath? Good grief, sir! Did you think I was longing to be raising children? I want exactly what you are describing. Adventure, disguises, uncertainty. And . . . to be working and travelling with you. For I *do* desire your company. I . . . I like you very well.'

Perhaps I liked him better than I wished to admit at

that moment. But it was true that I had no desire for wedding bells. I hadn't even thought of that. All I wanted was to be with him. 'Seriously, sir. Could Jenny and I not be useful to you? We can go to places and speak to people that you cannot. We wouldn't cost you much. We can live simply.'

Mr Charleton was frowning. I could see he was seriously considering it, and held my breath. The minutes ticked by in silence.

'It's often tedious work,' he warned me at last. 'At times it's extremely dangerous. And as Aphra Behn is your hero and your model, you already know that the pay is erratic and at times non-existent. You too might end up in prison for debt, writing plays to survive.'

'I know,' I agreed, sighing with relief. He'd as good as given in now. 'I'm prepared for all that.' There was another long silence.

'Sophia, what do you care about serving your king?' exclaimed Mr Charleton at last with some indignation. 'You barely know his name!'

'No, but truly, I care about preventing the kind of unrest I saw brewing at the Bath. That was not the sort of excitement I enjoy. The rest I can learn in time, can I not?'

'And your reputation? If you travel and work with me, it would be lost for ever.'

I laughed. 'Some time I'll tell you about the things I did whilst I was at the Bath. I never cared *that*,' I snapped my fingers, 'for my reputation.'

Mr Charleton was still holding my hand, a fact that had not gone unnoticed by me. He raised it to his lips now and kissed my fingertips, setting my heart pounding. 'Very well,' he said. 'This is a trial. We are friends and we need to trust each other. In future, our lives may depend on it.'

I nodded, excitement racing through me at the thought of all that lay ahead.

At that moment, there was a knock at the door and Jenny came into the room, neatly dressed in clean clothes and looking a little shy. I let go of Mr Charleton's hand to jump to my feet. 'Jenny, Mr Charleton says we may be spies too and work with him. Say you'll come along!'

Mr Charleton shook his head and laughed a little at my excitement. 'I'm a fool,' he said to himself. 'There's no doubt about it. Jenny, any picking of pockets without prior agreement, my girl, and it'll be the worse for you.'

'Is it true, sir?' asked Jenny, puzzled.

'It's true if it's what you want. And both of you please stop calling me sir! It makes me feel old, and I'm not. I think you should both know my name is Peter and please feel free to use it in private. As for our public appearances, I daresay we shall be using various names and identities . . . Good Lord, what have I agreed to?'

'Very well, Peter,' I said, ignoring his doubts and relishing the informality of his Christian name. 'Where are we going first?'

'You'll have to give me time to think. You've just turned my life upside down.'

'But in a good way?' I asked tentatively, wanting to be sure he wasn't regretting his decision.

'Time will tell,' he said but the warm smile that accompanied his words reassured me. 'First of all I think we need to go back to the Bath. All your gowns and personal possessions are packed and stored with Mr Allen, and we shall need them.'

I groaned at the memory of my hoops, petticoats, and high heels, but Peter held up his finger warningly. 'No protests! I choose the manner in which you will assist me. There's a certain man in London who's causing us some grave concerns. He has a young wife who could possibly be befriended. Jenny, we could possibly get you a job within their household. What do you say? Are you both willing?'

I looked at Jenny and saw her eyes gleaming with mischief. The possibilities were endless and utterly beguiling.

'We certainly are,' I replied.

HISTORICAL NOTE

The events of this story are based around the failed 1715 rebellion. During the summer of 1715, a large number of supporters of the Stuart heir to the throne gathered in Bath. Many horses were stabled outside the city and large caches of weapons and gunpowder were secreted in places like Slippery Lane. However, the rebellion was defeated before it really began, largely thanks to the vigilance of Ralph Allen, postmaster of Bath at that time, who is thought to have opened key items of correspondence between the rebels and reported them to the authorities. He worked with General Wade and as a result of their success he was given influence and power to reform the post office. This enabled him to make his first fortune which he used to open a quarry and market the sandstone of which almost all of Georgian Bath is built.

A few of the characters in the story are real people—Beau Nash, Ralph Allen, General Wade, Aphra Behn, and Alexander Pope for example. Most are fictional, notably Sophia and her family and Peter Charleton. The story is a work of fiction, based only loosely on the real events mentioned, and the placing of gunpowder in the cellars of the Guildhall is invented. However, I have tried to give as accurate and full a picture as possible of the daily life in Bath at that time for the wealthy and fashionable who flocked there in the summer months.

Marie-Louise Jensen (née Chalcraft) was born in Henley-on-Thames of an English father and a Danish mother. Her early years were plagued by teachers telling her to stop reading and stop writing stories and do long division instead. Marie-Louise studied Scandinavian and German with literature at the UEA and has lived in both Denmark and Germany. After teaching English at a German university for four years, Marie-Louise returned to England to care for her children full-time. She completed an MA in Writing for Young People at the Bath Spa University in 2005.

Her books have been shortlisted for many awards including the Waterstone's Children's Book Prize and the Branford Boase Award.

Marie-Louise lives in Bath with her two sons.